Dear Reader,

We are delighted to present you with three brand-new stories proving that, from the battlefield to the home front, love *can* conquer all!

Merline Lovelace will take you into the jungles of passion with "A Military Affair," the story of a U.S. Air Force sergeant whose recovery mission lands her in the arms of an ambitious photojournalist. After he's captured the story of a lifetime, will he take her heart, too?

The determined army lieutenant in Lindsay McKenna's "Comrades in Arms" believes a woman, especially one untrained in combat, can only be a detriment to his team. Until he faces the battle of his life—with her at his side.

In Candace Irvin's "An Unconditional Surrender," two passionate ex-lovers fight a mission side by side and learn in the flames of war what it means to be consumed by love.

We hope you enjoy this special collection of heroes and heroines who give their all for their country— including their hearts.

The Editors
Silhouette Books

MERLINE LOVELACE

A career air force officer, Merline Lovelace spent twenty-three years in uniform. She's served at bases all over the world, including tours in Taiwan, Vietnam and at the Pentagon on the Joint Chiefs of Staff. She has produced one action-packed sizzler after another and now has over forty-five published novels. Merline lives with her husband in Oklahoma City, where she is working on her next novel.

LINDSAY MCKENNA

A homeopathic educator, Lindsay McKenna teaches at the Desert Institute of Classical Homeopathy in Phoenix, Arizona. When she isn't teaching alternative medicine, she is writing books about love. She feels love is the single greatest healer in the world and hopes that her books touch her readers on those levels. Coming from an Eastern Cherokee medicine family, Lindsay was taught ceremony and healing ways from the age of nine. She creates flower and gem essences in accordance with nature and remains closely in touch with her Native American roots and upbringing.

CANDACE IRVIN

As the daughter of a librarian and a sailor, it's no wonder Candace Irvin's two greatest loves are reading and the sea. After spending several exciting years as a naval officer sailing around the world, she finally decided it was time to put down roots and give her other love a chance. To her delight, she soon learned that writing romance was as much fun as reading it. Candace believes her luckiest moment was the day she married her own dashing hero, a former army combat engineer with dimples to die for. The two now reside in Arkansas, happily raising three future heroes and one adorable heroine—who won't be allowed to date until she's forty, at least.

MERLINE LOVELACE

LINDSAY McKENNA

CANDACE IRVIN

IN LOVE AND WAR

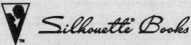

Silhouette Books

Published by Silhouette Books
America's Publisher of Contemporary Romance

SILHOUETTE BOOKS

IN LOVE AND WAR

Copyright © 2003 by Harlequin Books S.A.

ISBN 0-373-21835-4

The publisher acknowledges the copyright holders
of the individual works as follows:

A MILITARY AFFAIR
Copyright © 2003 by Merline Lovelace

COMRADES IN ARMS
Copyright © 2003 by Eileen Nauman

AN UNCONDITIONAL SURRENDER
Copyright © 2003 by Candace Phillips Irvin

Visit Silhouette at www.eHarlequin.com

Printed in U.S.A.

CONTENTS

A MILITARY AFFAIR
Merline Lovelace

* * *

To those who serve.
May you all come home safely.

Dear Reader,

My father, two sisters, brother and husband all served in uniform, as did I for twenty-three years. I grew up listening to my dad's tales of missions he flew during World War II. Those tales took on a whole new meaning years later, when I received orders to Vietnam.

So when you read this story, you'll understand why the theme is *very* close to my heart. Having served in a combat zone, I have only the greatest respect for the dedicated, incredibly skilled men and women who travel all over the globe to bring home America's fallen warriors.

All my best,

Maureen Lovelace

Chapter 1

"Raven One, this is Raven Three."

The call came through Tess's earpiece, soft and staticy in the stillness of the hot, steamy afternoon. Reaching for the radio clipped to the shoulder of her green Nomex flight suit, she keyed her mike.

"This is Raven One. Go ahead Raven Three."

"Unidentified nape at nine o'clock."

Nape. Her team's slang for naked ape, or human.

She spun around, her boot heels crunching on the crushed shells that constituted the only runway on this tiny atoll in the South Pacific. Blinking salty perspiration from her eyes, she searched the jungle edging the airfield.

"I make him at fifty meters," her team member radioed.

Seconds later, Tess spotted the figure moving through the dappled shadows. He was on the dirt track that led from town, if you could call the dozen or so thatched huts perched on stilts a town.

"I've got him, Raven Three."

Slowly, she brought her weapon to her shoulder. The high-powered scope fixed on the distant image and magnified it seventy times over.

She didn't particularly like what she saw. The nape was tall. Lean. Scruffy as hell. His cheeks and chin sported several days of dark, bristly growth. His tropical-flowered shirt flapped open above wrinkled tan shorts. He wore decent-looking boots, but appeared to be missing one sock. What knotted Tess's stomach muscles, though, was the camera looped around his neck.

The camera appeared ordinary enough. One of those digital jobbies that stored hundreds of images on one chip and downloaded directly to a computer. The kind every tourist seemed to have invested in these days. But the man who carried this one didn't look like your average tourist, which made Tess wonder just why the heck he was heading to the tiny airstrip and what he wanted pictures of.

The area threat briefing she and her team had received before departing Hawaii had stressed that relations between the United States and the government of the Namuoto Islands had improved considerably since its bloody, ten-year-long civil war had ended in 1998. But here, at the northern tip of the island chain, anti-American sentiment still ran high. Understandable, Tess supposed, given the U.S.-backed covert operation involving South African mercenaries that had failed so miserably and cost so many lives. The handful of residents on this tiny atoll had been less than welcoming when a plane bearing United States Air Force markings had swooped down yesterday.

Tess flicked a quick look over her shoulder at the C-130 Hercules she and her team were charged with protecting. The four-engine transport was parked at the far end of the runway, poised for a fast takeoff. Its crew waited in the shade of the wing. Edgy and anxious, they were sweating out the return of the recovery team that had climbed up the island's jagged volcanic peak to the crash site of the World War II-era Corsair.

The team should be starting back down the mountain any time now. They'd hacked their way up to the mangled wreckage of the single-seat fighter before noon. Their initial radio report indicated little had survived the crash and subsequent detonation of the plane's ordnance, not to mention six decades of scavenging by wild creatures. All they'd recovered from the site were a few bits of human bone. Still, those fragments represented a fallen warrior who'd served his country during a time of great crisis. It was Tess's job to make sure no one—including the small cadre of al-Qaeda-trained terrorists believed to be operating out of base camps in neighboring Indonesia—messed with the people or the plane sent to transport this fallen warrior home for long-overdue honors and burial.

Her glance cut back to the nape. He looked harmless, but she'd long ago learned never to trust appearances. Anyone in her line of work who did was asking for a bullet.

"I'm moving up for an intercept," she told her team. "Raven Two and Four, maintain your positions. Raven Three, back me up."

"Roger, chief." Danny Boyle's Alabama drawl drifted through her earpiece. "I've got you covered."

Tess lowered her weapon and tucked it into the crook of her arm. The M249 SAW—Squad Automatic Weapon—was outfitted with a Special Ops package, yet was still light enough to be carried easily and fired from the hip, even when loaded with a 200-round ammunition box. After six years as a military cop, Tess could take the SAW apart and clean it in six minutes flat. After three additional years as one of the air force's elite Phoenix Ravens, she could reassemble it again in her sleep. The butt of the weapon rested lightly on her hip as she crossed the clearing toward the nape.

The brutal training program every Phoenix Raven went through was designed to provide a working knowledge of everything from international law to unconventional and highly effective close-combat techniques. In what was touted as the equivalent of graduate program for supercops, instructors took law enforcement and security to the next level. In the field, however, the basic operational principle of every security force operative was to begin at the lowest end of the force continuum and escalate only as necessary.

In this case, Tess decided, she'd start with a simple command.

"That's far enough!" she shouted. "Stop where you are."

Relief zinged through her when the nape halted at the edge of the airfield clearing. Her mission prebrief had stressed that the Namuotan population consisted of four diverse ethnic groups who spoke some two hundred different dialects. She'd been warned to expect communications problems. Thankfully she found that this particular islander understood English. Either that, or he had a healthy respect for the SAW.

Keeping her finger light on the trigger, Tess approached him. He didn't appear any more reputable up close than he had from a distance. His black hair stood up in uneven spikes. Red shot through the whites of his eyes. His shirt looked as if he'd slept in it for the past week.

"Identify yourself, please."

"I'm Quinn. Peter Quinn."

Tess searched her memory for mention of anyone by that name in the mission brief and came up blank.

"What can I do for you, Mr. Quinn?"

He bent an elbow and made as if to dig into the pocket of his shorts. "I'm with the…"

"No sudden moves!" she snapped, whipping up the SAW. "And no reaching into any pockets."

"Look, lady…"

"It's sergeant. Staff Sergeant Teresa Hamilton, United States Air Force. Now turn around, plant your palms against that tree, and spread your legs."

Scowling, he looked her up and down. His reddened, whiskey-colored eyes took in every one of her five feet, two inches before fixing on the naturally curly auburn hair that tended to go wild in this steamy heat. She'd mashed her blue beret emblazoned with the Ravens' unit insignia down over the thick mane, but enough damp tendrils had escaped to frame her face and give her a deceptively fragile air. Fragile, that is, if you didn't happen to notice the lethal arsenal she packed on her slender frame.

The nape noticed it. He definitely noticed. She saw his gaze drop from her face, skim down her front, and linger on her expandable baton in its leather jacket. The Taser clipped to her belt. The cross-hatched grip of the handgun poking from her underarm holster.

Tess let him look his fill before jerking her chin toward a tall palm. "Turn around, place your hands on that tree, and spread 'em."

Swearing under his breath, Quinn turned. A whole lot faster than he should have, he realized in the next, blinding instant.

Fiery spikes drove through his skull and stabbed into eyeballs aching and sandpaper-rough from the home brew he'd swilled last night. Ten days on this dime-sized island and he still hadn't figured out what the locals put into their beer to give it such a kick.

Gritting his teeth against the pain lancing through his skull, he planted his palms against the scaly trunk and widened his stance. Not far enough for the gun-toting GI Jane behind him, evidently. Hooking a boot around his right ankle, she jerked his foot over another eight or ten inches. Off balance, Pete used the tree for support while she patted him down.

And up.

And down again.

A snide comment on her thoroughness popped into his aching head. It popped right out again when she slipped a hand inside his shorts pocket and felt around.

Christ!

His lower body went on instant alert, but he wasn't about to give her the satisfaction of knowing she'd gotten his attention. He stared at the tree trunk, determined to play it cool. Despite his best efforts, beads of sweat were trickling down his temples when she withdrew her hand.

"Was this what you were reaching into your pocket for, Mr. Quinn?"

Craning his neck, he aimed a glance over his

shoulder. A red lace thong dangled from her fingers.

How the hell did that get into his pocket? More to the point, who'd put it there? The faces of a dozen different women swam through his head, some young, some old and seamed, all smiling.

No, wait! Those faces were from the wedding feast yesterday afternoon. The thong must have come after, but he was damned if he could remember when.

"I was reaching for my credentials," he answered gruffly. "They're in my other pocket."

Her hand slid into his shorts again. Quinn swallowed. Hard. His reddened, sandpapery eyes drilled into the peeling tree trunk.

"You can turn around now."

He turned more cautiously this time, not wanting to set off another artillery barrage inside his skull. The rumbles from the last one died slowly as he watched her unzip the leather case he never traveled without. Inside were his Palm Pilot with the notes he'd taken the past few weeks, his passport, and the credentials that identified him as freelance stringer for Associated Press.

"You're a reporter?"

"Photo-journalist."

"Do you live in Namuoto?"

"No. I live in L.A., but I'm temporarily based out of Hawaii."

Her eyes were green, he noted, and decidedly unfriendly as she handed him back the case.

"What are you doing on this island?"

Even with the spikes pounding into his skull, Quinn understood her wariness. He'd covered the first six months of the war in Afghanistan, had seen the soldiers' reactions when they'd heard an American had been captured fighting with the enemy. Had seen, too, the dangerous minefield of politics, religion, tribal loyalties and old hatreds the soldiers had had to negotiate.

This wasn't Afghanistan, but Americans weren't all that welcome in these parts, either. The scars from Namuoto's decade-long civil war hadn't completely healed yet. It had taken Pete Quinn ten days and untold quantities of beer to worm his way into the locals' confidence.

"I came to Namuoto from Micronesia," he said in answer to her question. "I'm working my way across the South Pacific, attempting to follow the trail of arms supplied by terrorist organizations."

Her gaze went razor-sharp. "The trail led you here?"

He scratched at the bristles on his chin, wondering how much he should tell her. So far, all he'd sniffed out was a vague rumor of a cache stored in one of the caves honeycombing the volcanic peak. No one would verify the rumor, and the hours Quinn had spent scrambling up and down the damned mountain had been a waste of time and energy.

Well, not a total waste. He'd photographed the site where the World War II-era Corsair had plowed into the volcanic rock, thinking he might get a story out of it. He'd had no idea, though, that the U.S. had already requested permission from the Namuotan government to access the site. Hadn't known until he'd surfaced from a drunken stupor a half hour ago that a recovery team had landed this very morning and was already up on the mountain.

"The trail led me here," he admitted finally, "but it's gone cold. Stone cold."

"So what brought you out to the airstrip?"

The question surprised him. He would have thought the answer was obvious.

"I want in on the story."

"Which story is that?"

"The Corsair that augered into the mountain. It should sell well with all the interest in the Second World War these days. I heard a recovery team is already up at the site." He shook his head in disgust and ended up wearing a wince. "I can't believe I missed out on their arrival, but I've shot the site, so I'll get the team as they come down. In the meantime, I'll shoot the C-130 and interview the—"

"Sorry," she cut in, looking anything but. "This is a military affair. We brought a photographer along to document the recovery operation. No outside coverage is necessary or permitted."

"Hold on a minute, Teresa."

"It's Tess to my friends. Sergeant Hamilton to you."

She wanted to play hardball, did she? Fine by him.

"You're standing on foreign soil here, *Sergeant*. You have no authority to prevent me from taking pictures or writing this story."

"As a matter of fact, I have all the authority I need. The United States executed a repatriation agreement with Namuoto before we launched this mission. We're recovering one of our own. We intend to accord him the dignity and honors he's earned."

"You accord the honors, I'll document them."

Disdain filled her green eyes. Her lip curled. Not enough for a real sneer, but pretty close.

"My definition of rendering honor to a fallen

comrade doesn't include letting an AP stringer cash in on the story and splash it across the headlines before his remains are positively identified and his surviving next of kin notified.''

The scathing remark got Quinn's Irish up. ''You have a problem with how I make my living, lady?''

''Yeah, I do. In this particular instance, anyway. Sorry you stand to lose a few bucks, Mr. Quinn, but this story is off limits.''

Well, damn. He was usually more careful about pushing the wrong buttons when he went after a story. He could only blame his clumsiness on the home-brewed poison he'd swilled down last night—and the fact that Staff Sergeant Hamilton, United States Air Force, was pushing a few of *his* buttons. Shoving a hand through his hair, he tried for conciliatory.

''Look, I understand where you're coming from.''

''No, you don't,'' she shot back, her eyes darkening. ''You couldn't.''

Quinn's instincts started pinging, the way they always did when he stumbled on a story within a story. Ignoring the hammering inside his skull, he raked another gaze down the sergeant's face. His photographer's eye noted the skin stretched taut over high cheekbones, the tight set to her jaw.

There was more to this mission than Sergeant Quinn was willing to admit. Before he could probe deeper, however, she issued an ultimatum.

"No pictures," she said flatly. "No story. Now amble on back to town before I confiscate your camera."

The threat brought his simmering anger close to a boil. The sergeant must have seen *how* close. Casually, she brought the SAW's barrel up a few inches.

"Move it, Quinn."

His jaw locked. He threw another glance at the aircraft squatting at the end of the runway before zeroing in on the redhead again.

"You and I aren't done, Hamilton."

"Yes, we are. Move it."

Tess kept the SAW leveled at his backside until he disappeared around a bend in the dirt track that passed for a road. When she went to thumb the safety on her weapon, she discovered her hand was shaking.

Damn! She had to stop taking everything about this mission so personally. Had to stop thinking about her grandfather.

Despite the stern admonition, she couldn't quell a sharp stab of pain. She'd lost him just a few months ago. Larger than life, with a laugh that rumbled up from his chest, Big Mike Hamilton had been a hero—her hero—for as long as she could remember.

He'd also flown Corsairs during the Second World War. Right here, in the South Pacific. She'd grown up on stories of Pappy Boyington and his Black Sheep Squadron. Of dogfights over Tarawa, Iwo Jima, the Solomon Islands. Of all-out, diving attacks on Japanese warships. That could be one of her granddad's squadron mates up there on the mountain. His wingman. His friend.

No way would Tess allow anyone to cash in on this mission. "That includes you," she muttered to the slowly retreating reporter.

Not ten minutes later, she was forced to eat her own words.

The radio call came just as she was walking back to aircraft.

"Raven One! Raven One! This is Raven Five."

Her throat went tight and dry. That was automatic rifle fire she heard in the background. Slapping a palm to her radio, she answered the urgent call.

"Go ahead, Five."

"We're taking fire."

"From how many and who are they?"

"Sounds like ten, maybe twelve unfriendlies. No clue who they are, but they're packing some serious iron."

Tess's stomach clenched. A dozen or so heavily armed individuals against a team consisting of a forensic anthropologist, an odontologist, an explosive ordnance tech, a photographer, a mortuary affairs specialist and one Phoenix Raven.

"We've got good cover, One, but we're pinned down. We could use a little help up here."

"It's on its way."

She was already racing for the C-130, her mind churning. This could be a feint. A ploy to draw her and the rest of the security team away from the aircraft. She had to leave sufficient firepower at the airstrip to protect the plane and its crew.

"Three and Four," she barked into the radio, "you'll stay with the plane. Two, you'll go with me as far as the base of the mountain. You'll have to provide back-up for both sites as needed."

Boyle materialized at her side. "I'm with you, One."

"We'll take the RATT."

The Rescue All Terrain Transport was a souped-up dune buggy specially modified for rescue-type operations. The Ravens liked the vehicle's ability to climb sheer cliffs and plunge down ravines so much they'd modified a few for their own needs. The six fold-out stretchers had been replaced by side seats shielded by layers of Kevlar. A whole squad could squeeze in if necessary.

"I'll brief the aircraft commander while you roll out the RATT and fire her up," Tess told Boyle grimly. "Load her with the extra boxes of ammo."

"Roger that, chief."

Her boots crunching on shell, Tess raced toward the aircrew. They were standing now, alerted by the radio call from the recovery team. The aircraft commander's jaw squared at Tess's terse recap of her plan of action, but he knew better than to suggest he or any of his crew go along with her. They had their job. She had hers.

"I'll bring the recovery team down, sir. When I do, I hope you have this baby revved up and ready to roll."

"Count on it, Hamilton."

Her cool confidence took a hit when the RATT rumbled down the aircraft's rear ramp.

"She's loaded and powered up," Boyle told her, swinging out of the ATV's driver's seat, "but I can't get the navigational finder to lock onto the team's coordinates."

"What?"

"She's not taking a signal." Frustrated, he

pounded the instrument panel, as if a good, old-fashioned wallop would get the high-tech circuitry's attention. "We'll have to use our NavSat system."

"Which only works when we find a big enough hole in the jungle canopy to take a fix," Tess muttered.

She chewed on her lower lip. If they relied on the NavSat system they'd have to stop and get a directional reading whenever the canopy thinned enough to allow the satellite transmission. They didn't have time for that. She needed a navigator, someone who knew his way up the mountain, and she needed one fast.

Swinging into the driver's seat, Tess gunned the engine. "Climb aboard, Boyle. We'll go get us a guide."

The RATT threw up a plume of white dust as it sped down the crushed-shell runway, then cut across the clearing to the dirt track that led to town. Tess had made the trip into town earlier this morning, shortly after the C-130 touched down. She'd met with the island's headman and forked over the two thousand dollars the U.S. had agreed to pay to park its aircraft on foreign soil for a few hours, then returned with the beefy fisherman the headman had sent to guide the recovery team to the crash site.

She didn't intend to go all the way to town for a guide this time. She figured she'd find one tramping along the dirt track.

Sure enough, he'd made less than a mile when they caught up to him. He turned at the muted roar of the dune buggy, watched it approach. Tess hit the brakes and fishtailed to a stop a scant yard away from his scuffed boots.

"You wanted in on the story, Quinn? All right, you're in."

He cocked his head, clearly suspicious of her abrupt about-face. "Why the sudden change of heart?"

"The recovery team's taking fire."

His red-rimmed eyes went from suspicious to sharp with interest. "Who from?"

"From a dozen or so hostiles, identity unknown at this time. But whoever they are, they've got my people pinned down. You said you've been up to the crash site. I need you to show me how to get there."

"No problem. But I want an exclusive."

"Dammit, Quinn…"

Shoving his hands in his pockets, he rocked

back on his heels. "That's the deal, Hamilton. Take it or leave it."

She didn't have time to argue. "All right, all right! You've got your exclusive. Now get in the vehicle."

Chapter 2

Tess left Danny Boyle at the base of the volcanic peak. From there he could cover the recovery team's descent or hotfoot it back to airstrip if the C-130 and its crew came under attack.

"Keep your head down and your backside covered, Dano."

"That goes double for you, Chief."

As soon as Boyle had hauled out his weapon and extra ammo, Tess aimed the all terrain vehicle up the jungle-covered slope. Beside her, Quinn braced both boots against the floorboard and grabbed the roll bar to keep from being tossed out as the RATT jounced over the roots of giant strangler vines and dodged rotting tree trunks.

The tropical rain forest's dense canopy trapped the muggy heat and blocked all but a few stray beams of light. Green darkness surrounded them and the leafy underbrush was tough to penetrate. Making matters worse, the layers of thick, spongy vegetation had already swallowed the recovery team's tracks. By sheer luck, Tess spotted a broken fern leaf. A few moments later, she drove over a hacked-off vine. Without Quinn's terse directions, though, she would have lost precious minutes to backtracking and searching for additional signs of the route the team had taken.

All the while the RATT rattled up the steep slope, Tess monitored the recovery team's situation. They'd scrambled into defensive positions and were still pinned down, although Raven Five was pretty sure he'd taken out at least two of the unfriendlies.

"They're about twenty meters below us and to the east," he advised Tess. "I'll fire a smoke grenade to mark their position when you close in."

"Roger, Five. Between us, we'll generate a nice little crossfire."

She glanced at Quinn, saw he'd heard her end

of the exchange. Quickly, she filled him in on the rest.

''The jungle thins out when we hit the lava beds,'' he warned. ''We won't have much cover.''

''How far to the lava beds?''

''Another five minutes or so.''

''Are they navigable?''

''Only on foot.''

She was already starting to see proof that they'd have to abandon the RATT. Lumps of glistening black poked through the spongy vegetation, creating more obstacles to steer around. All too soon the lumps swelled to rivers of black and the dense jungle canopy thinned enough for the rattle of gunfire to penetrate.

Her jaw tight, Tess took the all terrain vehicle as far as she could before the jagged rocks made the way impassible. Cutting the engine, she swung out of the vehicle and took a quick fix on their position.

The cone of the volcanic peak loomed directly above. Below, she saw in a fast sweep, the jungle rolled all the way down to the sea. She spotted the white scar of the airstrip off to the east. To the west was the town and a minute slice of palm-lined beach lapped by frothy waves. Beyond the beach was the sea, an endless expanse of shimmering turquoise topped by cotton-candy clouds.

Blowing out a breath at the deceptive serenity of the scene, she turned back to survey the steep precipice. No doubt about it. She'd have to scramble up the rest of the way on foot. Ripping open a box of ammo, she stuffed extra clips into the zippered pockets on the arms and legs of her flight suit.

"Stay with the vehicle," she instructed Quinn.

"No way. You promised me an exclusive, remember? I'm going with you."

"The hell you are."

"If it'll ease your mind, I was with the 101st Airborne at Kandahar."

The fact that he'd spent some time in Afghanistan didn't cut it with Tess. "You had a whole division of rangers covering your butt at Kandahar," she pointed out acidly. "All you've got here is me."

Quinn couldn't help it. She sounded so tough and so damned superior, he had to pull her chain.

"You can cover my butt any time or any place you want to, sweetheart. The way you felt me up at the airstrip got me thinking we both might enjoy it."

Her eyes flashed, and she looked ready to put a

bullet through him on the spot. He must have some perverted death wish, Quinn decided. This slender, wild-haired Amazon was starting to turn him on.

Maybe it was the hair. The tendrils of dark red curled wildly around her face. From the look of the fat twist she'd stuffed up under her beret, the rest of it was thick and long and just made for a man to burrow his hands through.

Or it could have been her eyes. As vivid and green as the jungle, they looked out at him through a screen of red-tipped lashes.

The body that went with the hair and the eyes wasn't too shabby, either. She certainly filled out a flight suit better than any other airman he'd come across in his years of covering military operations. Giving thanks for the form-fitting Nomex, Quinn stopped the scathing retort he saw her getting ready to deliver with a dry observation.

"Right now, though, I'd think you'd have other things on your mind besides my backside. Like getting to the recovery team."

With an evil glare, she spun around and started up the treacherous lava bed.

As Tess scrambled up the jagged river of rock, the exchange of rifle fire above them grew louder. She took advantage of every scraggly palm and

fan-shaped palmetto, not so much to protect herself
but to keep the unfriendlies from detecting her approach.

Quinn dogged her heels, keeping up with more
ease than she'd expected. He had stamina. She'd
give him that. Even with all her conditioning and
rigorous training, her cheeks were puffing in and
out like a blowfish.

He also had the persistence of a dogfly and an
ego that wouldn't quit. She couldn't believe the
man had all but come on to her. Here. Halfway up
a damned mountain. With the rattle of gunfire
echoing above them.

Setting her jaw, Tess scrabbled for a hold on the
smooth, jagged rock. Sweat drenched the armpits
of her flight suit by the time she crouched in a
crevice of shiny black rock and searched the
craggy peak above through the SAW's high-
powered scope.

The team was up there, but hidden behind a wall
of rocks. She could see the unfriendlies, though.
They'd left their backs exposed, obviously not ex-
pecting an attack from the rear. Big mistake, Tess
thought with savage satisfaction. *Very* big mistake.

Signaling Quinn to take cover, she propped her
automatic rifle on a rock, cocked it, and keyed her
mike. "I'm in position, Raven Five. You don't

need to paint the bastards. I've got them in my sight.''

"Roger, One.''

"Keep your heads down.''

"Will do.''

The SAW spat fire. A feral smile curved Tess's lips as bullets traced a path across the rock and cut into the hostiles. They whirled, tried to pinpoint the new source of attack, and found themselves caught in a murderous crossfire. One went down with a scream. His pals dragged him behind a rock and tried to return fire.

At that point, Raven Five and the others opened up again from above. Tess heard the stutter of his automatic weapon accompanied by the bam-bam-bam of the handguns carried by the team members.

It didn't take the hostiles long to decide they'd had enough. They scrambled away, firing as they went. Gradually, the crack of rifle fire and the splat of bullets digging into rock died. Tess held her position, her muscles coiled and her finger on the trigger, until instinct told her it was safe to move.

She started to get to her feet. A scrabble of sound behind her had her twisting violently to face the threat. Quinn froze and stared down the barrel of her rifle.

"Sorry," she muttered, lowering her weapon. "I forgot you were there."

He blew out a breath. "That's the second time you've aimed that thing at my midsection, Hamilton. How about we don't go for three?"

"Fine by me. Just don't get in my way."

The response was a little less than gracious considering how he'd guided her through the jungle, but she was too wired to care. Her mouth set, she started up the slope.

The recovery team scrambled down to meet her. Dr. Peggy Courtland, a forensic anthropologist and the team's leader, gripped a blue steel Beretta in one sweaty fist.

"Boy, are we glad to see you, Tess."

"Same here, doc." Her gaze swept the small group. "Everyone here?"

"All present and accounted for. Except our guide. The guy turned tail and ran at the first shot."

"Anyone hurt?"

"A few scratches and cuts. Nothing that needs attention right now." Courtland's gaze went to Quinn, who had his digital camera to his eye. "Who's he?"

"A reporter."

"What's he doing here?"

"I'll explain after we get the team down to the plane. Let's go, folks."

The anthropologist shook her head in quick protest. "We can't leave our equipment behind."

"You'll have to. Whoever took those potshots at you might be re-grouping as we speak. Or they could decide to head down the mountain and take out the plane. We have to move out, and fast."

"You don't understand." She thrust a hand through her short, sweat-streaked blond hair. "When those guys attacked, we dropped everything and scrambled for cover. The remains we recovered are up there along with our equipment. We can't leave them behind."

No, Tess decided grimly. They couldn't.

That could well be one of her grandfather's squadron mates up there. She owed it to him, to every man and woman who served their country, to see he was brought home and laid to rest at last.

"I'll retrieve the box," she said curtly. "You folks start back down to the plane. Go with them, Travers."

The muscled Raven who'd accompanied the team didn't want to leave her. She could read the reluctance in his face. But, like her, he knew his duty. The safety of the plane and crew, including this recovery team, took first priority.

"You'll find the RATT parked where this lava rock gives way to jungle," Tess informed him. "Boyle is waiting further down, at the base of the mountain."

He nodded. "Let's hustle, people."

Tess had scrabbled up a good ten yards or so before she realized Quinn was behind her. Exasperated, she twisted around to blast him but he got off the first shot.

"Save your breath. I'm coming with you."

Her lip curled. No doubt about it this time. It was definitely a sneer.

"Is there anything you won't do for a story, Quinn?"

"If there is, I haven't bumped up against it yet. Better get it in gear, Hamilton. Unless I miss my guess, our daily deluge is only minutes away."

A quick glance over her shoulder had Tess stifling a groan. In the mere minutes since she'd last checked their position, the cotton-puff clouds had turned dark and threatening. Blown by a breeze that felt blessedly cool on her face, the thunderheads scudded in above a sea that was now gray and choppy.

Great! Just great! She had armed unfriendlies possibly lurking nearby. A thoroughly obnoxious reporter dogging her heels. And now, what looked like a first-class tropical storm about to dump on her. Muttering a curse that would have shocked even her salty-tongued granddad, Tess continued up the steep slope.

As Quinn had predicted, the sky split open just minutes later.

The rain didn't bathe the two climbers in cool, refreshing mist or drift down in gentle streams. The fat, bloated drops dive-bombed out of the clouds and hit with the force of hailstones. In the process, they made the rocks so slick that Tess slid down a foot or more for every yard she climbed.

The first time she slipped, her fire-retardant Nomex flight suit protected her knees. The second time, she sliced a palm on a razor-sharp outcropping of black rock. Cursing, she swiped the bloody cut against the leg of her flight suit and pressed on.

Quinn wasn't faring any better, she saw in a quick glance over her shoulder. Those wrinkled shorts didn't provide anywhere near the protection of her flight suit. Blood mixed with rain to run in pale-pink rivulets from a gash in his left knee, and he was sporting the beginnings of a nasty bruise on his right.

Home-based in Hawaii, Tess knew these tropical

storms blew over almost as fast as they blew in. She hated to delay retrieving the recovery box and heading back down to the plane, even for a few minutes, but they couldn't make much headway on these wet, slippery rocks. Wiggling around, she called back to Quinn.

"We'd better find a spot to hole up in until the storm blows over."

He looked up, blinking the rain from his eyes, and surveyed the steep grade above her. "Best I recall, there's a ledge a little farther up, with a good-sized overhang."

With the way her luck was going today, Tess thought grimly, the unfriendlies had taken shelter from the slashing rain on the same ledge.

Signaling Quinn to stay put, she crawled up another few yards. Her fingers closed around a loose piece of lava rock. With a hooking, over-arm throw, she lobbed it onto the ledge. Her finger tight on the trigger of her automatic rifle, she waited for a startled shout, a scrabble of boots, a burst of gunfire.

None came.

Relieved but still wary, she inched up and confirmed with a quick, visual sweep that the ledge housed no other inhabitants. None of the nape variety, anyway.

Grunting with the weight of her equipment, Tess hauled herself onto the rock shelf and collapsed. She lay on her back for a moment, panting, while the rain pelted into her face. As soon as she gathered her strength, she'd roll onto her side and give Quinn the all clear.

She should have known the blasted man wouldn't wait for her signal. Flexing an impressive set of muscles under his now-tattered shirt, he, too, hauled himself onto the ledge and collapsed. Right on top of her.

The breath she'd just sucked into her tortured lungs whooshed right out. She pulled it in again and waited for Quinn to roll off. Instead, he settled his weight more evenly over hers and pressed her into the rock.

"Well, well. Isn't this cozy?"

The nasty gleam in his whisky-colored eyes told her he intended to milk the awkward situation for everything it was worth.

"I wouldn't get too comfortable if I were you," Tess drawled. "You're in a pretty vulnerable position at the moment."

"Is that right?"

"That's right."

All it would take was one knee to the groin, one

twist of her hips, and she could send him over the edge. She knew it. He knew it.

Tess was tempted. Lord, she was tempted! The guy was *really* starting to get on her nerves.

And under her skin.

To her consternation, she felt little pinpricks of sensation at every point where his body pressed into hers. He packed some weight onto his tall, lean frame. She could feel him along every inch of her body. Disconcerted by the way her nerves jumped at every contact point, she shifted her hips and glared up at him.

"I'm not here to play games, Quinn. Don't think you're going to add another trophy to your collection."

"Trophy?"

"What else would you call that red lace thong? Unless, of course," she added with a saccharine-sweet smile, "you're into cross-dressing."

Her tone implied she wouldn't be at all surprised. Quinn answered with a wicked grin. "Nope, I'm not into cross-dressing. I am, however, into *un*dressing. Ever get naked and fool around in a tropical rainstorm, Hamilton?"

Tess knew he was goading her, knew he'd no more strip down and leave himself vulnerable to attack at this moment than she would. Still, the mere suggestion raised some pretty potent images in her mind. She'd fingered more than just a few loose coins when she'd slipped her hand into the pockets of his khaki shorts.

Sternly banishing the memory of his hard thigh and seriously impressive equipment, she blew out an exasperated breath. "Enough of this nonsense, Quinn. How about we get out of the rain and behind some cover before one of those unfriendlies lines us up in his gun sights?"

With an agility he'd already proven during the arduous climb, he rolled to his feet and reached down a hand to help her up. Tess wasn't too proud to take it. With the SAW and the extra ammo she'd stuffed in her pockets, her equipment weighed almost as much as she did.

The overhang provided some protection from the pelting rain. The fissures at the back of the ledge offered more. Most of the cracks were narrow, barely big enough for vegetation to take root and sprout, but one appeared wide enough to squeeze through.

"Looks like a cave of sorts," Tess murmured, examining the opening.

"It probably is. This whole mountain's riddled with them. I think the molten lava trapped air pockets when the volcano erupted who knows how many millennia ago. Every time the earth shifts, new fissures like these open up.''

She speared a glance at the drop beyond the ledge. From here, it looked a long way down. The idea of this narrow slice of rock shifting under her feet didn't particularly thrill Tess at the moment.

''Does the earth move often around these parts?''

As soon as the question was out, she wished it back. Quinn, of course, took it exactly the way it wasn't intended. His brows waggled. A lecherous grin creased his whiskered cheeks.

''Not often enough, sweetheart.''

''Oh, for pity's sake! Give it a break, will you?''

''I'll think about it,'' he tossed back, unrepentant, just before sticking his head inside the fissure.

''Quinn!''

She leaped forward, intending to hook the waistband of his shorts and jerk him back. Someone who'd gone into Kandahar with the 101st should damned well have more sense than to poke his mug into a cave that hadn't been cleared.

No one pumped a bullet into him, however, and Tess let her hand drop before she got into his shorts. Again.

''This one looks pretty deep,'' he announced. ''And dry.''

He wedged in sideways. Muttering under her breath at the risks he took, Tess followed.

"Move away from the entrance." His impatient order echoed hollowly from deep inside the dim interior. "You're blocking the light."

"Yes, sir. Right away, sir."

If Quinn heard the sarcastic reply, he didn't respond in kind. In fact, he didn't say anything at all for some moments.

Tess used the short interval to prop her weapon against the rock wall. Water dripped from her hair into her eyes. Rain had drizzled down the back of her neck. She felt as though she'd taken a bath fully clothed.

There wasn't much she could do about her soaked socks and boots at the moment, but at least she could get her wet hair out of her eyes. Pulling off her blue beret, she shoved it into the breast pocket of her flight suit. A quick tug released the plastic clip that held her hair up and off her shoulders. Using her fingers, she combed the fly-away tendrils back from her face. Once the clip was in place again and her hair semi under control, she squinted into the gloom.

"Quinn?"

He didn't answer. His continuing silence was starting to make her nervous. Quietly, she reached for the SAW and checked the safety. Her finger was inching toward the trigger when Quinn emerged from the darkness.

His shirt hung open, gaudy and tattered. His knee still trickled a trail of watery red. But it was the deep, tight grooves bracketing his mouth that stopped her breath.

"We may be in trouble here," he said grimly. "Deep trouble."

Chapter 3

Tess didn't like the sound of that terse pronouncement. At all. She searched the darkness behind Quinn but saw only shadows. Her glance zinged back to him.

"Just what kind of trouble?"

"Remember me telling you that the trail of terrorist-supplied arms I've been following had gone cold?"

"Yes."

"It just heated up. This cave is a damned arsenal."

"Great! Just what I needed to hear right now."

"Take a look."

He flattened against the rock wall to give her room to edge by. Her heart thumping, Tess squeezed past him and moved deeper into the dim interior. Barely enough light filtered through the narrow opening to illuminate the dark shapes stacked one on top of the other at the rear of the cave.

She couldn't read the Chinese markings on the cases, but from their size and shape she had a hunch they contained AK-47 assault rifles, 20-caliber machine guns and mortars. The smaller boxes had to be ammo.

Two larger crates lay off to the side. The lid of one had been pried open. Tess scooped out a handful of packing material and found herself staring down at the weapon U.S. intelligence officials had dubbed the Red Parakeet, Tweet for short. It was a Chinese knock-off of the U.S. Army's Stinger— a man-portable, shoulder-launched, heat-seeking missile. Despite its small size and simple "fire-and-forget" operability, the Tweet could knock a 747 out of the sky.

Or a C-130 transport.

The thought made her throat go dry. She scooped out more of the packing material and saw there were six of the missiles, securely mounted one above the other in special racks. Their launch tube lay nestled at the bottom of the crate.

Quinn materialized at her shoulder. "Are those what I think they are?"

"If you're thinking Stingers, you're close."

With a low whistle, he angled his body to let in as much light as possible and snapped a half dozen shots. Tess barely heard the digital camera's whirr. She was thinking hard and fast.

"I'll have to rig up some kind of delayed fuse," she murmured, more to herself than him. "Something that will give us enough time to get down the mountain before this stuff blows."

He lowered the camera. "Come again?"

"The guys who stashed this stuff here could return at any time. I'm not real keen about letting them aim one of these Tweets at our aircraft when it takes off."

"So you're going to blow the whole cache?" he asked incredulously.

"That's the general idea. I'd stack a few crates at the entrance of the cave and try to fire into them from a safe distance, but the angle's all wrong. I'd be shooting up instead of down."

"So what's the plan?"

"I'm thinking a delayed fuse of some sort. Or maybe…" Thoughtfully, she stroked her fingertips along a small, sleek missile. "Maybe I'll just generate a little heat for this baby to lock onto. Yeah, that would work."

"Christ, Hamilton, have you ever fired one of those?"

"There's a first time for everything. Besides, I hear they're idiot-proof."

"Oh, yeah?" Planting his hands on his hips, Quinn blew that theory all to hell. "Tell that to the kid from the 101st I saw loaded onto a chopper in a body bag. He managed to detonate his supposedly idiot-proof missile before it left the launch tube."

That didn't sound good. Not good at all. Tess didn't see any other choice, though. The missiles were the only option at this point.

"Look, I'm going to go up and retrieve the recovery box. Do me a favor and empty as many of these crates as you can. Stack them by the entrance to the cave, then make tracks down the mountain, okay?"

His jaw set. "No, it's not okay. It's not anything close to okay."

"What's your problem?"

"If you're climbing up," he said flatly, "I'm climbing up. So we'd *both* better start emptying crates. We'll set them ablaze on our way back down.''

"Have it your way," Tess snapped. She was tired of trying to save his scruffy hide.

The tropical storm ended as dramatically as it had begun. One minute, rain was sheeting down outside the cave. The next, the clouds parted, the sun blazed out, and Tess was steaming in her an-kle-to-neck flight suit. The heavy auburn hair she'd wrung out and clipped up came loose again. It straggled down and lay hot and damp on her neck as she emptied crate after crate. Between them, she and Quinn managed to make a sizeable mound at the entrance to the cave.

"I just hope this stuff burns long enough for us to get down the mountain," she worried.

"And hot enough for the Tweet to lock onto," Quinn muttered, throwing another crate on top of the would-be bonfire. "There, that's the last of them. Ready to climb?"

"Ready."

He hefted his camera. She slung the SAW onto her shoulder. They'd pick up the Tweet when they came back to light the bonfire.

With the sun beating down on her back, Tess found a foothold in the black rock and edged off the narrow ledge. The lava still felt dangerously slick in places, but was drying fast. She climbed swiftly, propelled by the gnawing worry that the unfriendlies might return with reinforcements at any moment. Quinn was right at her heels when she reached the spot where the recovery team had been ambushed.

Equipment lay scattered everywhere. Shovels. Picks. The acetylene torch necessary to cut through the wreckage. A laptop computer. A box of calipers used, Tess guessed, to measure bone fragments.

Ignoring the scattered equipment, she made straight for a gray knapsack and went down on one knee. To her relief, the small wooden recovery box was nestled safely inside.

Relief gave way almost instantly to a stinging combination of sorrow and regret. This was all that remained of a man who'd gone off to war in defense of his country. Maybe he'd left a young wife behind. And children who'd grown up with only a few faded black-and-white photos to shape their memories of their father. Parents who'd never known what had happened to the son they'd sent off to war.

Slowly, Tess pushed to her feet. Spine straight, shoulders back, wrist as stiff as a pine plank, she brought the fingers of her right hand to her brow. She held the salute for several seconds in silent tribute to a fallen comrade before slicing her hand down to her side.

Only then did the soft whir of Quinn's camera pierce her intense concentration. A snarl rose in her throat. She whirled, ready to rip the damned camera out of his hands and smash it against the rocks.

Quinn read the fury in her face. His own expression hardening, he issued a soft, lethal warning. "Don't even think about it."

"You're starting to piss me off, fella. You want to know what you can do with that damned camera?"

"I've got a good idea. You wouldn't be the first one to suggest it, either."

"Why am I not surprised?"

"What's your problem?" he countered. "We made a deal, remember?"

"The deal didn't include me," she spat, snatching up the knapsack.

Oh, yeah, baby, Quinn thought. *It did.*

More and more his gut told him Sergeant Tess Hamilton formed the heart of his story. Or maybe that was his libido talking. No doubt about it, the woman had snagged his interest. Not once, but twice. The first time when she'd poked her hand into his pockets. The second when he'd landed on top of her down there on the ledge.

He could still see rain slick on her cheeks. See the surprise in her green eyes, their dark red lashes spiked together with the wet. He'd had to battle the almost overwhelming urge to dip his head and take a taste of her full, ripe mouth.

Matter of fact, he was still battling the urge.

That surprised him, considering his tastes usually ran to softer, more cuddly females. He'd never tangled with one who probably knew a dozen different ways to inflict bodily pain using only her thumbs.

Wondering how it would feel if she applied her thumbs to one or two of his more strategic pressure points, Quinn looped the camera strap over his head. Maybe he'd give her a call when he got back to Hawaii. Catch her between missions and find out if she looked as sexy in civilian clothes as she did in that figure-hugging green bag. Better yet, find out how she looked wearing nothing at all. His gaze lingered on her trim rear as she stood with her back to him and radioed the C-130.

"Raven Two, this is Raven One."

"Go ahead, One."

''I've secured the recovery box. Has the team returned to the plane?''

''That's a rog, One. The gang's all here. We're just waiting on you.''

''Tell the aircraft commander to rev the engines. I've got one more little task to attend to, then I'll join you.''

When a bullet splatted into a rock just inches from his head, Quinn's vague plans for the future morphed into gut-clenching immediacy. The bad guys were back. It was time to get the hell out of Dodge!

The next moments were a frantic blur as he and Tess bumped and jumped back down to the cave. Quinn got in a couple of quick shots of her loading one of the thin, twenty-two-pound heat-seeking missiles into the launcher before he helped her set fire to the wooden crates.

''Okay,'' she panted, thrusting the tube at his chest. ''You take the Tweet and head down the slope. I'll cover you.''

Smoke billowed out from the burning crates. The air above cracked with the sound of rifle fire. Quinn's eyes stung and his heart thumped against the launcher, but he didn't budge.

''How about I cover you?''

"I'm a whole lot better shot than you are."

"Yeah, well, you haven't seen my pictures yet, lady."

It was a feeble joke, but the best he could do under the circumstances. He knew she was right, knew she was doing the job she'd been trained to do, but everything in him balked at the thought of leaving her.

Another fusillade from above underscored the danger of staying where they were. He was jeopardizing her as well as her mission by delaying the inevitable. Clutching the thirty-plus pounds of missile against his chest, he prepared to scuttle over the ledge.

Her fist gripped his arm. In full commando mode, she held him in place and issued one last instruction. "Get down to where the slope levels off and you have some cover. If I don't follow you within the next ten minutes, fire the missile."

"No way, lady."

Her eyes burned into his. "Think how many innocent lives these weapons could take. Think how many they may have already taken. Fire the missile, Quinn!"

Before he could answer, she spun around and let rip with the SAW.

''Go now!'' she shouted between bursts of fire. ''Now!''

She'd left him no choice. He went.

With the Tweet cradled awkwardly in his arms, he half stumbled, half slid down the lava bed. The jagged edges sliced at his calves. Bullets zinged down all around him. Quinn now knew exactly how the emperor must have felt when one of his more intrepid young subjects pointed out that he wore no clothes.

He was naked. Absolutely naked.

His blood hammered in his ears and his breath came in wheezing pants by the time the lava thinned and the jungle took over. He dodged behind a tree, whipped around and searched the rocks above.

The smoke from their bonfire was thick now, so thick it formed a hazy cloud. He couldn't see the ledge. Couldn't see Hamilton.

How long had it taken him to reach the trees? Three minutes? Five? Where was she?

His hands shaking, he swung the Tweet out and held it at arm's length. It looked simple enough to operate. The sight was at the front, right next to a square, boxy antenna. The arming mechanism consisted of a single lever. The trigger hung down from the barrel.

If he remembered right from those weeks he'd spent with the 101st, all he had to do was activate the antenna, aim it at the heat source, wait until it pinged to signal a lock, and fire. Once launched, the missile would look for the infrared light put out by the targeted heat source and follow it in.

That was the general idea, anyway.

Resting the launcher on his shoulder, Quinn sweated for another minute. Two. Three.

The breeze off the ocean caught the smoke, blew it down in gusts. He wanted to curse the gray blanket but knew it provided Tess the cover she so desperately needed.

His heart pounded out the seconds, the minutes. Where was she?

His muscles twitching at each crack of rifle fire, he pushed up the lever to activate the antenna. It hummed in his ear. Hands sweaty on the slick tube, he peered into the scope and aimed for what he hoped was the source of the gray smoke.

Suddenly, the launcher emitted a distinctive ping. Quinn experienced a second of sheer exultation. Damned if the radar hadn't locked onto the burning crates. His hand went to the trigger.

The next instant, it dropped.

No way he was firing the missile. And he wasn't

sitting here on his butt while GI Jane fought off a small army alone. Flicking the lever to de-activate the radar, he hefted the missile higher on his shoulder and started back up the slope.

He'd climbed maybe five yards when a figure in silver-green emerged from the haze of smoke above him. She had the gray knapsack slung over one arm, the SAW over the other. She'd lost the clip that held her hair. The damp, curling mane made a flag of dark copper against the glistening black rock.

Quinn was grinning like an idiot when she covered the last few yards toward him. The sight of several more figures plunging down out of the smoke wiped the grin right off his face.

"Fire the Tweet!" she shouted, racing toward him. "Now!"

The lever went up. The radar hummed. Quinn aimed, waited two agonizing lifetimes for the ping that indicated a lock. Fired.

He felt the jolt when the missile left the tube. Heard the hiss when the launch engine separated. Saw the trail of white smoke as the rocket cut through the sky in a graceful arc.

Then he dropped the launcher, grabbed Teresa's hand, and ran like hell.

*   *   *

The first explosion sounded like a deep, bellowing roar of outrage from Vulcan, god of the underworld. The second was even louder.

Tess spun around, saw the jagged peak come apart, and punched a fist in the air.

"Yes!"

Quinn didn't even bother to look. He was more concerned with putting as much distance as possible between them and any of their pursuers who managed to survive the shower of rock and debris from the disintegrating mountain. Yanking on Teresa's arm, he jerked her after him. Side by side, they dodged the humped roots of giant strangler figs and whipped around ferns the size of small houses. They'd traveled only a few dozen yards before her radio cackled.

"Raven One. This is Raven Two."

Pulling her arm free of Quinn's grip, Tess fumbled for her mike. She didn't key it fast enough for Boyle. He came back on, his Alabama drawl sharp with urgency.

"This is Raven Two, chief. Come in, please."

"Raven One here. Go ahead, Two."

"What in blue blazes is going on? From where we stand, it looks like the top of the mountain just blew off."

"That's what it looks like from here, too."

"Was that your doing?"

"Actually," she panted, aiming a goofy smile at the man chugging along beside her, "it was Quinn's."

"Come again?"

"The newspaper guy. Our guide. Look, I'll explain things when we get to the plane. Ask the a/c to have the plane ready to roll, will you? We may have a few unfriendlies hot on our tail."

"The props are turning as we speak."

Quinn didn't think he'd ever seen a more beautiful sight than the C-130 Hercules sitting at the end of the crushed shell runway. Its four turboprop engines stirred up clouds of white dust. The short, squat fuselage vibrated with restrained energy, like a champion quarter horse at the gate, ready and eager to run. The rear ramp was up, but he saw three or four figures spread out beside the gaping side hatch. They had their weapons at the ready and were scanning the jungle in different directions.

Beside Quinn, a now seriously gasping Tess keyed her mike. "Raven Two, this is…One. We're coming in…at…eleven o'clock."

The figures whirled, searched the tangle of trees. "We have you, One. Come home to papa."

When they burst out of the jungle and raced

across the clearing toward the airstrip, Quinn did the emperor thing again. He felt totally exposed, completely naked.

Like Tess, his breath was coming in gasps. A sharp little stiletto plunged into his side with every pant. But when he dropped back, intentionally lagging a few yards behind, it wasn't because he was fast running out of steam. It was to shield her back.

She wasn't having any of it. Whirling, she grabbed his arm and dragged him with her. They were within shouting distance of the transport when the crack of rifle fire split the air and a plug of dirt flew up a yard or so to the left.

"Down!"

Tess dropped to her knees, dragging him with her, then went flat on her face. Quinn's nose hit the dirt just as her team answered with a barrage of fire.

Over the whine of the Herc's engines, he caught the thud of boots. Within seconds, a small phalanx had planted itself between them and the jungle. Quinn wasn't stupid. He kept his head down. But the newsman in him had him reaching for the camera still looped around his neck.

Thank God for technology. He used to tote a monster Nikon, along with a dozen different lenses, various filters, and a month's supply of film. This little digital miracle with its quarter-sized spare disks had replaced two suitcases of equipment. Contorting his body, Quinn snapped off four quick shots before Tess shouted in his ear.

"Okay! Let's hustle."

They made for the open side hatch. Hands reached down to haul Tess up. Quinn provided an assist by planting both palms under her bottom and heaving. He flopped inside next and had barely rolled out of the way when the rest of her team vaulted in.

By the time he scrambled to his feet, the plane was already rolling. Tess was suspended half out the hatch, hanging onto a cargo strap with one hand and firing her SAW with the other. Her team crowded beside her and provided protective fire while the Herc gained power.

Quinn didn't let the opportunity pass. He got in several fantastic shots before the C-130's nose went up and the tail dropped. Grabbing at the cargo netting draped over a pallet of equipment, he held on until the jungle fell away, the rattle of automatic fire died, and the transport soared into the sky.

For several moments, the only sound in the hold was the roar of the engines and the whistle of the wind coming through the open hatch. Only after the loadmaster cranked the hatch closed did one of

Tess's crew let out a wild whoop. The others pounded her on the back.

"That was some show you put on, One."

"Yeah, it was."

Raking her tangled hair out of her face, she turned to the bristly-cheeked journalist. Her green eyes were alive with the thrill of having beat the odds. "Way to go, Quinn."

He didn't even try to fight the urge this time. Wrapping both hands around her upper arms, he hauled her against his chest.

Her jaw dropped. Her eyes widened in surprise. While her crew watched with varying expressions of astonishment, Quinn bent her back over his arm and covered her mouth with his.

Chapter 4

Having made the flight from Hawaii to Namuoto just yesterday, Tess knew the return trip would take sixteen hours, with a stop en route at Wake Island to refuel. Plenty of time to decompress after the wild events on the island.

Her first priority was to brief the aircraft commander and her team members on the stash of arms she'd found in the cave. Once the plane was airborne and on course to Wake, the pilot climbed out of his seat and came back to the belly of the plane to hear the details.

Pitching her voice to be heard over the roar of

the four turbo-prop engines, Tess gave him and the dirt-streaked team members a brief recap of what had happened.

"Let me get this straight," the pilot said with a grin. "You blew up the whole cache with a single Chinese Tweet?"

"Well, technically Quinn here blew it up. His hand was on the trigger. I just provided, uh, a few words of encouragement."

The eyes of everyone on board turned to the newcomer in their midst. Tess hid a smile at their varying expressions of disbelief. In his gaudy tropical shirt and wrinkled shorts, Quinn had that effect on people.

"I'll radio ahead to Hickam," the pilot told her. "They're going to want a full report when you land."

No kidding! Tess figured she'd spend the next week filling out forms.

Still hyper from their close escape, both the recovery team and the Phoenix Raven crew wanted to hash over events on the island. First, though, they conducted a simple, heart-wrenching ceremony.

"I'll take that," Dr. Courtland said, relieving Tess of the gray knapsack slung over her shoulder.

Her sunburned face solemn, the anthropologist

retrieved the wooden recovery box from inside the bag and passed it to the senior military representative on her team. The lieutenant stood at attention, the small wooden container in his hands, while the rest of the recovery team lined up on one side of a plain, coffin-like transfer box. The Phoenix Ravens flanked the other side.

With a nod, the lieutenant signaled for the lid to be raised. Slowly, step by deliberate step, he moved forward and placed the recovery container inside the larger box. Once it was securely nested in the foam liner, the lid came down. An American flag was unfurled with a snap and draped over the coffin.

The lieutenant stepped back. As Tess had done up on the mountain, he raised his arm in a slow, measured salute. A silent observer, Quinn was struck by the centuries of symbolism and tradition embodied in the gesture.

Sixty years separated the two warriors. One was young, black and dedicated to recovering the remains of fallen comrades. The other had died alone, consumed by a fiery crash and mourned by a family who'd never known where he rested all these years. Yet, with a simple salute, the lieutenant rendered the gratitude and respect of an entire nation.

The scene stirred emotions in Quinn's chest he hadn't felt for a long time. Admiration for a generation who gave everything in them in defense of their country. Respect for their sacrifices. A vague longing for the days when there were no shades of gray; there was only the sharp, clear white of duty. Honor. Country.

He stood back, well away from the small cadre, framing his shots with an artist's eye. The drone of the engines drowned out the quiet click of his camera's shutter. He'd get the names of everyone on the team later, enter them in his Palm Pilot. The device's memory contained names, dates, notes from the various interviews he'd conducted, outlines of the stories he was working. This one, he decided as he lined up another shot, would get top priority.

When the simple ceremony was done, the passengers in the back of the C-130 sloughed off their weapons, wrung out their wet socks, and tried to make themselves comfortable for the long flight home. One of the Ravens broke out a case of MREs—the army's ubiquitous Meals-Ready-to-Eat. Lifting the brown foil packages one by one, the sergeant read the labels.

"Okay, troops. Listen up. We have hearty beef

stew. We have cheese tortellini. We have chili macaroni and chicken with rice.''

Quinn put in a bid for chili macaroni and caught the package the security specialist tossed him. He'd dined on MREs during his weeks with the 101st Airborne and knew each meal pack came with an entrée, a side dish, dessert, crackers, cheese spread, a beverage powder, a spoon, gum and a towelette. Although his conscious mind balked at the idea of eating food that had been cooked and packaged as much as six or seven years ago, his stomach rumbled in eager anticipation.

He found a place on one of the fold-down web side seats. The friendly—and very curious—Sergeant Boyle hunkered down next to him.

''So where do you know Tess from?'' the sergeant asked casually, ripping open the foil of his MRE.

''From Namuoto.''

''You mean you never met before today?''

''No.''

Boyle hooked a brow. His glance drifted to his team chief, curled into one of the fold-down web seats.

''You two sure got friendly in a couple of hours.''

"Yeah," Quinn murmured, following the direction of his gaze, "we did."

And he planned to get a whole lot friendlier.

Staff Sergeant Teresa Hamilton had gotten to him in a way no female had in a long, long time. The woman had the heart of a lion and the body of a temptress. Quinn got hard just imagining all the ways to exploit that potent combination.

Digging his spoon into the package of cold chili macaroni, he started thinking ahead. To Hawaii and a breeze-swept hotel room. A steaming hot shower. Cool, clean sheets. A certain slender redhead stretched out under him.

Tess felt an odd sensation ripple along the nerves just under her skin. Seeking its source, she threw a look over her shoulder. She caught Quinn's gaze, hot and intense. She held his eyes for a long moment while the ripples intensified to became a river of pure sensation.

Shaken by its intensity, she jerked her attention back to her chicken and rice. This was crazy! She'd met the man all of…what? Four or five hours ago? In those short hours, she'd formed a less-than-favorable impression of his character, his morals and his motivation.

And yet…

He'd stuck with her, toughed it out up there on

the mountain. More to the point, he'd fired a Chinese-made missile and destroyed a store of arms that would have supplied international terrorists for years. That alone raised him several notches in her estimation.

And, she admitted with a funny little quiver low in her belly, he'd pretty well blown her away with that kiss. Obviously he'd been working on his mouth-to-mouth technique for a long time. No doubt he'd perfected it with Miss Red Lace Thong.

Fighting a traitorous desire to discover just what other techniques Quinn had perfected, Tess spooned out a chunk of chicken. She was halfway through her meal when Raven Three brought his over and joined her. Like Danny Boyle, Jeff Anderson made no effort to hide his curiosity.

"Funny thing, Peter Quinn popping up on Namuoto like that. I thought he was still in Kandahar."

Tess slanted the lanky Texan a quick look. Anderson had just rotated onto her team a few weeks ago following a tour in Afghanistan.

"Did you bump into Quinn at Kandahar?"

"No, but I heard a few tales about him."

"Like what?"

He hesitated, obviously unsure how much to spill after the lip-lock the journalist had laid on his team leader. Loyalty to one of his own won out. His warning was oblique, but definitely designed to give her a heads-up.

"Rumor is," he said with a shrug, "Quinn figured out how to get past more than one sweet young thing's veil."

Tess gave a small snort. "So tell me something I don't already know."

"Well... Do you know about Al Sharif?"

"Who or what is Al Sharif?"

"It's an isolated village in the mountains west of Kandahar."

She flicked a curious glance at Quinn. "What's our newsman's connection to this village?"

"It was caught between two vicious warlords," Anderson related in his slow Texas drawl. "They rounded up every male over the age of ten and forced them to fight for one faction or another. They also rounded up every pig, goat and sack of grain in the village. The women, children and old folks were left behind to starve."

"Nice guys."

"Quinn heard about the village and went in. Just him and a driver. They had to travel through a hundred miles of hostile territory and almost drove off a mountain road in a blizzard, but finally reached Al Sharif."

"Anything to get a story," Tess murmured.

"Yeah, well, in this case Quinn got more than a story. He sent back digital photos via a commercial news satellite. The stark photos convinced various relief organizations to organize an emergency airdrop of food and medicine. They sent in enough to get the village through the winter. Quinn probably saved two, three hundred lives. Back where I come from, that classifies him as an okay guy."

That pretty well tagged the man, Tess admitted silently. Pig-headed. Too prone to take risks. A pain in the butt about his so-called exclusive. But…okay.

"I was surprised to see him on Namuoto," Anderson continued. "What was he doing there?"

"Following the trail of al-Qaeda-supplied arms."

"The ones he blew up?"

"The very same."

The journalist's role in the dramatic events on Namuoto grabbed the interest of everyone on the plane. The recovery team drifted over to join him, as did the other Phoenix Ravens and the aircrew members not confined to the cockpit. Soon Quinn was in the middle of a lively discussion punctuated with offers to stand him several rounds of drinks when they touched down in Hawaii.

He also received an invitation from Dr. Courtland to visit the military's Central Identification Laboratory on Hickam Air Force Base.

"Our mission is straightforward," the blond, sunburned scientist said, "and unbelievably complex. Simply put, we want to find and identify the almost ninety thousand Americans still classified as missing in action and presumed dead."

"Hang on a sec." Dragging out his Palm Pilot, Quinn punched a few keys. "Ninety thousand?"

"If you want more exact figures, there are seventy-eight thousand still missing from the Second World War. Another eight thousand from Korea. About two thousand from Vietnam and a hundred and twenty from the Cold War era."

"Good grief! I didn't realize we had so many still unaccounted for."

"Most people don't," the lieutenant on the recovery team put in. "They also don't know our lab employs the largest staff of forensic anthropologists in the world. And the most qualified. Dr. Courtland and her colleagues hold the highest possible board certification."

"Tell me more."

Tess stayed where she was, her legs outstretched, her back curving in the web seat, as fascinated as Quinn by the recovery team's description of their state-of-the-art computers, radiographic imaging, odontology procedures and mitochondrial DNA testing.

She'd heard about the Central Identification Lab, of course. But until this mission she'd had no idea of the lab's scope or the utter dedication of its staff to recovering the country's lost warriors. Maybe, she admitted grudgingly, it wasn't such a bad idea for Quinn to do a story on the lab, give its people the kudos they deserved.

She just wished he'd give up the idea of making money off of the dead American they were bringing home.

The short, incredibly moving ceremony when they landed in Hawaii some sixteen hours later should have convinced him of the solemnity of the occasion.

Dawn was just breaking. Streaks of red flamed the sky above the Punchbowl, turning to gold as the transport taxied to its designated parking spot. Evidently, word of their arrival had been broadcast across the base. Despite the early hour, a crowd of military and civilian personnel had congregated at the flight line. At their forefront a USMC honor guard in full dress uniform stood at attention, waiting to render honors to their fallen comrade.

Tess felt a catch in her throat as the plane rolled to a stop and the flight engineer lowered the rear ramp. The sight of the American flag fluttering in the morning breeze straightened her spine and brought her shoulders back.

The red and gold flag of the United States Marine Corps flew beside the Stars and Stripes. The flag was weighted down with battle streamers. The colorful ribbons signified the major wars Marines had fought in, from the bloody conflicts on American soil to a host of foreign wars.

The American Revolution. The War of 1812. The Civil War. The Barbary Coast Wars. The Nicaraguan Campaign. The Yangtze Expedition. The First and Second World Wars. Korea. Vietnam. The Gulf.

As she swiped her palms down her flight suit to remove the worst of the dirt and blood and sweat, Tess wondered how many men and women had answered their country's call to arms during all those conflicts. She thought of her granddad, remembered his tales from the trenches and honored his memory along with that of the warrior they'd brought home. Shoulders back, chin high, she stood at attention with the others as the band struck up the Marine Corps Hymn and the honor guard marched forward.

From the halls of Montezuma
To the shores of Tripoli

The music called to mind two hundred years of sacrifice. Two hundred years of service by men and women who left their homes and their families to contribute to the defense of their nation. Her throat tight, Tess kept her gaze locked on the flags as a small phalanx marched toward the lowered ramp in rigid lock step.

"Detail, halt!"

The crisp command carried over the last strains of the hymn.

"Color guard, to the left, *harch!*"

The five men carrying the flags wheeled left, shoulder to shoulder, hip to hip.

"Funeral squad, forward, *harch!*"

Six white-gloved marines marched up the ramp, their cadence slow and deliberate. Following another series of commands from their leader, they halted beside the flag-draped casket. Each marine executed a razor-sharp turn. They stood at rigid attention while their leader brought his arm up in a solemn salute.

Slowly, so slowly, the six men lifted the flag-draped casket to their shoulders. Step by measured step, they carried their fellow marine off the plane.

The entire crew on board the plane and the assembled crowd remained at attention while the casket slid into the bed of a waiting hearse.

A moment later, the clear, clean notes of a bugle cut through the absolute quiet. Tess blinked furiously to hold back tears while the mournful call of Taps drifted across the morning air. Her throat was raw and aching when the last, somber notes died away.

A white-gloved marine gently closed the rear door of the hearse. The vehicle moved slowly across the ramp. The crowd parted to let it through.

A lost warrior had come home at last.

Chapter 5

After the heart-wrenching ceremony, the crew stand-down and mission debrief was definitely anticlimactic, but unfortunately, necessary. Tired all the way to her bones, Tess grabbed her gear and started down the ramp. Quinn caught up with her halfway to the crew bus.

"I need to fill in some details about the Phoenix Ravens for my story. How about you and I get together later?"

She angled her head, studying him through gritty eyes that were probably as red as his. She didn't have a clue how the man could look so sexy with his flowered shirt ripped to shreds, his hair styled by wind and rain, and his cheeks covered in black bristles.

But he did. He most certainly did.

"I'm staying at the Outrigger," he told her. "You could meet me there for dinner. Or better yet…" He waggled his black brows in an exaggerated leer. "I could come to your place. That way you could take a shower and slip into something comfortable."

"Like a red lace thong?"

"Christ, woman, don't give me a heart attack!"

She couldn't hold back a laugh. "You never let up, do you?"

"Nope."

Tess actually considered the offer for all of a moment or two. Now that she was back in Hawaii, though, she had a chain of command to answer to.

"I'd better check with the Public Affairs Office before I provide you any more details about the Phoenix Ravens. I'm probably in enough hot water as it is for letting a journalist in on this mission without proper clearance."

Not just for that, she discovered when a jeep squealed up to the flight line and her supervisor climbed out. Heavily muscled and tested by fire, Senior Master Sergeant Steve Jenkins wore his blue Phoenix Raven beret like the badge of honor it was.

"The squadron commander wants to see you, Hamilton."

"Before the team debrief?"

"Before the team debrief."

Uh-oh. She'd expected this summons, but had hoped to clean up and get her mind out of exhausted mode before she reported to the C.O.

"I suppose he wants the details of that little incident on Namuoto."

"You got it." Jenkins's glance cut to Quinn, then back to Tess. "He also wants to know how you ended up with an unauthorized civilian on your team."

Quinn stepped forward. "Look, if this is about me, I've worked with the military before. A quick call to my boss in Los Angeles will verify my security clearances."

"No, sir. This isn't about you." He looked to Teresa, his expression deadpan. "It's about the formal protest the White House received some hours ago from the President of Namuoto. Seems the search and recovery mission we sent into one of his islands turned into a search and destroy. The squadron commander would like a full report, Hamilton. Now."

"I'll come, too," Quinn volunteered. "I was part of that little fracas."

"Sorry, sir. At this point, the matter is strictly a military affair. Where can we find you if the C.O. wants your input?"

"At the Outrigger." He turned his attention to Tess. "About getting together later…"

"I'll call you."

Maybe, she added under her breath as she climbed into the jeep.

And maybe once she'd finished her report, had a shower and grabbed a few hours sleep, she'd realize scruffy, opportunistic journalists weren't really her type.

That's exactly what she might have done if her squadron commander hadn't taken a hand in matters.

Tess debriefed him and a whole room-full of other officials, some uniformed, some not. They listened intently to her report, took notes of the type and make of the arms she'd seen in the cave, and didn't appear all that concerned that she'd destroyed a good chunk of the island along with the arms. She was starting to breathe easier when the gaggle filed out and left her with her squadron commander.

"I've got enough to send off the initial Situation Report," he told Tess. "But we'll need to follow up with a more detailed report."

"Yes, sir."

"You'd also better get with this Quinn character and make sure there aren't any significant deviations between his story and ours."

Well. Nothing like having a decision made for you.

"I'll take care of that, sir."

"Good. That's all, Hamilton."

Nodding, she collected her gear and started for the door. The colonel stopped her with a few gruff words of praise.

"That was a helluva job you did there on Namuoto."

She tipped him a grin. "Piece of cake…for a Phoenix Raven."

"Yeah, right."

It took Tess two hours to complete the full postmission debrief with the rest of her team. Another couple to clean, inventory and turn in her equipment.

Her tail was dragging by the time she claimed her car and drove the short distance to the off-base apartment she shared with two other female sergeants. The rent for a condo ate a hefty chunk out of their paychecks, but they considered the spectacular ocean view from their fifth-floor apartment worth the bite. They rationalized the cost by the fact that the breeze coming in through the lanai saved a bundle on air conditioning. Plus, by supplying a great party pad, they could talk their friends into bringing the eats and drinks.

Tess loved the place. After a mission like this, the sound of the sea murmuring outside her balcony soothed away the jagged edges. Dumping her gear in her room, she headed for the kitchen.

Both of her roommates were at work, but one of them had left the remains of last night's pizza in the fridge. Blessing them both, Tess took the cardboard carton with her to the bathroom. Between bites of cold pepperoni and cheese, she scrubbed off Namuoto's dirt, shampooed her hair, and, as an afterthought, shaved her legs. *Not* because she wanted to impress Quinn with the short, swishy halter dress in a hot-pink Hawaiian print. Only because the strappy sandals that complemented the dress called for smooth, bare legs.

Her thick mane took too long to blow dry, so she just scrunched it into damp waves and left it loose. A few daubs of makeup hid the tired circles under her eyes. A spritz of her favorite perfume made up for the sweat she'd been forced to endure for the past thirty-six hours.

"There," she announced to her reflection in the bathroom mirror. "You're a whole woman again. Or as close as anyone in combat boots ever gets."

Tucking the initial report of the events on Namuoto into a straw clutch bag in the same dazzling pink as her dress, she went out into a breezy dusk.

She expected to find Quinn at the Outrigger's bar, regaling the patrons with his version of the explosion. Instead, a friendly desk clerk let drop that Petey had just gone upstairs and directed her to his room.

Petey, was it?

The clerk was young, dewey-eyed. Just the right age, size and shape for a red lace thong.

Tess stabbed the elevator button, both amused and more than a little chagrined. Not only had she shaved her legs, she'd resorted to a scrap of white lace of her own. Talk about lame!

She'd show Quinn the report, she decided as she marched down the corridor to his room. Get his chop on it. Depart the premises. That was the plan, anyway, until the blasted man opened his door.

Tess gaped. That was the only word for it. Her

jaw dropped. Her eyes widened. She flat-out gaped.

He must have just showered and shaved. The bristles were gone. So were the dirty, tattered shorts. Instead he wore only a towel draped loosely around his waist, the cotton stark white against the dark oak of his skin. Damp swirls of black hair shadowed his chest. His very broad, very muscled chest.

But it was his welcome that stopped the breath in Teresa's throat. He didn't say a word. Not a word. Just slid a hand under her hair, drew her inside, kicked the door shut, and picked right up where he'd left off on the C-130.

Chapter 6

Lord, the man could kiss!

Tess had already sampled Quinn's talent in that particular arena. That, she now realized, had just been a taste. A teaser.

This was the full-course banquet.

His mouth angled over hers, hard and hungry. The hand he'd tunneled through her hair held her head steady. The other wrapped around her waist. In response to his silent demand, she opened her mouth under his. He tasted of mint-flavored toothpaste, whiskey and hot, hungry male.

She braced her palms against his still-damp skin,

felt his muscles coil under her fingers. She could feel him against her thighs, her belly, her breasts. Tess wasn't prepared for the need that slammed into her. It caught her by the throat, sent her mind spinning.

She must have made some sound or given some other signal that told him he'd gotten to her. With a grunt of pure male satisfaction, he shifted his stance. The arm around her waist tightened, drawing her up against him.

Tess couldn't remember the last time she'd been plastered against six-feet-plus of solid male. Wait! Yes, she could. About eighteen hours ago, in the belly of a C-130. Then, as now, the experience had left her gasping for breath.

Pulling her head back, she dragged in some air and tried to clear the chaos this man was making of her senses. Quinn took that as a green light to go to work on her neck.

"Damn, you smell good," he muttered, nuzzling the spot just under her ear.

"Better than on Namuoto, anyway," she managed with a shaky laugh.

His tongue traced a trail from her ear to the curve of her shoulder. "You taste better, too. Not as salty."

"Thanks. I think."

He was too busy to pay any attention to the dry response. He'd just discovered the knot at the back of her neck.

"I have to say, this dress is a considerable improvement over your flight suit."

"Somehow I suspected you'd think so."

"Do these straps untie?" He tugged on the knot. "Well, what do you know? The gods are smiling on me. They do."

Whoa! This was going way too fast. Tess put a hand on his chest and pushed. It was like pushing against a solid, muscled wall.

"Quinn. Wait."

"Okay." He lifted his head and grinned down at her. "What am I waiting for?"

He looked as though he didn't have a worry in the world except getting her naked. He probably didn't, Tess thought wryly.

Suddenly, inexplicably, she didn't either.

It was probably a delayed adrenaline surge. A belated spike of excitement generated by the wild hours they'd shared on Namuoto. Whatever it was, it took Tess straight past cautious and hesitant to hungry. Going up on tiptoe, she slid her palms up the smooth planes of his chest and wrapped them around his neck.

"This, big guy. You're waiting for this."

He was more than willing to let her pull his mouth down to hers. This time she was the one who angled her head. She found his tongue with hers. She started the mating dance that soon had them locked together once more.

And, when her nerves were on fire and her belly tight with hunger, she snared a hand in his towel and tugged it loose. It pooled at his feet, cool and damp. Quinn filled her hand, hot and hard.

She tipped her head back, laughter in her eyes. "You sure you didn't pull a hitch in the military yourself, Quinn? You certainly spring to attention fast enough every time I touch you."

"I've never been frisked by anyone like you, Hamilton. You're— Ah!—" his breath hissed in as she slid her hand down his satiny length "—good at it," he finished through gritted teeth. "Very good."

"I get better with practice," she murmured, her own breath coming fast as he swelled in her hand.

She drew his head down again, locking her mouth on his while she tormented him—and herself—with slow, gliding strokes. A sweet, seductive feeling of power swept over her, fanning the heat already crawling through her veins. She reveled in the heady sensation…until Quinn abruptly reversed their roles.

"My turn."

Naked and proud as an ancient warrior claiming his prize, he swept her into his arms. She formed a fleeting impression of a sitting room decorated in rattan. Of cushions covered in red hibiscus jungle print. Of a bedroom dominated by a king-size bed on a raised platform.

Somewhere en route to the bed Tess lost one of her shoes. It took Quinn only a few seconds to deposit her on the mattress and dispose of the other, along with the knot tying the straps of her halter. He peeled her dress down to her waist, skimming the tips of her breasts as he did. Her nipples tingled at the touch, and hardened to tight little buds when he teased them with his teeth and tongue.

Tess arched under him, gasping as streaks of pure sensation shot from her breasts to her belly. Her womb clenched tight, so tight she raised up eagerly to let him work the hot-pink dress over her hips.

"Oh, baby…"

His awed reverence had Tess fighting a grin. "What is this thing you have about lace panties, Quinn?"

"It's called appreciation."

His hot gaze swept from the flat plane of her

stomach to the hair tumbling down around her shoulders.

"Do you have any idea how gorgeous you are?"

Now that, she decided, was exactly what every girl needed to hear after spending thirty-six-plus hours in heavy boots and a hot, sweaty flight suit. Smiling, she traced a fingertip along his jaw.

"You're not so bad yourself without all those bristles."

Not bad at all.

His hand made a slow trip from her breasts to her belly. She thought he'd hook a finger in her panties and pull them down over her hips. Instead, he slid his hand under the elastic waistband and found the damp folds between her legs.

Within moments, she was wet and gushing. Moments more, and she was ready, so ready.

"Quinn!" she gasped. "Any time now..."

"Yes, ma'am." His grin was wicked as he withdrew his hand and stretched out beside her. "We're here to serve. Just let me get some protection for you."

Tess decided not to tell him she'd brought her own. She always carried a condom in her purse, just in case. It had probably dried out and cracked months ago. Work had been seriously impinging on her love life.

But things were looking up considerably, she decided when he'd sheathed himself and kneed apart her legs. His whiskey-colored eyes smiled down at her as he positioned himself at her hot, wet center.

"Who woulda thunk it, Hamilton? You. Me. About to fire another missile."

"You're not supposed to make me laugh when I'm in this position! You're supposed to... Oh!"

A single thrust of his hips brought him inside her. Tess hooked her calves around his and took him eagerly, greedily. Hips lifting, muscles clenching, she strained against him.

His hard, sure strokes brought her swirling close to the edge. Pleasure spread through her in waves, surging, receding, pounding in again. Muscles clenching, she clamped her legs around him.

Burying his hands in her hair, he covered her mouth with his and quickened the rhythm. He drove into her now, one stroke after another, until Tess couldn't hold the crashing waves back any longer. Arching her back, she let the pleasure slam through her.

Quinn held himself rigid while she climaxed. Only after she'd drifted down from her high and lay limp in his arms did he pick up the rhythm once again. Slowly at first, then faster, until the friction and the incredible, glorious woman under him pulled a groan from the back of his throat and every ounce of strength from his body.

Since Quinn hadn't eaten and Tess had consumed only a couple of slices of cold pizza, he insisted on ordering from room service. While they waited for the broiled mahi-mahi, pineapple rice and white wine to be delivered, they got hot and sweaty again.

Only this time Tess was on top and Quinn was at the mercy of her busy hands and hot, clever mouth. The result was so spectacular and her ultimate climax so shattering that Tess abandoned her superior position to flop down at his side.

"I don't think I can ever move again. I *know* I can't get off this mattress."

"You don't have to," Quinn promised, dropping a kiss on her shoulder as he rolled out of bed to answer the knock on the outer door. "We'll have dinner here."

While he padded across the room to retrieve his towel, Tess cradled her head on her bent arm. The man had one tight set of buns, she decided. Tight and neat and intriguingly pale where his tan lines ended.

He also had one helluva technique. She was trying to remember exactly how she'd ended up naked and in his bed when all she'd been intending to do was get his chop on the report and…

Oh, Lord! The report. She'd forgotten all about the damned thing.

"Quinn," she called when the front door closed behind the room-service attendant. "Bring my purse in here with you, would you?"

He rolled it in on the cart loaded with covered dishes.

"Here."

Tossing her the straw clutch, he lifted the stainless-steel domes and sniffed appreciatively. "I've probably eaten every fish known to man in every hotel in the Pacific Rim, but no one—*no one*—does mahi-mahi better than the chef at the Outrigger."

As if to echo his sentiment, Tess's stomach gave a long, loud rumble. They'd eat first, she decided, then go over the details of the report. Setting the clutch aside, she curled her legs crosswise under her.

"Roll that cart over here where I can reach it."

Quinn obliged. Positioning the cart within easy reach of the bed, he dragged over a chair for himself and set to work on the cork in the wine. Tess found herself watching the towel wrapped low around his hips, wondering if the knot would come loose, hoping it would.

"So how did you get into the cop business?"

She dragged her gaze from his lap. "It was either law enforcement or aircraft maintenance when I joined up. Since I don't know one end of a wrench from another, I opted for a badge."

"No prior experience?"

"Nope."

The cork gave with a pop. Quinn filled two glasses and passed one to her.

"What do your folks think about your chosen profession?"

"My folks died in a plane crash when I was two. My grandfather raised me."

The pain she hadn't quite grown used to clutched at her heart. She missed Big Mike so much. His big, booming laughter. His sense of adventure. His endless store of war stories.

"I think my grandfather was prouder than I was the day I graduated from basic," she murmured. "He served, too."

"In the air force?"

"The Marine Corps. He was an aviator."

She took a sip of her wine, letting the fruity white glide down her throat while memories of her grandfather filled her thoughts. When she looked up, Quinn was watching her with a small, satisfied smile, as if he'd just solved a riddle.

"Your grandfather flew Corsairs, didn't he? In the South Pacific."

"Why would you think that?"

"Just a guess."

"Based on what?"

"A gut feel. I knew there was some reason you took this mission to recover the pilot's remains so personally."

His insight unnerved her. She didn't think she'd laid herself so open. Setting aside her wine, she picked up her fork and played with the mahi-mahi. Soft and succulent, the fish flaked under the tines.

"Well?" he asked. "Was I right?"

She lifted her gaze and locked on his. "Yes, my grandfather flew Corsairs during the war in the South Pacific. And yes, I took this recovery mission personally. That could have been his wingman up there on that mountain, Quinn. His squadron mate. So you understand why I don't particularly like the idea of you cashing in on his story."

"Back to that, are we?"

He, too, set aside his wine. His face was serious when he leaned across the table.

"I'm a journalist, Tess. That's my job. Like you,

I get paid for what I do. In my case, I get paid well.''

"So you're going to sensationalize this story and splash it across the front pages?"

"Give me some credit! I was there. I heard the band strike up the Marine Corps Hymn. I saw the flags flying. Do you think I wasn't as choked up as the rest of you when those marines carried that casket off the plane?"

"How could anyone tell what you were feeling? You had your camera to your face the whole time."

He raked a hand through his hair. "Why don't you wait until you read the article in tomorrow's papers before you pass judgment?"

"Tomorrow's papers?" Her fork clattered down beside her plate. "You mean you've already filed your story?"

"What did you think I'd do? Sit on it until it's old news?"

"I thought you'd at least have the decency to wait until Dr. Courtland and her team identified the remains and notified any surviving next of kin!"

"Gimme a break, Hamilton. I know what I'm doing."

"Yeah, I guess you do."

Shoving the cart to one side, Tess yanked the

sheet free of the mattress, wrapped the wrinkled cotton tight under her arms, and stood up.

"My boss sent me here tonight to make sure your report of the events on Namuoto didn't contain any glaring inconsistencies or differ substantially from ours. Since you've already filed your story, I guess it's a moot point. Now if you'll excuse me…"

She intended to sweep past him, grab her clothes, and march into the bathroom. He blocked her with a single sidestep.

"You want to run that by me one more time?"

"Which part needs repeating?"

"The part about your boss sending you here."

Her chin came up. She couldn't believe she'd tumbled into bed with an insensitive, opportunistic voyeur who filtered everything through a camera lens.

"What?" she jeered. "Did you think I came up here just to sample your admittedly spectacular bedroom technique? You're good, Quinn. Damned good. But not good enough."

His jaw locked. Hooking a finger in the sheet, he jerked her toward him. "I didn't hear any complaints a few minutes ago."

"Let me rephrase that. You're good in bed. And a sonuvabitch out of it."

Yanking the sheet free of his hold, she stalked past him. She was in and out of the bathroom in five minutes. Quinn still stood beside the cart, looking every bit as angry as Tess felt. She scooped her straw clutch bag off the bed and flipped it open. Her mouth set, she held out a sheaf of papers.

"Here's a copy of our initial report. It went over the wires a few hours ago. Let's hope it agrees with your story."

"Hold on a minute. I want to be sure I have this right. The air force has already sent in its version of what happened, yet you're pissed at me because I filed my story?"

"We're required by regulation to do an initial report of any international incident within twenty-four hours."

"Yeah, well, my deadlines are just as tight."

"Ask me what I think of you and your deadlines, Quinn."

"I don't have to. You've made your opinion abundantly clear."

Since he didn't seem inclined to take the report, she tossed it on the bed.

"Don't call me," she said by way of good-bye, "and I won't call you."

* * *

Quinn watched her leave, his jaw so tight he thought it would crack. He'd never met a woman who could rile him and rouse him at the same time.

She'd just about wrung him inside out with her busy hands and mouth. Then, when he was still feeling the aftershocks, she hit him again with that slam about his professional ethics.

Well, Ms. High-and-Mighty Sergeant Teresa Hamilton had one thing right. He damned well wouldn't call her. But that didn't mean she'd heard the last from him.

Stalking to the bedside phone, Quinn punched the number for the front desk. The sweet young thing who'd gone out of her way to make him feel welcome during his weeks at the Outrigger answered.

"Hi, Petey. What can I do for you?"

"I need a wake-up call for 5:00 a.m., sweetheart."

"You got it."

"And two copies of the *L.A. Times* delivered to my room by five-thirty."

"I'm not sure..."

"The Pacific edition hits the newsstands around four. You should have the hotel copies soon after that."

"Okay, I'll see what I can do."

"Good girl."

Rolling the table to his chair, Quinn polished off both helpings of mahi-mahi. The wine he left in the bottle. He wanted a clear head for what he had to do in the morning.

His stomach full, he dragged off the towel wrapped around his hips and dropped into bed. The sheets still held Tess's scent and the faint, sweet spoor of their lovemaking. Quinn fell into sleep with his face buried in the pillow and Tess Hamilton in his thoughts.

Chapter 7

Both roommates were home when Tess arrived back at their shared condo. Lani gave her a hug and a warm, welcoming smile. Joanna interrupted her scan of the contents of the refrigerator to hook an arm over the door and survey her roommate from head to toe.

"Okay, kiddo. Report. When did you get back from Namuoto and why are you looking like you just ran over the neighbor's pet schnauzer?"

"I got back this morning and it's not a schnauzer I wish I'd run over."

"Oh-oh. I smell man trouble."

Joanna popped the refrigerator door shut. The tall, sun-streaked blonde moved with the grace of a natural athlete. More than once, Tess and Lani had considered taking the scissors to her Spandex running shorts and sports bras. No woman should be allowed to look as good as this one did after a ten-mile run.

The fact that Joanna also had a love life that made her rooomates feel as though they'd just finished a long stretch on the dark side of the moon didn't help matters, either. Joanna went through more men than a virus.

Dropping into a chair, she draped her long, tanned legs over the arm. "All right, girl. Tell Auntie Jo. Who put that scowl on your face and why?"

Tess sank onto the couch with a sigh, kicked off her sandals, and propped her bare feet on the coffee table. "His name's Quinn. Pete Quinn."

Lani's dark eyes rounded. "The photojournalist?"

"You know him?"

"I've seen his work."

Since the petite brunette was a military photographer, Tess supposed she shouldn't be surprised.

"He's good," Lani said in a tone that bordered on reverence. "Really good. The story he sent back from Al Sharif last year won all kinds of awards.''

"He's also a self-serving, opportunistic jerk."

"Aw, cm'on," Joanna put in with a grin. "Don't hold back. Tell us what you really think about the guy."

"What I really think would take all night."

"All right. Give us the condensed version. Tell us how he got you into bed."

Tess's feet hit the floor with a plop. "What makes you think he did?"

"Oh, I don't know. It might be that thoroughly kissed look you're wearing. Or the fact that you've got your dress on inside out."

"What?"

She looked down at the wild pink print. It looked right-side out to her. Flipping up the hem, she examined the other side. Sure enough, the print was darker on the inside, but she was damned if she could see how Joanna had noticed the difference.

"You're wearing the tag on the outside of your strap," her roommate pointed out sweetly. "Not a big deal, you understand. I've come home with a few tags showing myself. But it does make one wonder..."

"Okay, okay. I had sex with the guy. That's all it was. Hot, meaningless sex."

The other two women exchanged glances, which told Tess she'd made her point a tad too vehemently. Deliberately, she tempered both her tone and her expression. She wasn't ready to admit those mind-blowing hours she'd spent in Pete Quinn's arms had constituted more than just sex. That he'd made her laugh at his silly jokes and almost weep with pleasure.

"I met him on Namuoto," she told the other two, knowing they'd never let her hit the sack until they'd wormed every detail out of her. "He was there researching a story and we sort of blew up a mountain."

Retelling the tale for the third or fourth time that day drained the last of Tess's reserves.

"I've got to get some sleep. I'm exhausted."

"I would be, too," Joanna purred. "Sounds like this dude you picked up on Namuoto is hot stuff."

"He certainly thinks so."

With that tart observation, Tess dragged herself off the couch and headed for her room. A quick shower washed away the residue of several hours of lovemaking. A thorough workout with her toothbrush almost—*almost!*—removed the taste of white wine and Quinn.

Pulling on a sleeveless, well-washed Phoenix Raven T-shirt cut off just below her breasts, she cracked the lanai door open to let in the breeze and dropped into bed. She expected sleep to come crashing down the moment she closed her eyes. Instead, the image of Quinn's clean-shaven face imprinted itself on her eyelids.

Damn the man, anyway. Why couldn't he possess even a few scruples? Tess knew the story about the recovered remains was a tear-jerker, sure to appeal to his readers. Still, after spending so many hours with the recovery team, Quinn should have gained a real appreciation for the sanctity of their mission. The bits of bone they'd brought home weren't just a story. They were all that remained of a living, breathing man, a marine who'd served his country and died in a fiery crash.

Angry and frustrated and bitterly disappointed in one Pete Quinn, Tess rolled over and thumped her pillow with a fist.

Damn the man, anyway!

The insistent buzz of the doorbell dragged her from sleep some hours later.

Grunting, Tess raised her head and peered

bleary-eyed at the sliding glass doors to the lanai. Dew from the ocean breeze misted the glass. Weak, hazy light filtered in through the open crack. It was morning, but just barely.

Turning her head, Tess squinted at the clock on the nightstand. Oh, God! It wasn't even 6:00 a.m. With a groan, she dropped her face back into the pillow. Her roommates could deal with whoever was at the front door.

She heard the flop of bare feet on the parquet floor. Joanna's cool voice raised in inquiry. The sound of the chain rattling off the slide.

She listened a moment more. There were no screams. No shouts. Nothing to rouse the cop in her.

She went back to sleep.

The next thing she knew, something fat and hard whacked her in the butt.

Her face came out of the pillow, her body twisted and her feet hit the floor all in one lithe spring. Shoving back her tangled hair, Tess stared in disbelief at the male facing her across the bed.

"Quinn!"

"'Morning, Hamilton."

Blinking the last vestiges of sleep from her mind, she took in the shoulders stretching the seams of a white knit shirt, the jeans riding low on lean hips, and the rolled newspaper in his right fist.

Fire came into her eyes. "Did you just smack me with that newspaper?"

"I did."

"Care to tell me why?"

"It seemed appropriate."

"You'll have to do better than that," she warned in a low growl. "Assuming you want to walk out of here with the same basic equipment you walked in with, that is."

A speculative gleam came into his eye. He slapped the newspaper against his open palm and issued a soft challenge.

"You're not wearing your riot gear, Red. Think you can take me?"

"I know I can."

A muffled sound from the door spun Tess around. Her accusing glance went to Joanna, who paid not the slightest attention to it, then to Lani, goggle-eyed and standing on tiptoe to peer over her roommate's shoulder.

"Did you let this jerk in?" Tess demanded.

"I did," the blonde replied breezily.

"Why?"

"He's got great buns."

Quinn shot her an amused look. "Thanks."

"You're welcome."

His amusement deepened. "You sound as though you might be an expert on the subject."

"I am. Believe me, I am."

"Excuse me." Ice dripped from Tess's voice. "Could you two take this conversation into the other room? Some of us would like to get some sleep here."

"I've got a better idea." Grinning, Joanna nudged Lani away from the door. "Lani and I will go put on a pot of coffee while you and Pete finish *your* conversation."

Pete. It hadn't taken Joanna long to get to his first name. Petey couldn't be far behind. Thoroughly irritated, Tess crossed her arms.

"Okay, what's all this about?"

He took a while to reply. Long enough for his gaze to make a slow trip from her tangled hair to the slice of bare midriff under her cut-off T-shirt to the sensible cotton panties she'd pulled on after her quick shower last night. They were *not* of the lace thong variety.

"This is about you," he said at last. "And me."

"There is no you and me."

"There was last night."

"Last night was fun, Quinn. The first part of it,

anyway. What came after our little roll in the sack kind of ruined things for me.''

"Yeah, I got that impression.''

He tossed the newspaper down on the rumpled sheets.

"Lead story, front page, continued on 7A. Read it, Hamilton.''

She seriously considered picking up the paper and tossing the damned thing over the lanai railing. She was in no mood to see the story about the as-yet-unidentified Corsair pilot splashed across the front page.

"Read it, Hamilton.''

"If that's what it takes to get you out of my bedroom,'' she muttered.

Giving in with something less than graciousness, she plopped down on the bed and unrolled the paper. The picture that leaped out at her had her gritting her teeth.

It was a profile of her, her automatic weapon to her cheek, pumping out a steady stream of fire. Dirt and sweat streaked her face. Her hair was a mess. The Phoenix Raven insignia stood out in stark relief on her blue beret, but that was the only thing in the picture that looked good.

She threw Quinn a withering glance. "Couldn't you have picked out a more flattering shot?''

"That one told the story I wanted. Read the text that goes with it."

Jaw tight, she started the first paragraph. The prose was stark, the descriptions of her team and their mission terse and unnervingly accurate.

Quinn had done his homework in the short hours after they'd touched down in Hawaii, Tess saw. No doubt he'd pulled most of the information about the Phoenix Ravens off the Internet. However he'd come by the facts and figures, he'd used them to good effect. Those first few paragraphs painted a dramatic picture of the air force's supercops.

Pulled into the story despite herself, Tess turned to page 7A. The pictures there were of the recovery team. Dr. Courtland with her blue steel Beretta in hand. The lieutenant rendering honors over a flag-draped casket in the belly of a C-130. The weary orthodontist carrying what was left of his gear to the crew bus after the mission.

The accompanying text went into detail about the mission, and the organization and operation of the Central Identification Lab. The article included profiles of the staff, statistics on the number of open cases they were still working, and poignant examples of field recoveries they'd conducted.

What it didn't include, Tess belatedly realized, was information or speculation about the remains they'd brought back from Namuoto. Quinn hadn't even mentioned the F-4 Corsair or the victim's branch of service.

Chewing on her lower lip, Tess read the last few paragraphs. By the time she'd finished them, the suspicion that she'd made a world-class fool of herself last night had morphed into absolute certainty. She blew out a long breath, closed the newspaper and looked up.

"I owe you an apology."

"Yeah, you do. You also owe me a follow-up."

"What?"

"My editor loved the piece on the Phoenix Ravens. Cops are hot right now. Military cops get double points. He wants a more detailed feature story on the training you go through and the kind of missions you fly. I put in a request last night to have you assigned as my liaison. It came back approved this morning."

Tess's jaw dropped. "Already?"

"Already. Evidently blowing up a stash of Chinese Tweets gets the brass's attention. They were only too happy to expedite the request." His mouth kicked up in a smug grin. "You're mine, Hamilton, all mine."

"For how long?"

"For the next three weeks." His grin took on a

wicked tilt. "Maybe longer, if you promise to dump those cotton panties and wear only that little lace number you had on last night."

"Well…" Tess tapped a finger to her chin, considering his request. "Okay."

She had the sensible cotton briefs off in two or three wiggles. A quick wad and a long toss sent them sailing through the open doors of the lanai.

"Consider them dumped."

Laughter lit up his eyes. "You're a woman after my own heart."

"Funny, until five minutes ago, I didn't think you had one."

Oh, yeah, Quinn thought as he tugged his knit shirt up and over his head. He did. And if he wasn't real careful, he just might lose it to a green-eyed, gun-toting GI Jane.

Epilogue

Three weeks and five months later, Tess stood beside Quinn on a windswept ridge overlooking the National Memorial Cemetery of the Pacific.

The cemetery occupied the center of Punchbowl Crater. The crater was formed from an extinct volcano known as Puowaina, Hawaiian for Hill of Sacrifice. Local legend had it that the Punchbowl was the site of many secret burials of Hawaiian royalty. It had also supposedly witnessed the sacrifice of offenders of certain taboos. Now it served as the final resting place for veterans of the Second World War, Korea, Vietnam and the Gulf War.

Tess couldn't imagine a more serene site for a

national cemetery. The city of Honolulu sparkled like a jewel below, hemmed in on three sides by Oahu's steep green hills. Beyond the city, the Pacific rolled in on turquoise waves. She needed only to turn a few inches to the right to pick out Pearl Harbor and the glistening white Arizona Memorial. The sight tugged at her heart, as it always did.

Slipping her arm through Quinn's, she brought her gaze back to the lush park below. The cemetery was so beautiful in its breath-taking simplicity. Only a round, flat expanse of green dotted with trees, a soaring marble monument, and wide stairs flanked on either side by the ten Courts of Honor—monuments to the thousands of Americans still listed as missing in action.

After today, there'd be one less name on the list.

She and Quinn didn't intrude on the solemn ceremony taking place at the base of the marble steps. This time belonged to the family of the man whose remains had been positively identified, and who was now, at long last, being laid to rest among his fallen comrades. His son was there, mourning for the father he'd known only through faded photographs. His grandchildren and great-grandchildren as well.

Tess stood silent, her throat tight and her thoughts on her grandfather. Big Mike would have liked Quinn. Tess certainly did, now that she'd come to know him better. In fact, she was pretty sure she was going to marry him. He'd asked her twice, the last time with just a hint of impatience.

She'd already admitted that she loved him. Several times. Once even out loud. He'd pounced on that like a dog on a steak bone and had started making plans to permanently move her into his bed. Not that they'd occupy it at the same time all that much. His job took him on the road almost as much as Tess's did. Where they slept didn't matter, though. No matter where she and Quinn had met these past five months or how long they'd had together before one of them had to jump on a plane again, they were home.

A little curl of warmth spread through her veins. She squeezed Quinn's arm. When he glanced down at her, she answered the question in his eyes with a soft whisper.

"Yes."

"Does that mean what I think it does?"

"If you're thinking wedding rings and honeymoons, it does."

His smile melted her heart. His hand right hand closed over the one she'd tucked in the crook of his left arm. Together, they turned their faces to the wind and their attention to the ceremony unfolding below.

* * * * *

COMRADES IN ARMS
Lindsay McKenna

* * *

To the men and women of our armed forces,
our National Guard and those in reserve service—
thank you for giving us the freedom that we enjoy.

Dear Reader,

It is an honor to be asked to create a story for the second military anthology in Silhouette history! Participating with Merline Lovelace and Candace Irvin makes this book special for me because we all served our country. Our services might have been different, but our hearts beat to the same patriotic tune. I'm very proud to be a part of this collection with my "sisters" from the military services.

Freedom should never be taken for granted. I have traveled the world over—Canada, Europe, Japan, Hong Kong, China, Australia, New Zealand and South America—and I now know what we have in the U.S.A. is something to cherish with our lives. I wish we could invite people of all countries to our own, to live here and experience firsthand the life that freedom bestows upon human beings.

"Comrades in Arms" is a story about hope. Set in Afghanistan, it shows how kindness and generosity can open up even the most tightly closed doors between very different people. I hope you enjoy it.

Sincerely,

Lindsay McKenna

Chapter 1

"Dave," Morgan Trayhern said, a note of warning in his tone, "I know you don't want a woman on your Special Forces team going into Afghanistan, but it can't be helped. No one on your team speaks Pashto, or any of the other dialects of that country." Running his fingers through his silver-flecked dark hair, Morgan eyed Captain Dave Johnson, who was looking very grim and unhappy as he stood before him in the small office at Fort Campbell, Kentucky, home of the Special Forces.

"Sir, with all due respect," Dave said, opening his hand in a plea, "she—"

"Captain Tara McCain."

"Er…yes, sir. *Her*… Well, this is unprecedented."

"So was 9-11," Morgan growled. He looked at his watch. In another five minutes, he had to leave and go help prep another Special Forces team that would soon be on its way to Afghanistan. It was September 29th, and the U.S. military had geared up to go after al-Qaeda who had been behind the attack on the World Trade Towers in New York City eighteen days ago.

"Yes, sir, I know…."

"Captain, you'll be meeting McCain on the tarmac in exactly thirty minutes. You'll be flying by Air Force C–141 Lockheed Starlifter to Afghanistan. Once you land, you'll be taken by CH53 Super Sea Stallion helicopter to a remote mountain village known as Tarin Kowt. There's a hotbed of Taliban there, along with U.S.-friendly Pashtun Afghan people. Your job is to get the leaders to tell you who is in the Taliban, who is in sympathy with Osama bin Laden, and where they are. You are then to call in air strikes or anything else you think appropriate, to either capture them or kill them. We want prisoners if at all possible. Without an interpreter, you are dead in the water, and we both know it. Now, Captain McCain has worked for

Perseus, my secret black ops company, which is linked to the CIA. She's a marathon runner. She has expertise in all weapons, up to and including the one you carry, the M–4 rifle. If you're worried about her keeping up, don't be. And if you're going to give me a hard time because she's a woman, you're barking up the wrong tree. Typically, in all our missions with Perseus, we have a male and a female teamed up to work together. Each gender brings its own unique qualities to the table—strengths that complement one another for the best success of any mission.''

Dave frowned as he held Trayhern's blazing blue eyes. When Morgan jabbed a finger in his direction, he almost felt it physically.

''I have years of studies showing that man-woman teams are a helluva lot more successful than same-gender ones. So get rid of your prejudice and get your team ready to rock. Got it?''

''Yes, sir, I do.''

Nodding, Morgan grunted, ''Good luck, Captain,'' and he reached out and shook the army officer's large, square hand. ''Bring everyone home safe and alive. Your families will be waiting for you.''

''Yes, sir,'' Dave muttered, releasing his hand. When Trayhern left, Dave scowled heavily and sat on the end of the olive-green metal desk, his arms folded against his chest. What was he going to do? He commanded the most elite of the U.S. Army's teams—a Special Forces A team. There had never been a woman on any of his missions—ever. He rubbed his wrinkled forehead. Dave understood why Tara McCain was coming along; they needed someone who spoke at least one of the major languages of Afghanistan. Now he wished mightily that he had taken advantage of the language classes the army had offered him two years ago, to learn Arabic. But he'd declined. What a fool he'd been.

Heaving a sigh, Dave acknowledged that his own actions and reactions toward McCain were going to determine how his ten-man team would respond to her. The urgency to get covert military teams on the ground in Afghanistan was paramount. Tiger 01, his team, had been given a plum assignment, and no one wanted to settle the score with the perpetrators more than his men. Thousands of innocent civilians had died in the attack on the World Trade Towers. Dave closed his fist, wanting to extract his own personal revenge.

It was 1500. His men were waiting for him at the operations area, near the tarmac where a huge Air Force C–141 was waiting to take the team and their supplies on the long, long journey to Afghanistan.

Pulling his dark green beret out of the epaulet on his left shoulder, Dave placed it on his head. The door was ajar, and he could hear frantic calls from other teams as they prepared to go to war. Dave slid off the edge of the desk, straightened his desert fatigues, and strode outside. It was time to meet this woman who was like an unspoken curse to his team.

Tara McCain stood just inside the Ops building, near the glass doors to the tarmac. Outside, a Starlifter was being hurriedly prepared for a number of Special Forces teams. Nervously, she licked her lower lip. Dressed in desert fatigues, her pack and rifle nearby, she waited. Morgan Trayhern had called her two days ago at the Pentagon, where she worked as an intelligence officer for the army. He'd begged her to go on this mission. How could she say no?

Tara watched the hundreds of men milling around in the terminal, their own packs and rifles resting on the shiny waxed floor. The din they made was low but constant. More than a few eyeballed her and she could see the question in their eyes: what was a *woman* doing here? Except for some of the air control and meteorology desk people, she was the only woman present. And she was the only woman dressed in combat clothes, so that made her stand out from the office personnel. Because her brown hair was short, those that glanced at her had to look hard to see that she was female. She knew that, at five foot nine inches tall, and weighing in at 140 pounds, she could probably pass for a man. The flak vest she wore over her fatigues effectively hid her breasts and other curves, so that, upon first inspection, she looked more like an eighteen-year-old youth than a twenty-seven-year-old woman.

From out of the crush of soldiers, Tara saw a man roughly six foot two inches tall coming toward her. His features were dark and set. He had narrowed green eyes, a square face, a crooked nose and a thinned mouth. His gaze was trained on her.

Instantly, her heart beat once in response to the searing look he was giving her. Dressed in battle fatigues, he wore a pistol around his waist, along with a tan web belt that contained essentials like extra magazines of bullets. The green beret shouted that he was one of the proud A team officers. Seeing the black embroidered captain's bars on his epaulets, Tara knew without a doubt this was her boss, Captain Dave Johnson, leader of Tiger 01. Her team. Her assignment.

As he slipped through the last barricade of men, Tara tried to brace herself. Johnson was clearly not a happy man. His mouth was pulled downward, his brow was furrowed and those thick black eyebrows were dipped in a V. Tara saw the warrior in this man as he walked purposefully toward her. He seemed more hunter than human. Still, she liked his eyes, even if they were narrowed. They were a beautiful forest-green, with huge black pupils, and she liked the alertness she saw in them. Widely spaced, they stood out against his darkly tanned, weathered features.

Out of habit, Tara's gaze flicked for a moment to his left hand. He wasn't wearing a wedding ring. But that didn't really mean anything; many men took off their rings on missions like this.

Girding herself, as he rapidly closed the distance between them, Tara ordered herself to relax, or at least appear that way even if her stomach was knotted. She reminded herself that she, too, was a captain, the same rank as Johnson, and that he did not have seniority over her. They would share the command, and Tara was glad of that. Judging from the thunderous look he was giving her, she guessed that anyone of a lesser rank he'd eat alive.

"Captain McCain?" Dave tried to keep his voice low and smooth, though he felt anything but calm. The large-boned woman before him was tall and proud looking, her shoulders thrown back. Morgan had told him that she would not advertise herself unduly as a woman for the duration of the mission. Dave could almost believe she could pass for a man, except for the soft fullness of her lips. And that was his undoing...her mouth. Even though she wore absolutely no makeup, Tara McCain was a damn good-looking woman, in his estimation. Her dark brown hair was cut short, hidden mostly by the red beret she wore. Her eyes were blue and thickly lashed and he found himself being pulled by her wide, arresting eyes as she looked up at him.

"Yes, I'm McCain," she answered, and offered her hand.

Dave halted, staring at her proffered hand. Her nails were blunt cut and he could see calluses on the palm. Still, she had a beautiful, graceful hand with long fingers. Mouth tightening, he reached out and gripped it. He was surprised at the returning strength. Okay, so she wasn't one of those cushy Pentagon types that never worked out.

"Dave Johnson. I'm the leader of Tiger 01."

"Nice to meet you." Well, maybe, Tara

thought, as she released his large, square hand. There was nothing pretty about Johnson, either in his face or his demeanor.

"I wish I could say the same."

"Excuse me?"

Dave stared down at her. He noted the steely glitter in her eyes, saw her mouth pursing with displeasure. "Look, I don't like this. I don't like the fact that I have to take a woman into a dangerous combat situation with my team, but I'm saddled with you. So we're going to make the best of it. My men are my family. We're tight and we've bonded over the years. You're a stranger walking into our unit, and I have to get you folded into my team's dynamic so we operate as one fluid machine. Got that?"

"Yeah, I got it, Captain."

Dave sighed and straightened. He dropped his hands on his hips and looked around, and then back at her. Anger was banked in her blue eyes. "Time's short, McCain, and I need to say a few things."

"Like you haven't already? Are you throwing down a red flag, Captain? You want me to pick it up? Maybe you're forgetting whose side I'm on. Well, you don't speak Pashto. I do. And I'm fluent in two other dialects of Afghanistan, not to men-

tion Farsi, the language of Iran. You won't have a
prayer of a chance without me acting as interpreter,
so if I were you, I'd be treating me far better and
with a lot more respect than you are presently. I
stand between you and the enemy, Captain. If you
can't understand the language, the only way you'll
know who's going to kill you is when they raise
their weapons in your direction, and by that time
it may be too late. So let's start again, shall we?
I'm not going to be bullied by you because you're
having a tizzy over a woman being on your all-
male team.''

Her low, husky voice flowed straight through all
the defenses Dave had erected. The blazing blue
of her eyes reminded him of Wyoming, where he'd
been raised. The sky over the Grand Tetons was
exactly that shade.

"Okay," he muttered defiantly, "so you aren't
the soft marshmallow I thought you were going to
be."

Tara almost smiled, but thought better of it.
"Don't count out marshmallows, either, Captain."

Managing a sour smile, he took a step back,
raised his head and looked around. "Okay," he
rasped, meeting her mutinous gaze, "I apologize,
Captain. I came on strong. Me and my team are

all uptight and eager to get the bastards who did this to our people.''

"Like I'm not?"

A sliver of a grin started. He swallowed it. Seeing the petulance and defiance in her oval face, those huge blue eyes slitted with silent rage, Dave realized she was a fighter, too. "Truce," he murmured, and held up his hand. "Okay?"

"We're on the same page, right? We're all going after the Taliban. We're a team. I'm going to dress like a man and keep my femininty subdued as best I can. I will be at your side at all times, Captain Johnson, when we interface with Afghan people. Right?"

"Right," Dave said, some of the anger going out of him. He looked down at her military pack and the M–4 rifle leaning against the wall nearby. "You ready to go?"

"Of course I am. How about you?"

Plucky. Feisty. A woman warrior. Okay, he could buy that. "Yeah, we're saddled up. All I'm waiting for is the Air Force loadmaster out there on the tarmac to give us the signal to board."

Tara eyed him warily. She saw his anger receding, replaced by open curiosity—about her. She wasn't too sure she wanted that kind of attention from him. Burned by another Special Forces offi-

cer in a relationship that had ended more than a
year ago, she had sworn never to get involved with
one again. Still, Dave Johnson was larger than life.
He had that kind of quiet, demanding charisma that
a good military leader possessed. It seemed to flow
naturally from him, and whether she liked it or not,
Tara was drawn to him. Unhappy with the stirring
in her heart, she tamped down her feelings. This
was not the time or place for such a thing. They
had an objective: locate the Taliban and destroy
them. Give Afghanistan back to the people, and
release the Afghan women from the terrible bond-
age they endured under that regime.

"Once we get on board, you and I need to go
over the mission briefing."

"Fine," she said.

"You ever been out in the field like this?"

"No."

"That's what I thought."

"It's not a sin, Captain."

"No, but it's a detriment to my team."

"I'll try not to be a pain in the arse to you."

"Oh, I have a feeling you're probably a pain in
the rear most of the time, Captain, but where we're
going, that may prove to be a positive."

"Glad you think so, Captain, because I won't

stand for insubordination from you or your enlisted men. Are we clear on that?''

''Don't worry,'' Dave said, ''my men will treat you like a sister.''

''I worry about *your* attitude, Captain.''

Shrugging, Dave said in a low tone, ''How I feel about you personally is never going to show out in the field, Ms. McCain. I can guarantee that.''

''Good, then we should land at Tarin Kowt one big, happy family, right?''

Grinning, Dave replied, ''Absolutely. But I don't think it will be too long before the village leaders realize you're a woman, even if you are wearing men's clothes.''

Tara knew that when they landed in Afghanistan, everyone would shed their military uniforms for local garb, so that they blended in. If they stood out they were much more likely to be spotted and shot by the Taliban.

''We'll have to take it as it comes,'' Tara growled back. ''I don't want to be targeted, either.''

''How do you think the local leaders will react to you being a woman?''

''Depends upon the leader. There's all kinds of attitudes and biases for and against women over there. Some who follow Islam treat women as equals, but they are few and far between.''

"Maybe we'll get lucky," Dave murmured.

"Let's hope so," she answered. "But I have my ways of getting through to people, Captain Johnson. If I need to, I'll get the man's attention and he will speak to me or else."

Dave could believe that. He saw the resolute look in her eyes, heard the determination in her voice. Minute by minute, he was being convinced that maybe, just maybe, this woman could handle herself. But she'd never seen combat, and that was a completely different situation.

"Are you leaving loved ones behind?" he asked. Maybe he shouldn't nose into her personal life, but it was eating at him. Did she have a significant other? Was she married? Dave knew little about her. He hadn't had time to read her file due to the speed and urgency of this mission.

"My parents live in New Hampshire. I was able to call them yesterday and tell them I was going undercover on a top secret mission, and that I'd contact them upon my return."

"I see… Any husband? Kids?"

"None of the above, Captain Johnson." Tara saw an emotion flicker across his face. Relief? No, that couldn't be. Why a look of relief? That didn't make sense to her. "What about you?" she challenged.

"Me? I'm from Wyoming. My parents own a cattle ranch that butts up against the Grand Teton Mountains. Ever been in that state?" He saw her face thaw. Tara was very attractive when she wasn't giving him that sour look. Of course, Dave realized, he was the one who'd put that expression on her face.

"Yes, mountain climbing is a hobby of mine." She held up her hands, showing him the calluses on her palms.

"That explains why your nails are short and your hands strong," he murmured, almost to himself.

"It does, doesn't it?"

Smart mouth. Plucky. He liked that. And he liked her a helluva lot more than he should. Scalded two years ago by a messy divorce, Dave had sworn off women in general. Rubbing his chest above his heart, he stated, "Well, where we're going, there's plenty of mountains."

"I hope your men are trained for them?"

He swallowed another smile. Now she was challenging *him*. "We've done some work in mountains, Captain McCain. I think we'll be able to keep up with you should we have to climb the face of one.''

It was her turn to smile, and her grin was wolfish, as if to say, *Gotcha!* ''Okay,'' she drawled, ''we'll see, when and if the time comes.''

''Is this show and tell time?'' He held out his hands to her, palms up.

Tara couldn't help but laugh. His palms were covered with thick calluses denoting how much time he'd spent roughing it out in nature. It was obvious he'd done his own share of mountain climbing.

Her laughter was like sweet, warm honey pouring into his heart. Surprised at the sensation, he caught himself smiling in return.

''Maybe you aren't going to be such a pain in the rear,'' he murmured.

''I was thinking the same thing about you, Captain Johnson.''

Chapter 2

Exhaustion pulled at Tara as she trotted through the hazy gold dusk of their first Afghanistan sunset. She was following on the heels of Dave Johnson, who was setting a helluva pace toward the village of Tarin Kowt. The CH-53 Sea Stallion had just disgorged them, and the billowing yellow dust churned up by the rotor blades as the aircraft took off practically choked them all. Dave had told Tara to tie her green bandana around her nose and mouth. Feeling a little stupid when she realized all the men on his team had done so already, she quickly covered her face and found relief from the suffocating dust.

Ahead, Tara could see several men coming out
to meet them from a large village of square mud-
hut homes. They all wore turbans and were dressed
in colorful, voluminous long-sleeved shirts, with
bandoliers of ammunition across their chests, and
dark-colored pants with leather boots. Each of
them had a rifle at the ready. Dave slowed a little,
raising his hand and gesturing for her to move up
to the front with him. Surging ahead, Tara followed him easily, until the rest of the team was
spread out in a semicircle. Directly behind her was
the radioman, Private Doug Seabert, of Tallahas-
see, Florida. He carried the most advanced communications gear in the world on his broad back
and thick shoulders.

Dave saw an older man wearing a cream-colored
turban, his white beard neatly trimmed, standing in
the middle of the awaiting party. He was probably
the ruling war lord or chieftain of this village.
Swallowing his fear, Dave wondered how these
men would respond to Tara. In the deepening dusk,
everyone's face was hidden in shadows, so it
would be difficult to identify her as a woman. She
had a low, husky voice that reminded him of aged,
mellow whiskey. Still, they weren't trying to hide
the fact that Tara was a woman, but they didn't
want to call attention to it.

Glancing to his right, he saw her move with fluid ease at his side, her M–4 in her hands, just in case. He'd been told that the warlord of the village, Chieftain Khalid Zaher, was anti-Taliban, and that he was also one of the most forward-thinking of the men who ran the country. Dave hoped so. Would he accept Tara as an interpreter? That would be their first huge test on this mission.

Pulling up, Dave raised his hand. His team automatically gathered in a circle around him as he halted a few feet from the group of Afghans. Seeing the suspicion in their eyes, he pinned his hopes on Chief Zaher, who was frowning directly at him.

"McCain?" Dave ordered. "Talk to them." He wouldn't use her first name; it would be a dead giveaway. In the military, the practice of using last names was common, anyway.

Swallowing, Tara stepped boldly forward. Dave noted that she was the same height as the thin, bearded leader, who stood with his arms crossed against his chest.

"*Salaam,*" she said, and then touched her brow, lips and heart, a respectful greeting for a person of the Islamic faith. Even though she wasn't a Muslim herself, the greeting would go far in setting the right tone.

Tara feared the leader would not like the fact that she was a woman. However, her face was coated with yellow dust and the bandana across her lower face and nose effectively hid the rest of her features.

"Ah, someone who speaks Pashto," Zaher said, and returned the age-old greeting.

Relief swept through Tara. Zaher seemed delighted, his chocolate-brown eyes dancing. "Chieftain Zaher, I'm the interpreter for this Special Forces A team. Our chief—" she motioned to Dave, who was standing at her shoulder, his M–4 pointed downward as a show of no hostility "—Captain Dave Johnson, has come to help you and your men make Tarin Kowt safe once more from the Taliban."

A booming laugh erupted from Khalid. The rest of his men joined in.

"Indeed? Well, we have just routed them from our humble village once again. They know that I hate them and their ways. We have been fighting them almost daily for years, to keep them out of here. They believe that our women are not to be educated and are only broodmares to advance our race." He turned his head and spat into the yellow dust at his feet.

From behind the half-dozen Afghans, Tara saw

another soldier appear. Blinking, she realized it was a young woman, very tall and thin. She was dressed exactly like the men.

"Ah, here is my daughter." Zahir held out his hand in her direction. "Come, Halima, come and let me introduce you to the men who are going to help us rout the Taliban once and for all...."

Dave blinked twice. He saw Tara give him a look of surprise. He swallowed his own reaction. The woman was dressed exactly like the chieftain's soldiers. She had bandoliers of ammunition crisscrossing her chest and the voluminous clothing she wore hid the fact that she was a woman. The only giveaway was her long, black hair, which flowed from beneath the white turban on her head.

"Halima Zaher. Freedom fighter for the true Afghanistan," Khalid proudly announced. "My eldest daughter fights at my side and risks her life so that the women of our village remain free to be educated, and not hidden in their houses as if in prison. Halima, meet McCain and Captain Johnson."

Halima bowed respectfully, grasping the old rifle in her long, thin fingers. "We welcome you to our land," she murmured.

Tara grinned, but no one could see it beneath her bandana. If the chieftain allowed his daughter to fight, he wasn't going to have a problem with her being a woman, either. Pulling off the bandana, she held Khalid's limpid gaze. "Just as your daughter fights for the true Afghanistan, the U.S. Army also allows me, Captain Tara McCain, to come and help your efforts, as well."

Chuckling, Khalid looked down at his daughter, who stood proudly at his side. "Ah, this is good! I have told Halima that the USA military has women in it. She did not believe me! Now she must."

Tara rapidly translated all that had been said. Relief was clearly etched in Dave's eyes.

"Ask the chieftain if we may come into his village," he told her. "We'll need accommodations. Ask him if my men can stay in his people's homes. Tell him we want to get out of our U.S. military gear and we'll need Afghan clothing. We'll pay for everything."

Tara translated all that to Zaher, who nodded.

"Yes, yes. Come, it is nearing darkness. You must be tired and hungry. We have little, but what we have, we share with you." He turned and gave rapid orders to his soldiers, who in turn went to Dave's men and gestured for them to follow.

Tara said, "Khalid will have each of his men take one of our team to a different house, to be fed, given space to sleep, and provided with Afghan clothing.''

''Great. Where are we going?''

Tara turned back to the chieftain. ''My chief would like to speak with you at length tonight. Will that be possible? There is much to discuss, honored Zaher.''

''Of course,'' Khalid said. ''Come, you two will share our humble house and food.'' He turned to Halima. ''I will allow you, my daughter, to find suitable men's clothing for Captain McCain.''

''Yes, my father, I would be more than honored to do so.''

Dave felt exhaustion pulling at him. Khalid's home was a bit larger than most, but then, he was a warlord, and very rich by most Afghan standards. There was one extra room available and it housed his weapons. They had dined on dates, goat's milk cheese, dried fruit and fragrantly spiced rice with lamb. Tara had remained at Dave's side at all times. The chieftain had his entire family, children included, sit around them in a semicircle in the carpeted living room, resting on large, colorful silk pillows with gold tassels. Huge silver platters of food had been set on the burgundy Oriental carpet. The servants who attended were quick, silent and respectful as one course after another was presented. Tara had whispered to Dave that if he didn't eat well, Khalid would be offended.

Rubbing his stomach because he'd overeaten, Dave finally saw the chieftain raise his hand. Everyone in Khalid's family, including his wife, Fazila, left them. Silence fell in the room after they had left. Khalid lit a pipe and smoked it for several minutes.

"Chief Johnson does not smoke?" he inquired, when Dave declined the pipe Khalid offered him.

Tara shook her head. "No, he doesn't, my lord."

"Pity. A good smoke after a good meal is like rain to the parched land."

"Yes, my lord."

"And was your leader satisfied with my humble meal?"

Tara grimaced inwardly. She turned to Dave and said, "Burp."

"What?" Dave replied with a frown.

"I said burp. You know, belch?"

He gave her a strange look. "Why?"

"Because in their culture, it's considered a sign that you liked the meal if you belch. Now, fake it if you have to, but do it. He's asking if you enjoyed his hospitality."

Dave kept his face carefully neutral. He placed his hand over his stomach and forced out a big belch. Instantly, Khalid smiled, making his dark, lined face look much younger than before.

"Excellent, excellent," the chieftain murmured. He put the pipe down on a silver tray and then drew himself up.

Tara forced a belch as well. Khalid nodded deferentially to her, a pleased look on his face.

"May we talk of why we're here?" she asked the chieftain.

"Yes, talk is welcome now, Captain McCain."

Tara launched into the game plan Dave had gone over with her on the C-141 as they flew long, endless hours from the U.S. to Afghanistan. She roughly sketched out what the team was here to do: locate Taliban and either capture them, which was their preference, or kill them. Most of all, the team wanted to learn where the regional leaders were hiding. She explained that Dave would need the close support, guidance and help of the chief and his men to accomplish all these things.

Dave enjoyed the low, mellow sounds of Pashto spilling effortlessly from Tara's lips. In the flickering light of the oil lamp, he could see she was tired. From where he sat, he could see dark circles beginning to appear beneath her glorious blue eyes.

Every minute, his respect for her was mounting. She had taken off her beret before dinner, and her smooth cap of dark brown hair outlined her skull. Halima had come over earlier, before the meal, to touch and inspect Tara's short hair. The young woman had looked sad, and Tara had smiled and said something to her in Pashto. Then Halima had taken off her turban and allowed her long, black hair, to flow over her shoulders, to below her small breasts.

Shifting his attention back to Khalid now, Dave watched the older man's wrinkled, thin face as he devoted his full attention to what Tara was saying. Dave thought he saw delight, anger and then a look that could only be interpreted as desire for revenge in the man's narrowed, dark eyes as she finished.

"You tell Captain Johnson that we will work together, as one force, to hunt down the leaders of the Taliban. They are in the neighboring village of Deh Rawod, which is twenty miles from here."

Tara turned to Dave, whose gaze was fixed on her. Skin prickling pleasantly beneath his hooded inspection, she managed a slight smile. "Good news," she told him, and repeated the chief's words in English.

"Ask him if we can turn in and sleep, okay?

Tell him we'll start doing serious planning tomorrow morning.''

"Of course…''

Tara felt uncomfortable. The room she was in was large, but most of it served as a weapons cache. There was a strip left, seven feet by four feet, for them to sleep within. They lay side by side on pallets, surrounded by many boxes of ammunition, grenades and other paraphernalia of war. This was the only room available. The darkness was almost complete. The window was open, allowing sporadic gusts of fresh air into the space. The huge wooden door, which hung on leather straps, was closed.

Sighing, Tara turned onto her back, resting her hands beneath her head. Dave was barely two feet from her elbow. She was still in her uniform, but had taken off her boots, as had he.

"Can't you sleep?" she asked, when she heard him shift restlessly.

He smiled a little and rolled over on his side, facing her. "No. Too excited. Hyperalert. I don't trust the Taliban, who are probably no more than twenty miles away, not to attack us here tonight.''

Tara nodded. Dave's closeness made her feel safer than she probably should. Still, his strong presence, his quiet charisma, which had immediately won Khalid's respect, was a comfort. "Do you think they will?"

"I don't know." Dave caught himself wanting to reach out and brush a strand of hair off her forehead. There was just enough moonlight spilling through the window for him to see her features. Outside, he could hear the bleat of goats and sheep in nearby corrals.

"I'm so tired I could die," Tara whispered, closing her eyes. "I feel stretched like a wire."

"Jet lag combined with the stress of living under the threat of combat," he murmured.

"You feel the same?" Tara opened her eyes and looked over at him. It was a mistake. Dave's eyes were hooded, and if she didn't know better, she'd say that was tenderness burning in them. Swallowing hard, she felt her heart take off at a gallop. Quickly lowering her gaze, she tried to ignore his nearness, his quiet, powerful masculinity.

"Maybe if we talk about home, it will help bring us down," Dave offered. He saw desire in Tara's eyes when their gazes locked for a moment. Desire? That was unexpected. Had she seen his wistful feelings toward her in his eyes? Hoping not, Dave scowled. He shouldn't be drawn to her at all. Not now, under these conditions.

"Does that do the trick?" she asked, chuckling softly.

"Yeah, usually does. I'll go first...."

Tara closed her eyes and pulled her hands from behind her head, settling them across her stomach. "Okay...you first," she murmured. Tiredness lapped at her. How desperately she wanted to sleep! And how she had to fight the urge to simply turn toward Dave, inch forward and snuggle in his arms.

"I was born in Barton's Junction, Wyoming. My family owns a cattle ranch at the edge of the Tetons, the most mountainous part of the state. I have two younger brothers and a sister. They all work on the ranch, helping out my parents."

Tara opened her eyes and, against her better judgment, looked over at him. She was surprised at how the tension had drained out of Dave's face as he lay there on his side, one arm propping him up. "You don't like being a cattle rancher?" she asked.

He shrugged and quirked his mouth. Picking at a thread on the Oriental rug beneath the pallets they rested on, he murmured, "My dad was in Army Special Forces during the Vietnam War. I was raised on the stories he told us, and I wanted to follow in his footsteps. I like the adventure."

"And you're the eldest son, right?" She smiled a little when his mouth softened. Tara found Dave's mouth absolutely mesmerizing. He had a full lower lip, the upper one slightly thinner. She could tell instantly from the way he held his mouth and the look in his eyes what he was feeling. Maybe he thought she couldn't interpret nonverbal signs, but that was her specialty, and Tara was finding it very easy to read him.

"Yeah, guess I fell into that trap, didn't I?" He chuckled.

"You're making a career out of the army? Put in your twenty and then go home and become a rancher?"

"Looks like it," he murmured, drowning in her wide eyes. Tara was incredibly easy to talk to. "I was only going to do six years, to fulfill my officer's commission, but...." He frowned.

"Uh-oh, real life intruded, right?"

Cocking his head, he studied her in the gathering silence. "What *is* it about you? I find myself wanting to spill my guts to you."

It was her turn to laugh softly. Opening her hands, Tara said in a quiet tone, "I'm mother confessor over in the intelligence section. Everybody comes to me and tells me their sad stories."

"You don't look like a mother confessor."

"No?" Tara found herself melting beneath his teasing grin. The way his mouth quirked caught her off guard once more. Fleetingly, she wondered how well he kissed. Very well, she bet. Suddenly frightened of the way her thoughts were meandering, she tried to remain immune to him.

"You're too young and pretty." He held up his hand. "I know, I know, that's not a politically correct thing to say to a fellow army officer...."

"But it's a nice compliment. Thank you." Tara felt heat scalding her neck and flowing up into her face. Thank goodness the semidarkness would hide her blush from him!

Dave realized he was letting his stupid heart lead his head. Hadn't he learned his lesson about women yet? But there was something guileless and trusting about Tara McCain. When he'd seen her soothing, low voice work its magic on Khalid, he'd felt an instant respect for her. The old chieftain was smitten with her from the looks of it, but that wasn't a bad thing, in Dave's opinion. It was better than Khalid having issues with her being a woman in the army.

Clearing her throat nervously, Tara tried to move on to a less personal topic. "You said you were going to spend six years in the army and then get out and go home. What made you change your mind?''

"Hmm? Oh, that. Well…" He scowled. "I got married.''

Tara grinned. "That's supposed to be a happy time. From the look on your face, it was a disaster.''

"It wasn't at first," he murmured. Why was he bleeding out his sob story to Tara? Dave couldn't help himself. Her liquid eyes were so wide and compassionate that he felt himself falling helplessly beneath her magic. "Wanda, my ex-wife, was a wild child. I guess what drew me to her initially was her free spirit. Sort of like Halima. She reminds me of that same type of rebellious personality.''

"That's not all bad. Being independent.''

Dave nodded. "Attraction of opposites, I guess," he said, staring blankly down at the dark carpet between them. He traced the flowery design with his index finger, lost in the pain of his past. "She was a lot younger than me. Actually, she was the daughter of an army major.''

"What attracted you to her?" Tara wondered what kind of women Dave liked. Obviously, the wild child variety, which wasn't what she was at all. Maybe she should feel relieved. Instead, she felt disheartened. Why?

"Loved to party. Wasn't afraid to be herself. She was full of life."

"I imagine she gave her parents a run for their money. Most army brats aren't rebellious. They toe the line and are conservative by nature."

"You got that right," Dave chuckled. "I think her father was relieved she was marrying me. It got her out of their household and into mine."

Tara saw the pain in his eyes as she met his fleeting gaze. He immediately dropped his eyes, slowly tracing the design in the carpet over and over again. "And life was good?" she prodded.

"For a while, yeah. We were married for three years and then it fell apart. The divorce was ugly. I *never* want to go through that again."

"I'm sorry. Any children?"

"No, thank goodness, there weren't."

Tiredness was stealing over Tara. She closed her eyes. "And how long ago was that?"

"Two years ago." Dave looked over at her. Tara's eyes were closed, her thick lashes resting against the planes of her cheeks. Fighting an urge to reach out and graze her skin with his fingers, he sighed instead and allowed the silence to lengthen between them. Five minutes later, he knew by the way her breasts rose and fell gently beneath the uniform that Tara had fallen asleep.

Sitting up, Dave drew the thin blanket up across her shoulders. He didn't want her to get chilled. September in this country brought hot days and cool nights. As he tucked her in, Dave had the wild, hungry urge to kiss those soft, parted lips of hers. No way. He couldn't. He just couldn't. It wouldn't be right.

Easing back onto his pallet, he frowned and pulled the blanket up to his waist. Facing the door, his M–4 rifle near his hand, he knew he had to separate these startling new feelings he had toward Tara from the mission that lay ahead of them. Tomorrow, everyone's lives would be on the line.

As he closed his eyes, Dave tried not to think of Tara as a target. The last thing he wanted was for her to be wounded or killed. His heart simply couldn't handle that possibility.

Chapter 3

"I think you've made believers out of the people of Tarin Kowt," Tara said to Dave as they sat in the all-terrain vehicle on a hillside above the village. It was nearly dusk. The October sky above them was pink and lavender. The sun had already set. Some thin, high cirrus clouds spread across the sky like a horse's tail.

Dave stirred in the driver's seat. "A week makes a difference, doesn't it?"

"Getting all the helicopter supplies, including food packets, in for Chief Khalid and his people made them believe your team is serious and here to stay."

"It's true. It has." Because he had not had many opportunities to be alone with Tara during daylight hours, Dave had driven up the dusty road from the village to a barren hill overlooking the small valley where Tarin Kowt nestled. He savored his time alone with Tara even though he knew he shouldn't. It was true they slept close to one another in the munitions room of Khalid's small home, and that was a special hell for Dave. He wasn't getting the sleep he needed because he wanted her in his arms.

"You've been part of the magic of this week," he murmured, cocking his head in her direction. Even in male Afghan clothes, Tara looked feminine to him. The thick frame of her dark lashes emphasized the beauty of her blue eyes. When her lips lifted and she grinned back at him, his heart skittered with need. For her.

"Let's give Halima credit, too. She's a real warrior, that one. And she can ride a horse like no one's business."

Laughing softly, Dave gazed out over the valley. They had the Taliban on the run, but it was never safe. Sitting too long on the hill could make them a target, drawing mortar or sniper fire. "Yeah, she was practically born on one." He started the engine and began the slow descent down the rocky, dusty yellow trail that served as a road. All around them the shadows of night began to creep over the barren, mountainous desert, creating perfect hiding places for Taliban soldiers.

"My butt's still sore from riding all day yesterday," Tara griped good-naturedly. "You sat on that horse like you were born to it. But then, you were raised on a Wyoming cattle ranch."

Yesterday, they'd ridden into the surrounding mountains with Khalid and his men in search of a Taliban leader. Halima had headed the column, for she knew some of their hideouts from sneaking up on them and locating them on a hand-drawn map she'd created.

Dave roused himself and stayed on the track. Getting off it might cause them to drive over a land mine. The mines left by the Russians a decade earlier were real killers of Afghan people. Khalid had given Dave and the team a map that indicated where known minefields were located.

"With a continual supply of gas and food," he told her as they bumped down the hill, "we'll be able to investigate that fortress that Halima says has tunnels."

"When are we going?" Tara allowed herself a moment to study Dave's rugged profile. Since coming to Tarin Kowt, he'd been busy eighteen hours a day, barely grabbing enough sleep in their tiny makeshift quarters to keep going. How she looked forward to those few hours with him. Oh, she would never admit it to him…. Tara found herself fighting hourly not to like Dave more than she should. She reminded herself that he was based in Kentucky, and she in Washington, D.C. A long-distance relationship just wouldn't work.

"Day after tomorrow, when we get new supplies."

"Is your boss in Kandahar happy with your progress?" Tara knew that Navy Seabees were coming in to make the small airport at Tarin Kowt accessible to larger aircraft. Right now, it was a yellow dirt strip just outside the village, and they were resupplied by helicopters.

"Yeah, real happy." Dave rubbed his chin, which was rough from a thick growth of beard. None of his men had shaved since coming to the country. They wanted to melt into the Afghan population as much as possible, to become chameleons so the Taliban couldn't single them out. That provided a modicum of safety—except in Tara's case; she couldn't grow a beard. During the day, though, she usually wrapped a white swath from her turban across her nose and lower face so that all that showed were her luminous blue eyes. And from a distance, no Taliban soldier could know she was

American, a soldier or a woman. Still, Dave lived in terror of her being hurt. He wasn't sure how he would handle it if Tara did get wounded—or worse, killed in the line of duty. His heart just didn't want to go there.

"Hey, tonight, when we get to our room, I have a special surprise for you," he said, grinning over at her before returning his focus to the road. They eased down the last slope and he picked up speed, heading toward the village, where a few oil lamps shone in the darkness.

Her heart speeding up momentarily, Tara smiled. "Oh?"

"Yeah, something special I ordered for you the last time I talked to the supply sergeant back in Kandahar." Absorbing her sparkling blue gaze, he felt his heart swell with joy. He was discovering he wanted to do little things for Tara. She never complained about the long hours, the choking dust, the lack of facilities or anything else. Truly, she made him proud she was an army officer. His men, too, had come to respect her, and were absorbing her into the "family" as a result. To them, she was like a little sister that needed taking care of, and she treated them all like big brothers. A lot of his fear that she wouldn't assimilate had been nothing but prejudice on his part, Dave realized.

Now, he was glad Tara was with them. It perked his men up. They enjoyed her company, because Tara could tease just as mercilessly as they could. Yes, with her special presence, Dave had seen Tiger 01 lighten up, laugh a lot more and relax, even though they were in combat conditions.

"I like surprises," Tara confided.

"Good," he said with another smile.

Tara had taken a cooling shower outside the house in a device that Sergeant Lovell had specially made for her and the team. The shower was a simple thing, but being able to wash the sweat and that fine, irritating dust off her body at the end of the day was a delicious feeling. It was the highlight of her evening. Aware of the degree of modesty required of a woman in Afghanistan, Tara had borrowed several of Halima's cotton shifts and they hung below her knees.

Toweling her freshly washed hair, she entered the house quietly and padded to the munitions room. The door was open. Dave had showered earlier. A sputtering oil lamp on a dusty table provided the only light in the tiny area. Shutting the door quietly, she turned and stepped around Dave, who was sitting cross-legged in his T-shirt and a clean pair of fatigues. His boots were off, his long feet bare.

"You look beautiful," he observed as Tara sat down on her pallet only feet away from him. Her hair was spiky from being rubbed dry with the green towel.

"Thanks…I don't know about 'beautiful,' but I sure feel wonderful getting cleaned up." Running her fingers through her hair, she found her small comb and quickly tamed the strands into place. Looking up, she smiled at Dave. "Okay, do I get my prezzie?"

"Prezzie?" He drowned in her luminous eyes, darkened by the night shadows. Only the dancing yellow light of the oil lamp allowed him to see her features.

"Yeah, that's what my family calls them—prezzies. Short for presents or gifts." She held out her hand. "Well?"

Laughing softly, Dave pulled out a small sack and handed it to her. "I'm afraid it isn't wrapped…." he said apologetically.

"Hey, we're at war," she murmured, taking the sack and placing it in her lap. Quickly opening it up, she gasped. "Oh! Hand lotion!"

Something warm and melting moved through Dave. The joy in her soft cry sifted through him like a sigh of pleasure. "It's not much…. I asked the supply sergeant if he could wrangle some. I saw your skin peeling and I knew you needed some protection…."

Without thinking, Tara rose up on her knees, threw her arms around Dave's broad, capable shoulders and kissed him on the mouth. It was a swift peck, meant to thank him from the bottom of her heart for his sensitivity and thoughtfulness. She'd never complained about her itchy skin, but he'd seen her suffering, noted it and had done something wonderful for her.

"Thank you, Dave," she whispered, her arms still around his shoulders, her knees touching his. "You are so thoughtful!"

Tara's unanticipated kiss unhinged him. When she remained so close, her eyes glimmering with unshed tears of gratefulness, he lost control. The driving need to touch her, to kiss her, overwhelmed him.

"I need you," he rasped, and, lifting his arms, he brought her fully against him. If Tara had hesitated, tensed or shown any interest in being released, Dave would have done so instantly. But she didn't. Instead, as he slid his arm around her waist and brought her into his embrace, her body folded and melted gracefully against his. When he looked

down into her uplifted face, saw her eyes huge
with desire, he knew she wanted him to kiss her.
He was old enough, experienced enough, to recognize the look of desire on a woman's face.

Leaning down, he slid his arm around her lower
back and captured her hips so that he could feel
the warm softness of her breasts and abdomen
against his body. As he brushed her lips the first
time, he heard and felt her sigh. Her mouth was
soft, beguiling, and as he moved his lips across
hers, he felt her smile. When her arms tightened
and she pressed herself more fully against him,
Dave shuddered with heightening desire. This time
he claimed her mouth, now wet and slick, with a
deep, searching kiss. She tasted minty, and he realized she'd just brushed her teeth. The clean smell
of Tara, that womanly fragrance, entered his flaring
nostrils and he drank it in like the starving man he
was.

And when she returned his hot, hungry kiss, her
mouth equally eager for contact, and her fingers
moving slowly across his skull, tangling in his
short hair, another, deeper shudder rolled through
him. He slid his lips across hers in a commanding
but cajoling manner. Breathing raggedly, Dave felt
her breasts rising and falling quickly against his
chest. How he wished they were naked! His mind

was turning to mush. His heart was banging like a sledgehammer in his chest. He wanted Tara. All of her. Now.

Running his hand upward, he moved his fingers across her damp hair, down her slender neck and then cupped her jaw, imprisoning her so he could tangle his tongue sinuously with hers. When he heard her moan as she arched against him, her breasts taut, the nipples hard and insistent against his chest, Dave groaned. Tara was just as needy as he. It was mutual.

He eased his mouth from hers and placed kiss after kiss on her broad brow, her closed eyelids, the soft skin of her cheek and down the slender column of her neck. The shift she wore covered most of her body, so Dave pressed a kiss on her partly exposed collarbone and allowed his fingers to move in a caressing motion across the fullness of her breast.

Tara moaned again.

Leaning down, he placed his lips against the fabric where the peak of her breast thrust upward. As he suckled her, she cried out softly in pleasure and her arms tightened around his neck. His heart arced in joy over giving her such happiness.

And then reality struck him. He couldn't make love to her here. At least, not now. Easing his lips from her hardened nipple, he found her mouth and kissed her deeply once more. Tara was vulnerable, the kind of partner he'd always wanted and never found. She was bold, hungry and equal to him in every way. Opening his eyes, he cradled her in his arms and reluctantly eased her away from him enough so that he could look into her eyes. Her fine nostrils were flared and her hands stroked his neck restlessly. Dave absorbed her touch as she slid her fingers through his short, thick hair, to his shoulders and back again in gentle, caressing motions.

Tara gazed up into Dave's dark, narrowed eyes, which burned like fire. Heart hammering, her lips tingling wildly from his passionate kiss, she found she couldn't speak. It was impossible. She could only feel. And then feel some more. When he lifted one hand to graze her hair, cheek and chin, she saw a sad smile shadow his strong, male mouth.

"You're thinking what I'm thinking," she said huskily.

"Probably. Wrong time. Wrong place."

"I know...."

He studied her ruthlessly, memorizing each nuance of her shadowed face. "But I'm not sorry it happened, babe. Not in a million years, if you want the truth."

Laughing breathlessly, Tara slid her fingers up the bristly stubble on his cheek. "Oh, I'm not sorry, either. Just surprised at myself. Normally, I'm not this spontaneous."

His lips curved in a feral smile. "Remind me to bring you another present tomorrow night."

Tara knew they must keep their voices down, and she clapped a hand over her mouth, squelching the sound of her laughter. Dave was grinning like an alpha wolf—at her. As if she was his mate. It made her feel extremely feminine and wanted. Desired.

Brushing strands of drying hair from her brow, he sighed. "This is mutual, right?"

"Yes..."

"I never expected something like this to happen, Tara."

"Neither did I. I wasn't looking for a man, to be honest."

"And I wasn't looking for a woman. Not after I got burned so badly by that divorce...."

Sighing, Tara snuggled into his arms and rested her head against his shoulder. "We can't have a full-blown affair under Khalid's roof. Islamic law is strict about that, and I don't think it would go over well under the circumstances. We have to sleep together because there isn't anywhere else for us, and he knows that. But to make love..."

"Yeah," Dave said grimly, "I agree with you. I don't like it, but I know you're right. We need his loyalty, and his trust. We can't go around breaking religious laws that would force him to view us differently."

Looking up into his dark, rugged face, Tara whispered, "I like being kissed by you, Dave. It was wonderful. Better than anyone else—ever."

Preening a little, he said, "Yeah? Really?"

"Yeah."

"You're not just saying it because of the hand lotion for your skin?"

"Oh! Get out of here!" She playfully hit his shoulder. "I'm not *that* easy, Johnson. Never was. Never will be."

Sliding his hand over her warm, firm arm, he said, "So, this attraction to me has been brewin' for a while?"

"Yes."

"Ever since I laid eyes on you at Ops, I've wanted you." He saw her lips part momentarily. And then that luscious mouth moved into a teasing smile.

"Yeah?"

"Yeah."

"I guess my attraction to you didn't hit me over the head at Ops," Tara admitted. She rested her hand against his chest. Beneath her palm, she could feel the heavy thud of his heart. "Over the past week, I've gotten to see you differently. The way you treat your men, the people here in the village. You're surprising."

"Not the Neanderthal you thought?" He chuckled, absorbing the feel of her fleeting touch as she ran her hand down his arm. He needed to touch Tara, to have this incredible contact with her. It fed his soul. It fed his heart.

Giggling, one hand over her mouth, she nodded.

Leaning down, Dave brushed her brow with a slow, warm kiss. He felt Tara sigh, felt her arm move around his neck to draw him close once more. Groaning softly, he whispered near her ear, "I'm starving for you, babe. You make me feel again in every way. I never thought another woman could do that. Never. But you have...." And he pressed several small kisses across her damp hair, her temple, cheek and, finally, her waiting mouth.

Cherishing Tara was so easy. Dave didn't want to stop kissing her, but he knew he had to. Sleep was a precious commodity, and neither of them ever got enough under the circumstances.

Easing away, he saw the tenderness burning in

Tara's eye. There was no question that what he saw glistening there was love—for him. That startled him as nothing else could. They hadn't known each other that long. Was it possible to fall in love so quickly? Dave didn't know. And he was scared—for them. And for the uncertainty of life under combat conditions.

"Whatever happens," Tara whispered as she touched his bristly cheek one last time, "no one can know of us. Or how we feel. Not even your men."

Letting her slip out of his arms, Dave eased her onto her pallet, next to his. "Agreed."

"Whatever we have, it will take the test of time, and I'm okay with that," Tara said, studying him in the silence. "Are you?"

"Yes. We need the time, babe. Especially me. I've been burned by a relationship before. I just never expected you to crash into my life and make me look at things differently."

"I wasn't in need of a man," she told him wryly. Tara took the bottle of hand lotion and opened it up. She knelt there facing him as she smoothed some onto her peeling face.

Dave watched her smile as the lotion began to lubricate her sunburned features. "Here, give me the bottle. I want to put it on your arms...."

Hesitating fractionally, Tara smiled. Giving him the bottle, she sat with her legs crossed beneath the shift. Lifting her right arm, she closed her eyes as his rough fingers slid provocatively from her shoulder downward. The lotion smelled of roses, and she reveled in the simple act he was performing. She absorbed the gentle, sliding touch of his strong fingers across first her right arm, and then her left. When he was finished, she opened her eyes.

"That was wonderful...."

"Maybe we can do small things like this for one another...." He handed the lotion back to her. Seeing Tara's eyes narrow with desire, he smiled slightly. "That is, if we can control our basic, primal needs."

Grinning, Tara set the lotion aside and lay down. Drawing the thin cotton blanket up to her waist, she faced Dave. "I'm the guilty party. I attacked you first."

Sliding down on his pallet, a mirthless smile on his mouth, he said, "I kind of like being hunted...it's a new experience for me. And I really like your feistiness, you know that?"

"Comes with being a female."

Dave reached over and touched the strands of her drying hair against her cheek. "A fighter by nature."

"Better believe it." She thrilled to his grazing touch and saw his eyes burn with desire—for her.

"And I was dead wrong about my belief that you might not be able to handle combat situations with us."

"My heart be still—an apology. Wow…"

"You really know how to pour salt in this poor guy's wounds."

"Yeah, my heart bleeds for you, Johnson. I remember the nasty guy who stormed up to me at Ops growling that I wasn't fit for combat duty."

Raising his brows, he sighed. "I guess I do have this coming…"

"In spades, so take your medicine like a good little boy, be gracious in defeat and I promise to stop pouring salt in your wounds, okay?"

Oh, the urge to raise up on his elbow and kiss that smart, feisty, smiling mouth of hers was nearly his undoing. "I'm really beginning to like women warriors."

Pleased by his lack of arrogance in admitting he was wrong, Tara whispered, "Go to sleep, Dave. It's taking everything I have not to scoot into your arms and do some really wild woman things to you…."

With a groan, Dave flopped on his back and put

his arm across his eyes. "Lady, you sure as hell know how to tease and tempt me...."

With a soft snort, Tara muttered, "And you don't think I don't feel the same way? I'll see you in my dreams, okay?"

Lifting his arm, he peeked at her grinning features. "Yeah, it's the only safe place for us to work out our torrid fantasies with one another, isn't it?"

Squelching laughter, Tara couldn't wipe the smile off her face. "Good night, Captain."

"Yeah...right...good night, Captain..."

Chapter 4

"Happy Thanksgiving," Tara murmured to Dave as they sat in a deep crater from a bomb dropped by a B-52 bomber a week ago. Dressed in her Afghan soldier outfit, a turban on her head and her M-4 rifle nearby, she crouched with him on the chewed-up dirt at the bottom of the depression where it was safe. Right now, the rest of their team was out on a mission to the hills surrounding Deh Rawod, a hotbed of Taliban soldiers.

Dave grinned and spooned up a bite of food from his packaged MRE—meals ready to eat. "Not exactly the turkey day I would like to have had."

Tara nodded. "Hey, this is better than nothing, under the circumstances. At least that supply sergeant was thoughtful enough to give us turkey MREs."

Dave smiled and continued to eat. The day was cool, and the walls of the crater around them provided a modicum of protection from both the wind and possible snipers. "If you were home right now, what would you have done for Thanksgiving?" he asked, studying Tara's sunburned features and peeling nose. He hadn't been able to get her another bottle of lotion and that bothered him. It was a small thing, but important to him. Her face had turned several shades darker from being exposed to the merciless Afghan sun in this mountainous desert. He himself looked more like an Afghan every day, with his dark beard and skin turning tobacco-brown from the constant outdoor activities.

Tara sighed and leaned back on the soft dirt, the flak jacket chafing her skin as it always did beneath the vertical striped white-and-brown shirt she wore. "I'd probably go home for the holiday. I have a lot of leave saved up. I'd help my mom make the turkey. I make a killer stuffing, Johnson. You'd pig out on it."

"I'll bet you do," he murmured, watching her

half-closed eyes, the MRE resting on her stomach as she lay back in the crater. Their nights together in the small munitions room hadn't lasted much longer. Halima had taken it upon herself to invite Tara to her room to sleep, a far more comfortable situation, and more in keeping with Muslim tradition. Tara had had to accept, so Dave was left without her warmth and her sense of humor. Maybe it was just as well, he supposed, because he found himself itching to touch her, to kiss her whenever the opportunity presented—which wasn't often. First and foremost, he had a team to run and a mission to complete. Whatever he and Tara shared came last, and he knew she was in accord with that. Still, he could see desire and sadness in her eyes sometimes, and that made him yearn for her even more.

Today they had an hour to themselves—a rarity. Dave was hungry to simply be with Tara. He felt far more than lust for her, he'd come to realize over the past three months. Something much deeper was taking root between them. Tara was touching a chord of need in him that had never been struck before she'd walked unexpectedly into his life.

"Ugh, I'm stuffed," she whispered, and sat up, resealing the MRE pouch. She wasn't about to litter the Afghanistan desert with her leftover food wrappings. Turning, she got up on her knees, opened her fifty-pound pack and put the empty container away.

"I could eat another one," Dave said. He watched as she turned and plopped down again, her legs crossed and her elbows resting on her knees. His gaze moved to her mouth.

"You're double my size," she laughed softly, "so I'm not surprised."

"Come here, you got some leftover cranberry sauce on the corner of your mouth."

Easing toward him, Tara gave him a mischievous smile. Placing her hands on his broad shoulders, she leaned closer, her knees pressed against his leg. "Do I? Or is this just a ruse, Johnson?" Thrilled as he gave her that hooded, dark look filled with desire, Tara drowned in his forest-green gaze. Oh, how she looked forward to these rare, beautiful moments with him! Sliding her hands around his neck, she leaned forward as he raised his right hand.

"No, you really do...dress you up, can't take you anywhere, McCain. What am I going to do with you?" He liked the easy banter and teasing that had developed between them. With one gentle swipe of his index finger, he removed the offend-

ing red sauce at the corner of her smiling mouth.
Heat suffused his lower body. How many times
had he ached to make love to her? So many…and
yet he couldn't. The time and place wasn't right,
and they both knew it. Dave lived in a special hell
on earth because of it, and he saw the same need
for him in Tara's eyes.

Holding up his index finger as she eased back
on her boot heels, he said, ''See? It wasn't a ruse.''

''You're right. For once you're being honest,
Johnson.'' And she chuckled. Releasing him, she
cupped his hand and guided it to her mouth. Moving her lips over his index finger, she sucked off
the sauce. Instantly, the look on his face changed.
Feeling his raw desire for her, she licked his finger
one more time and then released it. Even here they
weren't really alone. An Afghan soldier or group
could appear soundlessly out of nowhere, and if
they were caught being intimate, it wouldn't go
well. They didn't want to jeopardize the connection that Dave had been able to forge with Chief
Zaher.

''What a tease you are.''

''Me?'' She touched her heart and grinned. ''*I'm*
a tease? Dude, you're the pot calling the kettle
black as far as I'm concerned.''

Putting his own MRE aside, Dave met her chal-

lenging smile. "I like the blue fire I see in your
eyes. I like what you're telling me without saying
it."

Looking around before she did it, Tara reached
out and tenderly grazed his bearded cheek. The
dark hair covering his lower face gave Dave an
even more dangerous quality. "I miss our time together, too."

"Yeah, war doesn't exactly help lovers out, does
it?" His skin prickled pleasantly where she'd
touched him.

"No, it doesn't...." Tara frowned as she rested
her hands on the thighs of her dark brown cotton
pants. How much she wanted to speak to Dave of
what lay in her heart. She knew that what she felt
was love, but she was afraid to admit it. They simply hadn't the time for the kind of intimate con-
versations she craved. At times she saw a look in
Dave's eyes that she thought was more than just
desire. Was it love? Too afraid to ask, she tried to
be content with the present.

Just then, she heard the noise of several all-
terrain vehicles approaching.

"The guys are back," Dave said. Reaching
over, he touched her chin and gave her a tender
smile. "I like what I see in your eyes, babe. Just
hold on to it for both of us, okay? We aren't al-

ways going to be here in Afghanistan. At some point, they have to rotate us back stateside."

Nodding, Tara absorbed his unexpected touch. "I will, Dave."

He rose to his feet, his M–4 in his right hand as he looked over the lip of the crater. "Promise?" In the distance, he could see five vehicles speeding toward them, two men in each one, their mission complete. The yellow dust rose lazily into the noontime sky behind them.

"I promise...." And Tara stood up, brushed off the seat of her pants and picked up her rifle. Placing it over her left shoulder, she scrambled out of the bomb crater and onto the flat plain. Brown, desolate-looking hills rose before her, backed by higher and higher ridges and finally the razor-sharp, craggy mountains.

Dave had run ahead to meet his returning team members. Tara looked around. A solitary path wound along the plain at the base of the hills. Bombs had been dropped here last week because the area was a known minefield, and they needed this land for staging another strike against the Taliban hiding in caves in the mountains above them. After the bombing, Dave's team had diligently gone over the entire area in search of any last mines that might not have gone off during the brutal pounding and explosions caused by the B-52's.

The wind was chilling, and Tara pulled her tunic a little tighter as she walked. Dave had taught her to walk in his footprints, just in case there was a land mine they hadn't found. His team had to go over the area one more time today, to make very sure there were no mines left before the troops and equipment began massing tomorrow.

A sudden gust of wind rose, slamming a thick, stinging cloud of dust into Tara's face. Automatically, she raised her hand and closed her eyes. It was strong enough to force her to take a step to the left, off Dave's path.

Click.

Tara froze. *Oh no!* Blinking, her eyes watering and her vision blurred, she jerked a look downward. There, barely visible, was the round metal edge of a land mine. And she had stepped on it.

Terror snaked through her. Heart slamming against her rib cage, she froze. Dave was fifty feet ahead, his attention on his team.

Sweat popped out on her brow. Grasping the nylon web strap of the rifle on her left shoulder, she cried, "Dave! I've stepped on a land mine!"

Whirling around at her cry, he stared at her,

wide-eyed. Tara was standing there, her lips parted, terror written on her features.

"Don't move!" he roared, and sprinted back toward her. His mind whirled with questions of how she'd found one. He thought they'd gotten them all. *Damn it!*

Gasping for breath, Tara continued to stare down at her right foot, which rested on top of the mine. Afraid to move, she barely glanced up when Dave came running toward her, yet the look of worry and anxiety on his face struck her deeply. If she moved her foot at all, the mine would explode. It would kill her instantly, or at the outside, blow off her leg and leave her limbless. Sobbing for breath, Tara tried to calm down.

Dave skidded to a halt ten feet away from her. "Just take it easy," he rasped, blinking the sweat out of his eyes. "Don't move, babe. God, don't move at all. Let me see...." He followed his footprints back to where she had stepped off the path then got down on his hands and knees very carefully and gently. The least vibration might set off the mine.

"Why didn't you follow my prints?" he demanded, breathing hard as he leaned closer. Digging into the yellow dust with his outstretched fingers, he located the cold metal of the land mine squarely beneath Tara's booted foot.

"I—I tried, Dave," she whispered raggedly, her voice off pitch with terror. "A gust of wind came up. It was so strong it knocked me off the track. I'm sorry…sorry…"

"Shh, it's okay. It's okay, babe. Just stay where you are. I see the mine. You're okay for now. As long as you keep the same amount of weight on it, it won't blow up. Whatever you do, don't shift your body. Hear me?" He wiped his mouth as he nailed her with a look meant to make her understand that if she moved, she would die.

"Yeah…yeah, I know. You drilled me on this," Tara rasped.

"Hold on…I've got to alert my men. We have to get you out of this…." And he turned, moved away and then slowly unwound and stood up. His team had stopped their vehicles a hundred feet away and were dismounting. Dave hurried back toward them.

Tara could hear his voice in the distance; could hear the terror barely concealed in it as he gathered his team around him. She saw them all turn toward her. The stricken looks on their features only made her more fearful. Oh God, how was she going to get out of this alive? And what if one of them tried to help her and the mine went off, anyway? It would kill him, too.

Raising her hand slowly, Tara wiped her mouth, which felt cottony and dry. Suddenly, she was dying of thirst, but her water bottle was back in the crater with her pack. With her heart pounding in her breast like a runaway freight train, all she could do was stand helplessly and wait. Dave quickly gave orders and his men dispersed and went back to their packs, which were still in the vehicles.

Tara knew another strong gust of wind whipping down from foothills could make her lose her balance. The least movement would cause the mine to detonate. She'd be dead.

Suddenly, as she stood there, she realized she didn't want to die. Watching Dave trot back toward her, his long knife drawn and in his right hand, Tara wanted to scream out in fear. But she didn't. Instead, she swallowed hard, several times.

"Take some deep, calming breaths," Dave told her as he approached. Seeing the fear in Tara's huge blue eyes, he tried to keep his own voice low and soothing. It was nearly impossible. She was hunched over, her fingers tangled in the webbing of the M-4 rifle on her left shoulder. Her loose Afghan clothing whipped about in the inconstant breezes.

"Yeah...okay. What are you going to do, Dave?"

"First, I'm going to check the land around you to make sure there are no other mines. Then," he said slowly, as he got down on his hands and knees, "I'll carefully remove the sand from around the mine you're on."

"Oh God..."

"I know, I know, babe...just take it easy. Don't panic on me. Just stay exactly where you are and we'll get you out of this...."

She watched with wide eyes as Dave began to slide the tip of his knife into the sand, an ever widening circle around where she stood. Lifting her head, she saw Sergeant Burt Lovell approaching, carrying his own knife in his hand. His face was dark with worry, too. The rest of the team was staying back out of harm's way.

"Burt?" she called.

"It's okay, ma'am. Me and the captain have done this before. We'll make it go twice as fast. We need to make *sure* there're no more mines near you. Just take it easy, okay?"

Jerkily nodding, Tara watched him get down and go to work as Dave was going. *Breathe,* she ordered herself. *Slow, deep breaths. You're still alive, Tara. You're still breathing....*

"Gusts are coming!" Private Doug Seabert called out to them.

Oh, no! Tara tensed. The first gust struck. It slapped at her. *Don't move. Don't move.* Shutting her eyes tightly against the thick, yellow dust, she bit back a cry. *No movement. None!*

"You're doing fine," Dave called to her. He was now twenty feet behind where Tara was standing. Lovell was going the opposite direction, probing the earth with his knife. Trying to get a handle on his escaping emotions, Dave wanted to scream. Tara could die. Oh, God, he couldn't let that happen! Why hadn't he told her he loved her? Right now he couldn't. His men couldn't know of their relationship.

Tara felt her muscles beginning to shake. She was so tense and rigid that the muscle groups were beginning to complain.

"Dave...I'm starting to tremble. I can't stop shaking...."

He looked up for a moment. Tara's eyes were narrow with fear. "Try to relax. You can relax but keep the same weight on that leg. It's okay, try it. You won't blow us up. You've got to relax your muscles or you'll get so tense that your trembling could set it off. Understand?"

"Yeah...yeah, I understand...." Fresh fear shot

through Tara. How was she going to relax and yet stay steady enough that the mine didn't detonate? She had to try.

Dave finally met Burt on Tara's right side. "No more mines?"

"No, sir, none. We're good to go."

"Okay, go fetch that wooden plank you found. And I need a rock that weighs as much as she does."

Burt slowly rose to his full height. He slid the knife back into its sheath. "Yes, sir, I'll be right back."

"Find the right rock, Burt. You know what to look for. Have Seabert bring me the plank."

"You bet. I'll be right back...."

Tara watched the sergeant leave. She heard Dave get up, then come around in front of her, his brows drawn down, his eyes narrowed. "W-what are you going to do? How can you help me out of this?"

"We'll get a piece of wood and a rock that weighs as much as you do." Kneeling down, he used the tip of the knife to begin removing sand, just enough to expose the land mine Tara was standing on.

Confused, she watched his very slow, careful movements. Heart pounding, she whispered rawly,

"Oh, Dave, I'm so scared. I'm sorry I stepped off the path...."

"Hush, babe, you didn't do it on purpose. The wind here is bad. There's been more than a few times we've all been knocked sideways by it."

"Y-you could have stepped on this mine...." Tara closed her eyes for a moment.

"Yeah," he rasped grimly as he smoothed the sand away from the metal rim. The mine was round and rusty, and he recognized it as a Russian-made one.

"I thought you and your men cleared this area yesterday?"

"Most of it," Dave corrected. "Not all of it. We had gone over this area, but we must have missed this one. We don't have a mine detector with us. All we have are our knives and our eyes. We screwed up."

Tara shook her head. "You're all doing the best you can, Dave. I don't blame you or anyone."

He sat back on his heels and looked up at her, close enough to reach out and touch her. "I blame myself. I don't want anything to happen to you, babe."

Seeing the love for her burning in his eyes, Tara sobbed. She pressed her hand to her lips and forced herself to remain very still. "Oh, Dave, I love you. I should have told you before, but I was afraid...."

Holding her tear-filled gaze, he whispered raggedly, "And I love you, Tara. Never forget that. Now, just hold on. We'll get you out of this in one piece. No way are you going to die. I just found you...."

Dave saw Burt coming back, staggering beneath the weight of a huge white rock. Tara weighed around a hundred forty pounds, and the sergeant had to estimate as closely as possible that the stone was that same weight, or more. Was he right? Dave didn't know. Eyeballing the boulder that his sergeant struggled with, he thought it probably came close.

Tara saw Private Seabert approach with a rectangular piece of old, dried out planking. It wasn't more than two feet in length or a foot in width.

"Give it to me," Dave ordered Seabert, "and then back off. I don't want anyone else hurt if we don't do this right."

Nodding, Seabert said, "Yes, sir..." and handed him the plank.

Dave set it carefully at his side. He was kneeling on Tara's right side, the land mine mere inches away. He would be the one to do the dirty work. No one else.

"Okay?" he asked Tara, looking up into her tense face. He noted that two tracks of tears wound their way down her dusty cheeks.

"Y-yeah, okay."

"I'd reach out and pat you, but I don't want you to move," he teased her quietly.

"Right now, all I want to do is fall into your arms, Dave, and be held by you."

"Hold that thought, babe...." And he swung his gaze toward Lovell, who was huffing toward them with the boulder in his arms.

Tara watched, barely breathing, as the sergeant carefully placed the boulder behind her right foot, about six inches away from the exposed land mine. She listened as Dave quietly gave the sergeant instructions.

"Okay, Tara," Dave said, looking up at her, the plank in his hands. "Here's what I'm going to do. I'm going to gently ease the edge of the plank beneath your right heel. You're going to have to allow me to slide it slowly in between you and that mine. All the while, you're going to have to maintain the *same* weight on it. Once the plank completely covers the mine, Burt is going to roll the boulder forward on the exposed edge of the planking. As he does so, you're going to have to slowly slide your foot forward, giving him more and more room to roll the boulder up on the plank. The mine won't go off if *more* weight is on it than was there previously, it will go off if there's *less* weight. Understand?"

Swallowing, her voice scratchy, she asked, "How does Burt know the rock weighs as much as me?"

The sergeant briefly smiled. "Ma'am, I think this rock is about a hundred and sixty pounds, by my estimate."

"What if you're wrong?" Tara rasped.

"Then we all die," Dave told her quietly. "Don't worry, Tara. This rock is heavy enough. You need to listen to me now, and do exactly as I say, when I say it. Are you ready?"

No, she wasn't. Tara felt a lump rising in her throat. She felt her muscles shaking. Still, she struggled for calm. "Yeah, I'm ready. Let's do it...." How brave she sounded. And how scared she was!

Dave inched the plank forward. Beads of sweat trickled into his narrowed eyes. For a moment, everything blurred. He eased the plank beneath Tara's heel. "Okay, here it comes...." And he nudged it forward one slow, torturous inch at a time.

For the next five minutes, Tara felt as if her life was over. But the plank was smooth from age and weathering, allowing it to slide friction-free beneath the sole of her boot. She tried to remember to breathe, but kept holding her breath.

Dave maneuvered closer to Tara. The plank was

now in position between her foot and the mine. "Okay, Burt, roll that rock up on it…and be nice and delicate about it…."

Tara saw the other team members watching them, saw the fear and anxiety on every face. Their expressions mirrored how she felt. Hearing the crunch of sand as the boulder was eased up on the lip of the plank, she froze.

"Good…good," Dave murmured. "A little more now…yeah…we got it on the edge. Good…"

Tara heard the relief in his voice. Some of her fear abated because he sounded so positive. Every joint in her lower body ached. She was beginning to tremble in earnest from the hips downward. The crunching sound started again. She felt the boulder come up against her heel.

"Okay, babe, I want you to slowly ease your foot forward about two inches…."

Tara realized Dave had slipped and called her by the endearment. She knew the sergeant had heard it. Right now, that wasn't important. As she carefully slid her boot forward, she found it easy to move along the smooth planking.

"Great," Dave whispered. He was holding the board down with both hands, using his full weight to keep it steady. The mine wouldn't go off under the circumstances unless it was very old. Not all

Russian land mines were state of the art, he knew. Many went off without reasonable cause. Breathing through his mouth, he watched Burt roll the boulder forward, until it met the heel of Tara's boot.

"Excellent, excellent," Dave whispered. "Okay, Tara, this is it. I want you to slide your foot forward and off the plank. We've got the boulder on it now, plus my weight. Go ahead…move. And once you do, get as far away from us as fast as you can. Understand? Run to the team. They're a safe distance away."

"But…what about you and Burt?"

"We'll be fine. Just do it, Tara…*Now!*"

Holding her breath, she slid her boot off the plank. Instantly, she heard the grinding of the boulder rolling forward.

Rushing away, she raced toward the team, who gestured for her to run to them.

Panting heavily, she stopped and turned around once she reached them. Her knees were wobbly and she found herself swaying dizzily. Someone took her M–4 off her shoulder. Another man helped her sit down in one of the all-terrain vehicles. Her gaze, however, was riveted on Dave and Burt as they knelt over the mine. Hands pressed against her heart, she felt raging fear for both of them. What if the rock wasn't the right weight?

What if, as Dave eased his own weight off the plank, the mine exploded?

Seconds seem to drag like hours for Tara. She watched as Dave slowly inched back, lifting his hands away from the plank. The banked terror in both men's faces turned to relief as they slowly got to their feet and backed away.

Within a minute, it was all over. The boulder stayed on the board, unmoving. She saw Dave turn, sling his arm around Burt's shoulders and slap him with hearty congratulations on the back before they both jogged forward. The entire team broke out into a cry of victory. Someone handed Tara a bottle of water. She thanked him and drank deeply, her throat parched.

As she lowered the bottle and wiped her wet lips, she saw Dave's gaze pinned on her. Oh, how she wanted to fly to his arms, but she knew she couldn't. Tara sat there on the verge of tears, battling them back. This team deserved her courage, not her sobs. Another time, she would cry and release this backlog of fear from her brush with death.

Right now, as Dave approached, she wondered what would happen next between them. In the midst of a terrible situation, they'd both confessed their love for one another.

Chapter 5

"We're home," Tara said as she walked back into the operations building where her life-changing mission had started nearly three months before. No one heard her say it because the families of the returning Spec For teams were surging around the heroes of Afghanistan. Dave had gotten separated from her by the crush of wives, children, parents and siblings who were joyously greeting the weary warriors.

It was 0300 in the morning, but Fort Campbell's Ops building was bulging with loved ones who would have their men home for Christmas, which was two days away.

Shouldering her pack and rifle, Tara moved slowly through the jubilant crowd, her gaze pinned on the double doors that would lead outside to the snowy darkness. They'd had snow at Tarin Kowt before they left, and now here.

Tara forced back her tears as sadness filled her. Her time with Dave was at an end, she knew. Because he had been assisting the team that came in to replace them in that corner of Afghanistan, he hadn't been able to devote any personal time to her. Tara understood and accepted that; a new team coming in had to get to know the lay of the land, the procedures and protocols that had been established.

"Wait!"

It was Dave's voice rising above the din of noise. Tara halted near the doors. She saw him moving toward her, his green beret on his head, his face smooth-shaven once more and a glint in his dark eyes. Instantly, her heart speeded up. The look he gave her lightened her soul and made her hope again.

"Let's get out of here," he said with a grin as he pushed opened the brass-and-glass door for her.

Outside, Tara breathed deeply of the cool, refreshing air as they carefully moved down the concrete steps. Families were still coming and going, but the crowd had thinned.

"Over here," he said, and pointed to a stately elm that stood in the center of the snow-covered lawn. He hefted his bag and rifle as he walked alongside her.

Tara dropped her pack near the gray trunk of the tree. Its girth was wide, indicating how old it was. Snowflakes twirled lazily out of the darkness above them. Straightening, she saw Dave drop his pack, too, and sling the M–4 over his left shoulder.

"This is a great night," he told her with a grin, his breath a white mist in the frosty air.

"Yes, it is…." Tara smiled faintly. She leaned against the tree, feeling exhaustion threading through her. "It's great to be home…."

"Speaking of which," he said, lowering his voice so that only she could hear, "we haven't had time to be together in the last couple of weeks." Dave saw her lashes lift, revealing those heart-stopping blue eyes of hers. Since the incident with the land mine, he'd sworn to himself that he would treat every minute with her as if it were the last. Mouth tightening, he whispered, "Tara, I want you to stay here, with me…. I know you have thirty days leave coming. Stay here, babe…let's explore what we have. Give ourselves the time we need under less pressured circumstances to see if it's genuine. I know it is, but we need to do this for ourselves.'' He stopped himself from reaching out to touch her cheek. Her hair had grown longer, the dark strands framing her oval face—a face he loved fiercely. Searching her eyes, he said, ''What do you think? What do you want to do?''

''I wasn't sure, Dave. About us.... You know— wartime romance and all...''

''Listen to me,'' he rasped, coming closer, his head inches from hers. ''If that mine situation brought one thing home to me, it's that what I feel for you is real and deep. And lasting, Tara.'' How he needed to kiss her! The last time had been two weeks ago, and he ached to crush her warm, soft mouth beneath his. To feel her strong, womanly arms come around his shoulders as she pressed herself wantonly against him.

''I thought you might want to go home to your family?''

He shook his head. ''I'll call them. They'll understand. How about you? Your family?''

''Well...I had wanted to be with you. I was going to phone them, too....''

Heart lifting with relief, he looked around. They still couldn't be too familiar with one another; showing affection for a fellow officer in public just wasn't done. "That's all I need to know. They've got you billeted at the BOQ, Barracks Officers Quarters?"

"Yes."

"I'll walk you over there. It's not far from here. And then I'll get a lift home to my apartment, which is off base. How about I pick you up tomorrow, say, at 1500? That will give us both a chance to sleep in and get over this jet lag. Pack your bag, because you're moving in with me, babe. We're going to celebrate Christmas together...."

"This smells so good," Tara said as she cut into the thick, juicy portion of baked turkey. Dave's apartment was small but surprisingly warm and comfortable. It was 1600, late afternoon, and he'd dropped by the BOQ to pick her up, then had brought her home. He'd made a complete turkey dinner for them all on his own, which surprised her. Most men didn't know how to boil water, much less cook.

"Like it?" Dave sat at her elbow at the small rectangular table, which was beautifully set with a white linen tablecloth. A bright red poinsettia graced one corner. The gleaming silverware, white china and goblets of crimson wine added to the festive atmosphere. In the background, Christmas music played, inspiring warm feelings in Dave. Tara was his family now…or at least he hoped so.

"Yes," Tara murmured. Looking at the fluffy mashed potatoes slathered in thick, dark brown gravy, and the chestnut stuffing, she added, "Did you sleep at all? This feast didn't just appear out of nowhere."

He grinned. "I got up early," he admitted. "Helluva change from eating MREs out in the Afghan desert, isn't it?"

Chuckling, Tara said, "Sure is. Sand in every bite. We've probably eaten enough dirt to last us the rest of our lives." She drank in how handsome he looked in civilian clothes. The winter storm was still blanketing the Midwest, and Kentucky now looked like a picture postcard. Dave wore a bright red sweater, a college-style white shirt beneath it, the collar starched and pressed. The jeans he wore fit his lower body to perfection, and Tara had to squelch the urge to run her hands across his hips and down his hardened thighs. Dave simply invited a hands-on approach, and she felt another kind of hunger stirring in her.

"I like the look in your eyes," he confided in a conspiratorial tone. As he passed her the small bowl of cranberries, their fingers touched and he met her shy smile. Dave thought Tara looked incredibly beautiful in her pale pink angora sweater with its cowl neck. The tan slacks she wore flattered her lower body, reminding him of the delicious curves he'd memorized with his hands on those few, precious nights they'd spent together at Khalid's home.

"I guess I'm hungry in other ways, too," Tara confided. She felt heat moving up her neck and into her face. Seeing an understanding glint in Dave's green eyes, she placed the cranberry bowl on the table between them.

"You're dessert to me, no question."

"And vice versa."

"It's been hell waiting," Dave said as he sipped the burgundy wine, "but worth it."

Frowning a little, Tara finished off her meal and put her plate aside. "Dave, you know I have to leave after thirty days. My job is in Washington, D.C."

Picking up the plates, he stood and took them to the small kitchen, setting them in the sink. "Yeah, I know."

"Kentucky is a long way from D.C." Tara got up and followed him into the kitchen as he ran water over the plates and set them in the dishwasher.

"I'm working on that," he murmured. Turning

toward her, he wiped his hands on a nearby towel. "Right now, the most beautiful gift I've ever been given is standing in front of me...." And he stepped forward and placed his arms around Tara's shoulders. Grazing her chin, he raised it and looked down into her worried gaze. "Love always finds a way, babe. Believe in that."

Closing her eyes, Tara moved against him and slid her arms around his waist, her head pressed against his chest. Just the soothing sound of his heart beneath her ear calmed some of her anxiousness. "I want to, Dave. I really do...."

Kissing her soft, clean hair, he marveled at the glossy reddish strands mixed in with the darker ones. "Listen, if we could save your life after you stepped on that land mine, anything else is a piece of cake, believe me."

Laughing, Tara raised her head and melted beneath his dancing green gaze. His smile was careless and boyish. "You know what I'd like to do right now?" she said playfully.

"Name it and it's yours."

"I want to go outside and make a snowman. I love making them."

Dave nodded. They needed to work off this meal, anyway. "Let's go do it...."

* * *

As daylight changed to darkness, the snow stopped falling. By the time the snowman, a substantial specimen, was built, Tara saw the moon rising above the naked branches of the trees in front of Dave's apartment. Her breath a white mist, she laughed as he came over, wrapped his arm around her shoulders and admired their mutual work.

"Great teamwork." The snowman had a green beret on its head, a red scarf around its neck and twigs for arms. Tara had found just the right size stones from around the edge of the building to make its eyes, nose and mouth. "A Spec For snowman," he exclaimed.

Laughing, Tara said, "He looks ready to enlist, Captain."

Pulling her against him, Dave murmured, "The last two hours flew by. Look at that moon. She's beautiful." And he pointed upward into the dark sky. The moon was past its first quarter, shining like a silvery lantern and casting shadows around the yard where they stood.

"Every full moon was dangerous for us over in Afghanistan," Tara whispered. Absorbing Dave's nearness, the feel of his arm across her shoulders, she saw him lose his smile and nod. The bright light of the moon made them targets when they roved around at night looking for the Taliban. The dark of the moon was always their friend, she had discovered.

"I know… Hey, let's go in. I want to love you, Tara…."

Closing her eyes, she smiled softly and pressed her cheek against his shoulder. "Yes…."

In the bedroom Tara found a queen-size bed with a downy quilt of white across it. Her heart raced with anticipation as she stood near it, with Dave next to her, his hands on her hips as he looked down into her uplifted face. His fingers moved to the hem of her sweater and she felt him begin to slide it upward. The moonlight shafted through the gossamer lavender curtain panels, casting beams across the oak floor where they stood.

The fine prickle of the sweater grazing her flesh as he lifted it over her head made her shiver. Beneath it, Tara wore a pale pink silk camisole and no bra. As she watched Dave place the sweater over a straight-backed chair nearby, she smiled at him.

"My turn…" She stepped boldly up to him and eased his red sweater off.

"I like this," he murmured wickedly, and allowed her to open his shirt, one button at a time. When he saw her fingers tremble slightly, he leaned down and gently teethed her earlobe. For a moment, she didn't move. Smiling, he knew he'd found a delicious spot that gave her pleasure. With his mouth against her temple, nuzzling soft, silken strands of her hair, he breathed in her fragrance as a woman.

"Keep going...." he rasped near her ear.

Laughing softly, Tara said, "You're making this tough, Dave!" And he was. His mouth trailed a series of soft, provocative kisses across her brow, and then he teethed her earlobe once more. The prickles came again, wild and electric. Finally, she divested him of the shirt. It fell in a heap at their feet.

Placing her hands on his hard, flat stomach, she felt the warmth of him and the strength of him. Sliding her palms upward, she ran her fingers through the short, dark hair across his massive chest, making him groan. Tara closed her eyes and felt her knees weakening as his large, square hands grazed her breasts beneath the camisole.

"Just getting to touch you," Dave breathed, as he worked on the closure on her slacks, "is grace to me. You know how you go through life trying to do right by others? You get burned so many times and you wonder if it's all worth it." He opened his eyes and drew back to drown in Tara's vivid blue gaze as the slacks fell with a whisper around her ankles and feet. Helping her step free of them, he felt her hands settle on the waistband of his jeans.

"Grace," Tara said. "I like being seen as grace in your life."

"I never thought I had any," Dave murmured, easing out of the jeans and pushing them aside. Gripping her hand, he led her to the bed. "Until now. Until you came into my life, babe." Lying down, he brought Tara alongside him. Her legs were long and strong. Moving his palm from her hip down one firm, smooth thigh, he added in a deep, husky tone, "You're my gift, you know that? I knew it from the first moment I saw you, but I fought it." Shaking his head, he began to ease away the camisole from Tara's body. "Stupid me." He grinned crookedly as he rolled over to look at her breasts for the first time.

Tara couldn't speak as his roughened hand slid reverently around the curve of her breasts. Instantly, her nipples hardened and she moaned, pressing herself against him. Before her mind turned completely to mush, she pushed the boxer shorts he wore down his hips. Dave helped by removing them and casting them aside. All that was left were her silken panties, which he turned his attention to next.

Wild tingles moved provocatively over her skin when he slid his index finger beneath the band. As he flattened his hand against her belly and eased the panties down her legs, Tara felt a hunger she'd never experienced before. She looked up and saw him smiling down at her, like a man who was proud of the woman he loved. The moment he settled his hand on her rib cage and caressed the curve of her breast again, she sighed.

"You saved my life…." she whispered tremulously, arching against him, wanting more. "I could see how much you loved me then, Dave. I saw it in your eyes. I heard it in your voice…."

Leaning down, he kissed her lips, which parted beneath the onslaught. The tension of her body against his, the warmth, the insistent movement of her hips, made him groan once more. Tearing his mouth from hers, he rasped, "I love you with my whole heart and soul, Tara. I always will…."

Moving her hand across his hip, she explored the lower part of his body, committing it to memory as he kissed her more and more deeply. Their breathing was rapid; their hearts raced erratically. Lost in pleasures, Tara allowed the need she'd felt for Dave all these months to rise within her.

Boldly, she curved her slender leg around his thicker, stronger one and pulled him on top of her.

As their hungry mouths broke apart, she smiled up at him. His eyes were narrowed and feral looking, those of a hunter who had his prey in sight. They were focused on her, and she felt her heart explode with primal love for him. "Love me, Dave. Love me with everything you have because that's what I'm about to do with you...." And she slid her hands up to his head and drew his mouth down to hers.

Arching her hips demandingly against his, Tara felt his length and hardness press against her. The sensation was dizzying, dazzling. Closing her eyes, meeting his strong mouth with her own, she felt him slide his hand beneath her hips and raise her slightly, just enough to allow him entrance. The moment was exquisite, their journey a heartbeat away. Breath suspended, Tara opened her eyes and looked into his.

"Yes...." she whispered. "Yes...now..." Her lips parted and she threw her head back as she felt him slide powerfully into her liquid, heated depths. The joy of their meeting was like a sudden thunderstorm, washing the world with wild, vivid color, motion, feeling and sounds. The movement, the rhythm established between them was like a potent ocean tide coming into shore, pounding, pulverizing. Tara tasted the sweat of Dave's temple as he leaned down, his head next to hers, his powerful body covering hers with each pumping movement. Reaching upward, she slid her fingers across his bunched, damp shoulders, found his mouth and thrust her tongue deeply into it.

In that moment, he tensed and so did she. The wild, throbbing heat that exploded deep within her body moved outward like an expanding rainbow arcing across the sky. She tore her mouth from his and her cry of joy punctuated his low snarl of pleasure. He gripped the sides of her head and held her captive to prolong their mutual passion. As Tara spiraled downward, feeling the delicious weakness that followed her climax, she fell into his strong, awaiting arms. They collapsed together, perspiration running in rivulets where their bodies met and molded, their breathing chaotic and swift. Closing her eyes, Tara turned her head, her lips near his ear.

"I love you, Dave Johnson. I love you with every fiber of my being. Never forget it... never..."

"Merry Christmas," Dave told her as he handed her a small, red foil wrapped gift tied with a silver ribbon. They were sharing hot chocolate and Danish pastries the next morning near the open fireplace. The white sheepskin rug on the hearth was from New Zealand, and Tara looked pretty as a picture sitting on it, clothed in a fleecy, pale lavender robe that outlined her strong, feminine form.

Looking up, she took the gift. "I never expected anything, Dave...."

He sat down next to her and picked up his mug of hot chocolate. "I know you didn't. Go ahead. Even though it's only Christmas Eve, you can open it." He grinned at her over the rim.

Laughing, Tara set her own cup on the wooden floor next to the rug. They'd slept after their lovemaking, and then, shortly before dawn, he'd loved her again. The experience was so beautiful it had made Tara cry. There was an incredibly tender side to Dave, and he'd given her that gift as dawn broke on the horizon. Body still glowing from his touch, she crossed her legs beneath the robe.

"When did you have time to get me a gift?" she wondered as she quickly tore off the wrapping.

"Oh, well...you'll see," he told her enigmatically. Tara's hair was soft and mussed, her lips well kissed and her cheeks pink. It was her eyes, that soft, doelike gaze when she looked at him, that made Dave feel like Hercules and not just an ordinary man. She made him happy. Fulfilled.

Opening it, Tara gasped. "Oh! This is lapis lazuli, isn't it?" She held up a gold necklace that had an oval pendant of the blue gemstone dangling from it.

"Sure is," he answered. "Made by the old jeweler in Tarin Kowt. You remember him? An old man in his seventies? Habib Osmani?"

Gazing down at the beautiful, feminine piece of jewelry, Tara whispered, "Oh, yes, I do remember him. He was such a dear old man. I always thought of him as the village grandfather. Everyone loved him. He was so kind to others, and generous...."

"I asked him to make you this," Dave told her in a conspiratorial tone, putting his arm around her shoulders. "Do you like it, babe? It's supposed to match the color of your eyes...."

Moved beyond words, Tara smiled up at him. "Oh, yes, Dave, I love this! I like the fact that he made it. It's as if he'll always be a part of us...."

"I was worried..."

"I love it...like I love you, darling...." She held it up to him. "Put it on me?"

Getting up, Dave moved around to her back and fastened the necklace around her throat. The deep blue stone settled between her breasts, over her large, giving heart. "There."

Touching the stone with her fingertips, Tara turned and moved into his awaiting arms. The fire popped and crackled pleasantly in the background. The sun was peeking out, the sky a pale blue outside the frost-covered windows. Nestling her head against his warm chest where his robe had opened, she closed her eyes. "I love you so much, Dave...."

"I know," he whispered. Easing his one arm from around her, he dug into the pocket of his terry-cloth robe. "I have one more gift for you, babe. Here it is...."

Opening her eyes, Tara laughed briefly. "What is this?" He handed her a neatly folded sheaf of papers that had been stapled together.

"Something I hope you like as much as I do...." And he kept her cradled in his arms as she opened them.

"Oh! Oh, Dave!" Tara gasped, sitting up abruptly and turning around. She looked at the papers again to make sure she hadn't misread them, and then up at him as he grinned wickedly at her.

"I—is this for *real?*" she asked, holding the sheaf up to him.

"Official orders, babe. Sure, they're real."

Blinking, her heart pounding, Tara reread them

again. "It says I'm to report here, to Fort Campbell, Kentucky, on January 22 to put a language lab together to teach Special Forces A teams how to speak Pashto."

"That's right. And it's a two-year assignment." He reached out and touched her bright red cheek. "That means, among other things, you'll be here with me. We'll have time together, Tara...if it's what you want?"

Blinking back tears, she sniffed and read the orders yet again. Her mind spun. How had Dave managed to pull this off? Wiping her tears away with trembling fingers, she whispered, "Oh, yes, that's what I want, Dave. To be here with you. To make a go of what we discovered in Afghanistan...."

"Good," he murmured, pulling her back into his arms and cradling her head against his shoulder. "This gives 'comrade-in-arms' a whole new meaning, doesn't it?" And he smiled down at her.

"Yes, and how appropriate, darling...." She waved the papers helplessly. "But how? How did you do this? I *know* you had a hand in this, Dave."

"Guilty as charged," he said, kissing her temple, her cheek and then moving his lips tenderly across hers. He tasted the salt of her tears—tears of joy. Lifting his mouth away, their noses nearly touching, he said, "I called Morgan Trayhern before we left Afghanistan, from Kandahar. I told him I loved you, and asked if it was possible for him to move heaven and hell to get you out of the Pentagon and to my part of the country.'' He grinned as he watched her luminous blue eyes widen like those of a child. ''He said he'd get it done, that love between a man and a woman was of national importance.''

''Whose idea was it for me to set up a language lab here?''

''Mine,'' he admitted, proud of the idea.

''Between you two men, I didn't have a chance.''

''Did you want one?''

Chuckling, Tara shook her head and placed the orders aside. Moving her hand up the nubby material of his robe, she drowned in the joy she saw burning in his forest-green eyes.

''Not a chance, Captain Johnson. All I want is you. What we have. And the time to explore one another even more.''

''Oh, yes, for a long, long time,'' he agreed, his smile widening when he saw the deviltry shining in her eyes as she leaned up to kiss him.

''Forever...'' Tara breathed against his mouth. ''Forever, darling....''

* * * * *

AN UNCONDITIONAL SURRENDER

Candace Irvin

* * *

For CJ Chase.
Thanks for all the incredible critiquing, CJ,
but mostly for the wonderful friendship.
I wouldn't want to travel this writing road without you.

Acknowledgments

As usual, my ideas fall well out of my range of experience
and expertise. I'd like to thank the following folks
for loaning me theirs. The cool stuff is theirs,
the mistakes are all mine.

Lieutenant Commander Michael J. Walsh, USN (Ret.).
Thanks, Michael, for planting the original idea
and feeding me enough information to help it grow.
Captain Norton A. Newcomb, U.S. Army (Ret.), Special
Operations Intelligence. As usual, Tony, you know exactly
what I need to know before even I do. Thanks for willingly
sharing it when and where you can. SSG Frank M. Risso,
U.S. Army (Ret.). Thanks for the fantastic crash course
in army artillery. Special Agent Scot Folensbee, DSS.
You're a new friend, Scot, and a blisteringly awesome
source. Thanks for all your help with the Diplomatic
Security Service. Stay safe out there! Finally, a special
thanks to my agent, Damaris Rowland, and my editor,
Allison Lyons, for believing I could do it.

Dear Reader,

A year ago, a friend and I discussed a modern twist on an old-fashioned evil: slavery. I knew then, I had to write about it. Still, I wasn't sure I could weave so heinous a crime into a romance novel. According to the U.S. Department of State's 2002 Trafficking in Persons Report, annual victim estimates range from 700,000 to 4 million women, children and men, many of whom are bought, sold and transported for sexual exploitation. The latter became a main plot thread in "An Unconditional Surrender."

In this story, Delta Force Captain Jack Gage is reunited with his former lover, U.S. Army Captain Danielle Stanton, when she's thrust into the clutches of a black-market slave trader half a world away. Together, Jack and Dani must work through past problems to complete their present mission. And once Dani's safe, Jack won't settle for less than a future with her—and the complete, unconditional surrender of her heart.

For more information about trafficking persons, check out my Web site www.candaceirvin.com, and follow the hyperlinks.

Candace Irvin

Chapter 1

If the road to hell was paved with good intentions, Jack Gage figured he ought to be banging on the devil's door any moment now. Despite his imminent welcome at those fiery gates, Jack condemned himself to remaining motionless in the southernmost corner of Rurik Teslenko's dank, claustrophobic hovel. Not an easy task given the force with which the stocky bastard dragged his current "crop" of Croatian slaves into the room before shoving them up against the opposite wall. According to Rurik, the trio of terrified girls were fresh in from Sarajevo the night before. What kind of man preyed on women from the city of his birth, much less his own ethnic group?

Unfortunately, Jack knew the answer all too well. Rurik Teslenko was not the only Bosnian Croatian, much less the only man, lining his pockets through the kidnapping and selling of young women. Nor was Rurik's impatient customer the only "peacekeeping" United Nations soldier out shopping for his personal, shamefully young, sex slave. Even if the Swede opted not to purchase a girl from this dark-haired collection, someone would. Jack could only hope he'd be able to accomplish his increasingly hairy mission before the next batch of salivating bastards showed up. For the moment, his relief eased out as the camouflaged giant across the room shifted his scowl from the girls to Rurik.

"I told you, I want a *blonde.*"

Rurik shrugged his shorter but equally burly camouflage-clad shoulders. "I had a blonde. Unfortunately, there were…complications." Rurik dug his fingers into the snarled mane of the closest girl. The final, muted rays of day bled through the window behind them, highlighting the fresh surge of terror in the girl's eyes as Rurik dragged her close. Eyes that had already been blackened by someone's eager fist. Eyes that had seen sixteen, seventeen years tops. Old, by Rurik's criteria.

Bile roiled through Jack's gut, magnified by the soft whimper that escaped the girl's swollen lips as Rurik thrust her otherwise pale face toward the Swede.

"For you, sixteen hundred *markas*."

Eight hundred U.S. dollars. For a sixteen-year-old kid. As vile as the transaction was, Jack kept his trap shut. Too much depended on his silence. Too many lives.

American and Bosnian.

Dust kicked up as the Swede spat on the concrete floor.

The gold cross Rurik wore around his neck flashed along with his gaze as he shoved the girl back to the line. "Fine. Come back next week. I will have another blonde. Fourteen hundred *markas* for your trouble."

Dark-blue eyes narrowed suspiciously. "No more than fifteen years—and a virgin?"

Rurik nodded. "I give you my word."

Any man who knew the Bosnian slave-trader well enough to warrant a private showing at his country compound also knew that despite his unsavory profession, Rurik Teslenko was worth his word. Still, the Swede held Rurik's gaze for a good

ten seconds before he jerked an answering nod. A
moment later, the Swede spun about and strode
across the stifling room. The four Bosnian thugs
flanking the entrance to the hovel stiffened as his
scuffed combat boots reached the bullet-riddled
door.

"Let him go."

Jack eased out his breath as two of the flanking
thugs followed the UN soldier out. One less customer along with two less goons in the room just
might allow Jack to ease Rurik out of this scorched
hovel and across the dilapidated dairy farm-turned-
terrorist compound he'd arrived at less than an
hour before. If Jack was really lucky, he and Rurik
would return to their now cooling mugs of coffee
in the main house along with their discussion con-
cerning another illegal transaction Rurik had also
expressed interest in. Weapons.

"How about a trade?"

Jack turned to his Bosnian contact, once again
at the trembling line of girls, nudging them several
steps forward, one by one. Jack had no idea if any
of them spoke English. Not that they needed to.
Rurik's body language was universal enough.

"No thanks."

His distaste must have shown because Rurik
grinned, showing off a quarter of a century of non-

existent dental work as he chuckled knowingly. "Ah, I see. You did not tell me in Mostar that you preferred boys, my friend." That damned decaying grin widened. "Since you have joined us, however briefly, I suppose we can send someone into Sarajevo to accommodate you."

The hell they would. "I like women just fine, Rurik. Women. Not boys." Jack flicked his gaze to the nauseatingly battered trio, careful to keep the true extent of his disgust from showing through. "And not barely pubescent girls. *Women.*"

"Women, eh?" Another inch and that smarmy grin would split the man's ears. Apprehension snapped along Jack's spine as Rurik turned to the door once more, to the burly goon who served as his right hand. According to army intelligence reports, Youssef Ben Adnan had endured the siege of Sarajevo along with Rurik a decade before. Once again, Rurik opted for body language—unfortunately, this time in a private dialect only Youssef seemed able to translate. Until Youssef turned and left.

Damn. The cook.

Sullen, subdued and up to her dark, dour bun in her master's illegal activities, the compound's cook was not his type. But she was definitely a woman.

Still, from the brief glimpse Jack had gotten of the kitchen earlier, she also appeared vital to keeping the rest of the slaves in line until they were sold. Surely even Rurik wouldn't degrade the one woman he seemed to trust simply to ingratiate himself with some shady American artillery sergeant? But then, "Sgt. Jackson" wasn't just any shady American artillery sergeant, was he? Not to Rurik. Jackson was the sergeant who'd saved the bastard's life in Mostar by knocking him out of the way of an incoming bullet. Was Rurik looking to repay the debt now?

The odds grew as Rurik turned his back on the girls completely, motioning the remaining thug to take over as he crossed the room. The odds quadrupled as Rurik slapped him on the shoulder and nudged him toward the bullet-riddled door.

"Come, my friend, join me in the kitchen."

Despite the dread congealing in the pit of his stomach, Jack allowed Rurik to guide him out of the hovel and down the grassy knoll. He forced himself to focus on the ancient farm, instead, once again cataloguing the dilapidated buildings as discreetly as he could. A cluster of four more bombed-out crofts lay to the left, two leveled to their permanently blood-stained foundations. The compound's main but singed two-story thatched house lay directly ahead, backlit by a now fiery setting sun. A huge pocked and scorched concrete slab still divided into cattle stalls lay to the right. But it was the massive intact dairy barn to the left and slightly behind the house that captured Jack's attention. And the armed thug standing guard.

What he'd give to knock that guard aside and slide those enormous double doors apart. But as Rurik turned to shove the significantly smaller door to the main house open and gesture him inside, Jack knew what he wouldn't give. His integrity.

This might be his first assignment with Diplomatic Security, but it wasn't his first time undercover. Hell, this wasn't even his first time selling to Rurik. The fact that this particular cover had survived their last brush four years before had been too perfect to pass up. But while Jack had been forced to abuse his fair share of unsavory tactics during his previous career, he'd never come close to raping a woman. He wasn't about to start now. If it came down to it, he'd accept a complimentary night with the taciturn cook—and hope to hell she didn't spill the beans regarding his sudden case of erectile dysfunction the following morning.

But what if she did?

Adapt and overcome. The motto slammed through his brain as it had so often during his seven years with Delta Force. Rurik had yet to consider that like the Swede, he might have his own list of preferences. Jack considered voicing them as he and Rurik turned into the narrow hallway that led to the kitchen at the rear of the house. He changed his mind at the last moment, unwilling to allow the thug that far into his head, much less his heart. Despite the fact that eleven months had passed, it was still too blessed raw. Unfortunately, the insidious ache had already locked in by the time Jack stepped into the humid, oversized kitchen.

She locked in. For a split second, Jack was terrified he was hallucinating. Even as the wave of instant, blinding rage swept through him, along with the punch of sheer, gut-wrenching terror, he knew he wasn't. This was no dream, it was a living, breathing nightmare. *Jesus, Mary and Joseph, no!*

That woman was *not* Dani.

But she was. He blinked, struggling to take in the matted, light-brown waves tangled halfway down her back, the deep purple bruise marring the curve of her left cheek. The shredded, once-white shirt with its sweat-stained tails tied now between her braless breasts—because the buttons and sleeves had been torn completely off. The matching sets of goddamned rusted *shackles* that were clamped about the cuffs of her jeans and slender wrists. It was her all right, Captain Danielle Stanton, U.S. Army. The woman he'd loved and then lost was in Bosnia. And she was Rurik Teslenko's slave.

For the first time in his career Jack had no idea what to do, much less what to say. If he opened his mouth, God only knew what would come out. Given the fury still blistering through him, the bone-chilling terror, the odds were overwhelming it would be something that would get Dani killed. For her sake alone, he managed to slow his frantic gaze—but not before he spotted the mottled bruises roping Dani's throat as she turned away to hide her own stunned reaction. She'd been *choked.* From the twin bloodred, almost black, splotches at the base of her neck, damned near to death. *By whom?* A split second later his stomach bottomed out. Ice-cold terror surged into its place. Sweet Mother in Heaven…had she been raped?

Acid seared though his gut once again, this time eating a path straight up to his heart. Before Jack could move—hell before he could think—Rurik flicked his gaze to his right-hand man. Youssef responded immediately by shoving Dani and her brimming pail of water toward the cook and the stove at the far side of the kitchen. The force caused her bare feet to tangle with the rusting links of her shackles, sending water sloshing over the rim of the plastic pail and onto the immaculate stone floor. The flat of Youssef's hand swung up and out—

"*Wait.*"

Youssef, Rurik, Dani, hell, even the cook froze. Unlike the others, Dani didn't turn to face him. Thank God. At least one of them was thinking clearly. Adapting. If he didn't get his brain in gear within the next two seconds, they'd both end up dead. Given her military specialty, he could only assume that like him, Dani was undercover—or had been before Rurik and his bastards had gotten hold of her. And if he blew that cover...

Fortunately, Rurik had chalked up his stunned reaction to something else. Lust. Once again that decaying grin split wide. "You are...interested in this one then, yes?"

Interested? He'd been *interested* in General Stanton's daughter since he'd been a green twenty-one-year-old cadet at West Point. Since Dani had been as young as the girls out in that croft at the time, he'd wisely nailed his mouth shut. Admitting the extent of that interest to General Stanton a decade later had damned near ended his career. Admitting that interest still existed now to Rurik could well end Dani's life.

Somehow, Jack managed to hook his elbow on the island counter. "Personally, I like redheads, especially if they come with green eyes." He stared at the light-brown waves for several moments, then shrugged. "The length of her hair might be a plus, though...if it didn't look like a family of rats had moved in."

"Agreed. But it can be combed, even dyed. Besides, she speaks English. You would be able to understand her."

"You trying to drive your own price down or what?"

Rurik laughed at that. Loudly. Figured. Somehow, none of the goons he'd met this evening seemed the type to engage in bedroom chatter. Not that he and Dani had engaged in much conversation themselves the one and only night they'd spent in the same bed. Maybe if they had—

Don't go there, buddy. Not here and not now.

Rurik flicked his gaze to Youssef once again— and, again, Youssef lurched forward. But this time the thug wrapped his fist around Dani's hair, using the bulk of her matted mane to drag her back to the island, directly in front of him. Both Rurik and Youssef ignored the sloshing bucket as it hit the floor, focusing on him, instead. Dani did not. She kept her gaze welded to the shackles at her feet as if she still didn't quite trust herself to look at him. He knew the feeling.

Given what they both knew he'd have to do to pull this off, he wasn't sure he trusted himself. Jack pushed off the counter, risking his cover more than he'd ever thought possible as he slid the fingers of his right hand about Dani's painfully slender neck, directly over the bruises. Using his thumb, he nudged her chin up, frowning as she finally met his gaze.

"She stinks."

The criticism earned him another grin—from Rurik and his deadly sidekick. "We may not have running water restored yet, Jackson, but we do have baths. I will send the other girls up with water for the tub." Rurik waved his hand. "And, no, before you mention it, her eyes are not green."

True. But neither were they basic brown like his. Instead, they were the most incredible shade of soft blue he'd ever seen. That first year after his dad's death, not much had succeeded in burning though the fog of his grief. But these eyes had. Even then, he'd noticed the color shifted depending on Dani's moods. It wasn't until this past year—their first undercover assignment together—that he'd discovered just how dark and stormy her eyes could turn when Dani was aroused…or royally pissed. They were storming now. And she was definitely not aroused.

Rurik chuckled. "I do not think she likes you."

No bombshell there. "You said she speaks English. Where's she from?" To Jack's surprise, silence greeted the question.

Son of a gun. For all the evidence of abuse marring her body, Dani Stanton hadn't even given up her nationality. If only her father could see her now. Jack masked the surge of fierce pride and swung his gaze to the men in time to catch Rurik's shrug.

"Based on her accent…Canada, perhaps. Though she may be American. You all sound the same to me."

Jack ignored the dig. "Did you at least catch her name?"

Again, silence. But this time, he swore Youssef flushed.

Jack covered the second surge of pride with a taunting chuckle as he returned to Dani. "Damn, Rurik. This must be some woman if neither of you have been able to get so much as a name out of her, despite your impressive—" he managed to smooth his thumb casually down her battered neck "—persuasion."

Youssef growled a string of base Arabic and stepped toward him. Right then, Jack knew whose hands had left these marks on Dani's throat. Who would pay. Unlike the pride, Jack embraced the rage. He released Dani and stepped forward as well, not stopping until he was squarely within Youssef's personal space.

"Enough!" Rurik jerked his chin toward Dani. "You want the woman or not?"

He kept his gaze fused to Youssef's. "How much?"

"Four hundred. But I keep her when you leave."

The amount slapped Jack back to reality, as did the rest. There'd be time for vengeance later. Right now his only concern was getting Dani out of Rurik's possession and into his—and there was only one way to accomplish that. That bullet in Mostar notwithstanding, Rurik was first and foremost a businessman. Though there was a chance the debt would help with the price. He hoped. Jack forced a snort and took his first step away from her. "I hope that's four hundred *markas,* not dollars."

"Dollars. For that, the woman will be at your sole disposal for the duration of your stay."

"Four *hundred* dollars?" He shook his head and took another step. "Christ, Rurik, it's not as if she was beauty-pageant material, even before your buddy Youssef got ahold of her."

Dani stiffened. From the renewed steel in her gaze, she was ticked. Good. But if she didn't pick up on his unspoken request soon and get downright pissed, they'd be in deep kimchi. He only had three hundred bucks on him. Given the beating Dani had already suffered, he couldn't risk a trip to Sarajevo and a bank to collect the rest. And there was still his mission.

"Three hundred...and if I like her, I take her with me when I leave." He'd already told Rurik he'd recently arrived for a mythical two-year rotation with a UN artillery unit. If he was lucky, Rurik would simply assume he preferred to keep the same sex toy around the entire time he was stuck in Bosnia. Relief flooded Jack as the bastard nodded.

"Six hundred, and *maybe* you take her if I am pleased with the other work you do for me."

"Six hundred? You offered the Swede a virgin for seven."

Rurik shrugged. "You wanted a woman, not a girl."

"A woman, yes." Jack stalked forward and grabbed the curve of Dani's chin, using it to twist her face beneath the stark light shining down from the bulb at the ceiling. "A battered and bruised hag, no." He jerked his fingers from her jaw and shoved them down the V of her shirt, determined to ignore the heat that gusted through him as Dani's breasts filled his hand. He almost succeeded—until the memory slammed in.

Her, him. On his bed. That sultry, perfect late-August night. These same sky-colored eyes damned near smoke-blue with passion. These gently bowed lips, swollen and slick from his greedy kiss. Dani's fingers sliding through his hair, down his neck, digging into his shoulders. Her husky moan swirling into his ears as she urged him up over her. Him—hot, hard and excruciatingly ready as he plunged deep inside her.

The memory shattered beneath Rurik's crude chuckle.

Red-hot rage blistered though Jack, incinerating his body's instinctive reaction to Dani's flesh after all these months. He tucked his free hand behind his back and clenched his fingers to keep from shaking with renewed fury. To keep from throttling them. God as his witness, Rurik and his goon would pay for tainting what until then had been his most precious, private memory. But most of all, the men would pay for what they'd done to the one woman who for a brief night had been the very center of his world. Jack allowed the barest breath of his roiling disgust to show through as he ordered his hand to fondle Dani's breasts in front of the bastards.

"Hell, she's already sagging."

She spat in his face.

Thank God. Jack wrenched his hand from her shirt and backhanded the good side of her jaw. A fraction of his strength, the smack was ninety percent noise and show. Fortunately Dani had worked undercover long enough to know it was coming. She rolled with it, allowing the illusion of force to send her slamming into the whitewashed wall. The solid whack to the back of her skull left no doubt in Jack's mind, that groan was real. He stalked forward grabbed her hair, using it to pin her as Youssef had done. Unlike Youssef, he sealed his lips to her ear as he seized the shackles at her wrists, spinning her with him—toward the island counter and away from the men as he asked, "You okay?"

"Finish it."

For a split second he was afraid the cook had caught on. But the woman turned to the stove and busied herself with a large iron pot. His breathing still raw and much too shallow, he wrenched Dani around with him once more as he faced Rurik.

The yellow grin split wide. "Three hundred to keep a hag that it appears you, too, will have to persuade?"

Jack shot his own grin toward Youssef. "Unlike your lackey, I'm up to the task." He was rewarded with another Arabic curse.

Rurik ignored it. "Three hundred it is."

"And if I like her, I take her when I leave."

"Agreed."

"Done." Jack shoved Dani to the bucket. "Go bathe, woman. Then wait for me in my room." He forced himself to turn away and shift the Beretta at his hip to tug his wallet from his camouflaged pocket. Pulling out the three largest bills, he tossed them to Youssef, earning another scowl as the man caught them. "Now, you two ready to discuss why you brought me here?"

Another of those blasted, decaying grins. "Tomorrow."

"Dammit, Rurik, I—"

The man tsked softly. "You Americans. Everything must always be your way, in your time. Our business can wait, my friend. Tonight is for pleasure." Rurik clapped him on the back, chuckling as Dani wrenched the bucket off the floor and stalked across the kitchen, slamming the wooden door smartly behind her. "Though I do not think your new slave appears pleased with the change to her sleeping arrangements."

Now there was an understatement. He might not have a clue as to what Dani was doing trapped on this bombed-out dairy farm in eastern Bosnia, much less how he was going to get her off safely, but Jack did know one thing. No matter how many times he'd relived that sultry summer night in his mind this past year, she sure as hell hadn't. Nor did she ever intend to repeat it. In fact, he was the last man Danielle Stanton ever intended to sleep with again. She'd told him so herself.

Chapter 2

She was naked. Clean, but naked. God help her, it was a state she'd give just about anything to fix, especially now, and not because of Youssef and the rest of Rurik's leering, groping goons. Because of him. U.S. Army Captain Jack Gage. Or had Jack made the major's list? She didn't know. She'd refused to look. Not that Jack would refuse to look—at her. If given the chance.

Dani grabbed Zorah's hands, furious with herself as the plea tumbled out. "Leave my clothes. A robe, a towel, a blanket." Something to preserve her shredded dignity. *"Please."*

"I cannot." Zorah shook her head sadly as she tugged her fingers free. Without missing a beat, the woman nudged Dani down into the tepid water until her shoulders were flush with the back of the claw-footed tub. Only then did Zorah splay the bulk of her hair over the edge of the weathered porcelain and step behind her to work the snarls free. "I am sorry, but Youssef says you must go to the man as you were born."

Youssef. One more reason to hate the bastard. As for the other one? She might owe Jack for sparing her another round with Rurik's henchman, but gratitude would never absolve Jack of his own debt. Much less, his betrayal. She still couldn't believe he was here. When she'd walked out on the man eleven months before, she'd known she'd see him again. She'd just never expected it would be in Bosnia, a day after she'd been kidnapped outside a women's clinic in Sarajevo. Then again, given Jack's relationship with her father, she shouldn't be surprised. Who else would Daddy send in to clean up after her? After all, according to the all-knowing General Stanton, Jack Gage was the best. At everything.

Dani winced as Zorah's comb hit a particularly large snarl. Yeah, she might have been incarcerated at Miss Porter's School for Girls by the time Jack arrived, but she'd been old enough to realize Daddy had gotten what he'd always wanted. A ready-made son. So what if her father had inherited a twenty-one-year-old Jack by default after a war buddy died in a car crash? Jack was the boy her father had taken under his wing when he was still a colonel and Jack a cadet at West Point. Jack was the boy her father had had over for weekend dinners and Army football tailgate parties, while she was stuck a hundred miles away. And, of course, Jack was the boy her father had tapped to follow in his hallowed Delta Force footsteps. His daughter, on the other hand, had to slink off to a civilian college and claw her way to an ROTC scholarship without Daddy Dearest's unfailing support, much less more than a cursory acknowledgement on commissioning day.

But the humiliation hadn't ended there, had it? Years later, she'd had the honor of standing on the wrong side of a barely cracked door in the Army's Special Operations Command headquarters at Ft. Bragg while her brand-new SOCOM general of a father had the nerve to discuss her with her brand-new special ops lover. A lover fresh from the first mission they'd completed together. Hell, fresh from their smoldering bed.

Even now the memory of the devil's bargain her

father and lover had struck had the power to burn through her. She'd been a fool to hope her father could ever change. More so to think his naturalized progeny would be any different. Her patience with Zorah's rhythmic combing expired, Dani sat up. She stepped out of the tub as Zorah set the comb on the chipped vanity. Neither of them bothered to drain the water. With the ancient well out behind the barn the only source of clean water for miles, the rest of the girls would be shuttled through the bathroom before anyone dared to pull the chain on the rubber stopper. To think, up until last night she'd actually thought her life stunk.

Lina.

Don't. Dani shoved the guilt aside and clung fiercely to hope instead. Until she had proof to the contrary, Lina was alive. Probably inside the dairy barn. Why else had Rurik posted a guard at the doors? Maybe Jack knew something. Maybe Youssef had bragged. Either way, Jack would be able to help her find a way to keep the other girls from falling victim to the same fate. The piercing hope purged the impending indignity of padding down the hall, past God only knew who, with nothing but a collection of purple bruises to conceal herself.

She blew out her breath. "I'm ready."

To her surprise, Zorah touched her arm.

Dani blinked, stunned to see the bleached towel in the woman's outstretched hand. "Are you sure? Youssef will—"

"—not know. Not if you lay the towel out to dry before the sergeant—before he…" Pity filled the woman's dark-brown eyes, softening the lines a decade of war and not-quite-peace had etched into her forehead and about her otherwise attractive mouth. "Return the towel when I come for you in the morning."

"I will. If anyone complains, I'll tell Youssef I insisted." A glimpse in the mirror assured her she needed a nice fat bruise on the right side of her jaw to balance out the lump on her left, anyway. Jack's hand had left the barest splotch of red. While her jaw was grateful, her cover might not be. They might have fared better if he'd struck harder. Dani wrapped the towel around her torso and tucked the end between her breasts, then dragged her hair in front of her shoulders to cover the rest of her exposed flesh. What she could. "Thank you, Zorah."

Dani padded down the hall alone, reaching the door at the end far too quickly. Sergeant Jackson's door. Evidently Jack had revived an uncompromised cover he'd used in and around Sarajevo and after the Bosnian civil war—that of an artillery sergeant of low morals. Given Rurik's collection of ethnically diverse thugs, it made sense. Sergeant Jackson had been known to steal weapons and ammo from NATO bunkers and then funnel the goods to all three sides within the Bosnian conflict: Croatian, Serb and ethnic Muslim. If the money was good, Jackson didn't care who bought. And no one would question the shady sergeant's interest in female slaves. Not with a shameful number of UN peacekeepers up to their tarnished blue helmets in the practice.

A practice she was supposed to be investigating—not joining, especially on the unfortunate end.

I told you so.

Dani slapped the phantom recrimination aside and shoved the bedroom door open. Before she could step over the threshold, an iron hand whipped out, locking about her wrist and jerking her inside the room, straight into a brown, T-shirt-clad chest. Before she could protest, Jack's hungry mouth crashed on to hers, swallowing her gasp as his tongue invaded her mouth. He consumed her second, deeper gasp as he ripped the towel away. He dumped the towel at his combat boots and replaced it with his hard, muscular arms. She was dimly aware of his body shifting as well, as if he was subtly using his length and bulk to shield her now-naked flesh from…who? Rurik?

The coarse chuckle behind Jack confirmed it.

Jack ignored it, appearing to lose himself to lust as he raked the fingers of his right hand through the length of her damp hair to knead and cup her breasts. The pad of his thumb scraped her nipple. To her utter humiliation, it stiffened. She responded by jerking her right knee up as she slammed her hands into the man's granite chest—for Rurik's amused benefit, as well as her hijacked pride. Unfortunately, Jack had eight inches of towering height and a much thicker set of muscles on her. He used every one of them to his advantage, too.

She was pinned. All her futile resistance had done was settle her intimately between Jack's thighs as he sealed her back against the wall. The chill sent goosebumps rippling down her body—until Jack shifted again, this time bracing his forearm to the wall above her head so he could gain deeper access to her mouth. Just like that, the months seared away. The numbing loneliness and constant heartache that had dogged her since, followed. They were back on Jack's bed, tangled up in his dark-blue sheets, sweat slicking their bodies as they fed the frantic need within each other. She could hear his hoarse encouragement, feel him driving in and out—feel herself clamping around him as she'd tried to keep from splintering into a million pieces because it was just too damned soon. *He'd* felt too damned right.

The memory had burned in so completely, she clutched Jack's shoulders as he tore his mouth from hers, instinctively protesting as he scraped his lips and scruffed jaw across her cheeks—until she felt his ragged breath in her ear.

"Dani…he's gone."

The fantasy evaporated as quickly as it had flashed to life. Unfortunately, the traitorous desire didn't. Unspent passion continued to race through her veins at double-time, every drop still headed low, to her core, as she struggled to regain control over her errant lungs. It didn't help that Jack's breathing was as harsh and unsteady as hers. Or that his biceps were rigid with restraint as he pushed off the wall. Off her.

Despite the curtain of hair concealing her breasts, the chill returned. The goosebumps followed. A disloyal flush seared them off as Jack's still-smoking stare followed the tide to her waist, then lower. *The jerk.* She didn't care if he'd spent the past year so deep undercover that an eighth of an inch of ankle peeking out from beneath a burka would've turned him on. Because of some bastard's jollies, she was the one standing here, stark-naked and exposed, beneath her ex-lover's stare, not him.

Somehow, she managed to infuse the steady cool her skin and nerves lacked into her voice. "May I have my towel?"

Jack's gaze snapped up, his confusion at her anger unmistakable as he blinked off his own remaining passion. What had he expected? Open-armed gratitude? Or was he honestly waiting for her to part another set of limbs?

"Well? I had to beg for that scrap of cloth. May I have it back…or do you plan on making me beg too, *master?*" She'd never know where she found the nerve to casually rake her hair behind her shoulders, much less stand there as her nipples puckered beneath his dark, riveted stare, but it worked.

The unflappable Jack Gage actually blushed. He stunned her again by peeling off the T-shirt to his camouflage fatigues, thrusting it into her hands as he spun away to lock the door. She wasn't about to turn it down. She donned the shirt in two seconds, disconcerted to discover Jack's lingering warmth and subtle musk had enveloped her as well. At least the differences in their heights allowed the hem of his shirt to skirt the upper portion of her suddenly pathetically weak thighs. Now if she could just scrounge up a pair of—

"Here."

Dani snatched the ball of gray from mid-air, donning the running shorts as Jack crossed the room to switch on a small AM radio. As luck would have it, one of Sarajevo's more modern and erotic *sevdalinkas* filled the room as he stepped away from the dresser. The folk song's refrain of unrequited passion grated across her nerves as Jack turned to stuff a spare uniform into the duffel bag at the foot of the bed. A twin bed. Great.

Could this case get any worse?

She should have known better than to ask. Definitely not before she risked her first real look at Jack since he'd strolled into that kitchen half an hour ago. Eleven months might have passed since she'd located her spine, locked it into place and walked out on this man, but he hadn't changed a bit. He was still as gorgeous as ever. Jack's thick black hair was still cropped on the army-long side, lightly tapered at the sides and back of his head. The morning-after scruff covering his strong cheeks and square jaw added just the right touch of rogue his singleton Delta assignments usually required. And his body...

Despite her attempts to prevent it, her breath bled out. Without his T-shirt, it was toe-curlingly obvious every inch of Jack's torso was still honed to perfection. He closed the duffel and straightened. She heeded the warning, bracing herself as Jack turned and caught her gaze. It was a good call. Damned if his eyes didn't still remind her of deep molasses. And damned if they didn't still have the power to suck her right in, to make her wish she could spend her entire life right here, just like this, lost in this dark, sweet craving.

But the longer Jack's densely lashed gaze held hers, the more she was forced to admit the preceding months had wrought changes in him. There were fine lines at the corners of his eyes now, as well as beside his lips. Last winter, when Jack had turned thirty-one, his temples hadn't contained a hint of silver. They did now. But there was something else too, something she couldn't put her finger on. Whatever it was, it was consuming him. She was certain of that when he stepped forward, then faltered to a halt.

She stiffened as it slammed into her. Fear. Jack was afraid of something. Had something happened after she left the kitchen? *Lina.* Or was it one of the other girls? Apprehension surged into panic as he took another step, then stopped.

"Dani?"

She swallowed carefully. "Yes?"

"Did they—" He broke off and this time, he swallowed. Hard. "Were you—" She swore she could feel him choking on the rest. On the terror. He reached out and trailed his thumb down her cheek, the pain in his eyes deepening to agony as he reached the marks Youssef had left on her neck. She knew what he was trying to ask, what he needed to know. He closed his eyes. This time, he didn't even attempt to voice the words. But she could hear them. His heart was screaming them.

Had she been raped?

"No."

His lashes flew open.

She stared into the shock and the disbelief—the blinding hope—and reached up to squeeze the hand still cupping the curve of her neck. "I swear, no one touched me. Not like that."

"How? Why?" For the second time in over a decade, Captain Cool flushed. Amazing. He cleared his throat. "I don't understand. I know these men. You're not as young as Rurik and Youssef prefer, but you're not—"

"—exactly a sagging hag, either?" The sarcasm

dripped out before she could stop it. Regret slapped into her as the tide spreading up his neck deepened to scarlet. She had no right to throw what had transpired in that kitchen in his face. She'd worked undercover long enough to realize Jack had had to establish up front he was as much of an asshole as the rest of Rurik's goons. It was the only way to protect both their covers. If she was lucky, it would also protect her from Youssef's rutting interest. "I'm sorry. That was uncalled for. I realize how you've scripted this—*us*—and so far, it's working."

Especially that kiss. Rurik had to have bought it. She had. That was the problem. Eleven months and one hell of a betrayal later, and Jack still had the power to affect her. Fortunately, there'd been enough adrenaline flowing through both their veins at the time for her to blame a hundred kisses on.

"Dani, I—"

She stiffened as he reached for her, deliberately ignoring the hurt washing into those dark pools as she quickly stepped out of his reach. She covered her body's infuriating need to crawl right back into those rock-solid arms with a shrug. "Really, I'm fine. Other than the fact that my cheek still hurts and my neck—" Just like that, the desperation ripped in. The sudden, overwhelmingly primal need for *air*. She closed her eyes instinctively, dragging her breath in slow and deep as she struggled to convince herself that she still could. Through the entire agonizing draw, she could still feel Youssef's thumbs clamping down on her windpipe, still see the bastard's satanic grin as he squeezed off what he'd hoped was her final breath. It was the last thing she remembered before blacking out.

She opened her eyes as Jack growled.

"I swear, I'll kill that son-of-a-bitch if he so much as touches you again." The fury throbbing within his voice was dangerous. Almost as dangerous as that kiss had been. It seduced her. Promised an unconditional love and support that would never be there. Not for her. Not from him. She'd discovered that the hard way. But at least the memory of the shame had succeeded in erasing the terror of this morning.

"Yeah, well. Take a number." She took another step, increasing the distance between them along with her resolve as she forced a smile. Pleased with the result, she even managed a shrug. "At least you bought me before the jerk made good on his promise to complete the job. Daddy should be thrilled. Hell, he might even put you up for another medal."

She wasn't sure what she'd expected. Denial? Anger? After all, she'd never confronted Jack or her father about what she'd overheard. Frankly, she'd been too ashamed. But what she hadn't expected was this pregnant silence. Even through the final, lingering notes of a Kalesijski Svuci ballad, she could hear it. Oh, God. Had something happened to her dad? "Jack...what's wrong?"

"Your father. He doesn't know you're missing. As far as I know, no one at SOCOM does."

She sucked in her breath as the panic crashed in. It didn't make sense. Her father wasn't some dime-a-dozen Pentagon general. He was the Special Operations Command's *commanding* general. If her father didn't know she was missing, who the hell did? How had Jack even known where to look for her? She reversed her progress, closing the distance to ensure their conversation stayed beneath the grating folk song that kicked in next. "I don't understand. I thought that's why you were here— to track me down when my transmitter didn't go live."

"Nope. But I did send a text message to my own contact though my cell phone when Rurik headed downstairs to settle a scuffle between his men, just in case. Hamid's a Bosnian foreign service national investigator. He's a good man. I dealt with him in

Mostar after the war. Hamid's probably already passed the update to your commander. You still with Executive Support?''

Bemused, she grabbed the set of dog tags off his duffel as she nodded. They matched the fictitious Sgt. Jackson.

''Good. That'll make it easier to consolidate our backup.''

''Fine by me.'' The cell phone Jack carried was bound to be encrypted. It wouldn't even arouse suspicion. A shady artillery sergeant with a secure phone in his possession and a 9 mm Beretta strapped to his hip was one thing; an International Red Cross worker with either was another. But if Jack hadn't been sent in after her, what was he even doing back in Bosnia?

As he had more than a few times during the husband-and-wife murder-for-hire case they'd worked together in the States eleven months earlier, Jack read her mind. ''Weapons.''

Damn. ''Rurik's buying?''

He nodded. ''Word on the street is the man's attempting to coordinate an all-out attack on the U.S. embassy in Sarajevo. Unfortunately, he hasn't ordered anything yet. When he does, I'll have a better idea of what he's already got. Together with his wish list, we should gain some insight into his plans.''

Dani sucked in her breath. This was big. Very big. And very dangerous. No wonder her father had sent Jack. It didn't matter if the man was disarming a bomb with five seconds left on the clock or stalking his way through the sleazy underbelly of the terrorist world that thrived on constructing them, Jack Gage was always cool. Always in control. She might have spilled half that bucket of water when she'd spotted him in the kitchen, but what she'd lost in liquid, she'd gained in hope. With Jack on the job, she was all but on her way back to Ft. Bragg.

The bucket. The water well. She fused her stare to Jack's. *"The barn."* Like Rurik's plans, it was huge. Large enough to hold a tank if need be—or worse. And it was under armed guard.

He nodded. ''I know. I saw the patrol on the way into the house. Did you get a look inside?''

''No. But I might be able to the next time I'm sent for water. Maybe in the morning.'' Zorah had already informed her that as Sgt. Jackson's personal slave, Dani was expected to serve his every desire from tonight on. That meant she didn't dare leave the room until sunrise at least. Not with every man waiting to see how long Jack would keep her abed. Among this rutting crowd, if she left the room early, it would be a direct reflection on Jack's manhood. From the way Jack had shifted his stare from the claustrophobic twin bed to the blaring radio, she knew he was thinking the same thing. He was also remembering.

Another bed, another night. Two exceptionally eager lovers. They hadn't parted until dawn then, either. Both of them exhausted from lack of sleep and four hours of near-constant exertion. The alarm had startled them out of the latest leg of their erotic marathon, forcing them to bring the night to a mind- and body-shattering end. A quick, mutual shower ensued, followed by what had to be a record donning of camouflage BDUs for both, then a soul-searing kiss at her car door—seconds before he'd promised a replacement for the makeshift meal they'd forgone as well as the *now that we admit we're attracted to one another, where do we go from here?* conversation that should have followed.

If it had, they might have been able to save themselves the awkward tension pulsing between them now.

He cleared his throat. The terse, familiar sound snapped her back to the utter humiliation that had come after that steamy night. She turned, pacing the length of the tiny room even though she knew she'd be forced to turn around when she reached the door and head back to the bed. Back to Jack. She filled her lungs with air blessedly devoid of his unique musk and slowly retraced her steps until she reached the side of the bed. Despite their painful past, they had the present to deal with.

Rurik. For Jack's undercover mission, as well as hers.

"I'm working the M.A.S.H. case. Two female sergeants from the 42nd Field Hospital disappeared a week ago. They'd been assigned to NATO for almost eight months. For the last six, the sergeants had taken to volunteering at a women's health clinic in Sarajevo. The last time anyone saw them, it was dusk. They were en route to their barracks from the clinic on foot."

His brow shot up. "At night? Not smart."

She shrugged.

"What about you?"

"Apparently not so smart either."

He grabbed her hand. "You went out alone at night in Sarajevo?" He would think the worst, wouldn't he?

She jerked her fingers from his and stepped away, anxious to reclaim the distance she'd yielded. "I said not so smart—I didn't say stupid."

Then again, maybe he and her father were right. She shoved Lina's sobbing from her head and skirted Jack's imposing torso, wrapping the metal chain to his dog tags around her left hand as she sank on to the mattress. "My cover's with the International Red Cross. I stopped by the clinic yesterday on my day off and told the staff I wanted to help. Everyone seemed so sincerely committed to helping the women regain their dignity that by evening, I was reconsidering my initial suspicion that someone on staff was involved in the sergeants' disappearance. Until it was time to go."

The mattress sagged as Jack added his weight. "What happened?"

"Everyone pitched in, cleaning the exam rooms for the next day. By the time I finished, I was exhausted. I walked out with two locals without my purse." Okay, so she *was* stupid. She'd also been subsisting on a thirty-six-hour jet lag followed by twelve hours of manual labor. Still, she should have known better. The screw-up had cost her. But not as much as she'd cost someone else. "A couple blocks away, one of the nurses noticed. They waited while I headed back. But when I rounded the last corner, Youssef slammed his fist into my jaw. Before I could recover, he'd stabbed a needle into my arm. That's the last I remember." Until she'd woken to Lina's sobbing.

Jack shook his head. "I don't understand. If Youssef struck you, how do you know someone on staff's involved? Anyone could have injected you with that needle."

"I recognized one of the girls from the clinic. She was treated a good six hours before I was kidnapped, yet we both ended up here." Dani sighed. When she'd woken on the floor that morning she'd noticed her watch missing, so she'd decided to make a move for the emergency transmitter hidden in her shoe—until Lina's struggle with Youssef changed her mind. In her lingering, drug-induced fog, she decided to take Youssef on instead. She'd never get those moments back now. She'd never know whether tripping the signal as she was supposed to would have made a difference. Would backup have arrived in time?

Dammit, *don't.* She'd been so out of it, she'd been little more than a punching bag herself. There was no way of knowing if she'd even have been able to trip the transmitter.

But she hadn't even tried, had she?

"Dani?"

She stiffened. Not from Jack's touch on her arm, from the note in his voice. Like his fury toward

Rurik on her behalf, his concern for her was far too seductive. She didn't doubt it was real. It just hadn't been enough. It still wasn't.

"I'm fine." She shifted from his touch, dragging in her breath as she tried to ignore the hurt in his dark eyes. All she succeeded in doing was filling her lungs with his scent. Lord, did she have it bad! Less than an hour in Jack's company and here she was, wanting him again. She couldn't help it. For the first time in almost a year, Jack was in the same room as her, close enough to touch—even if he *was* staring at her as if he was afraid she was about to break. There were so many questions she wanted to ask, so many things she needed to know. Unfortunately, not a single question crowding her heart concerned their respective missions. They had to do with him. With them.

Had he missed her? Had he wondered where she'd spent this past Christmas—and, more importantly, the day after? Or had Jack already found someone else to celebrate his birthday with by then? Had he been too busy torching those dark-blue sheets of his with her replacement to even care that she'd kept her vow?

The lack of oxygen from Youssef's attempted strangulation must have affected her brain. Either that or her guilt over Lina's death had affected her heart. Because she finally raised her head and stared directly into that dark, simmering gaze. Before she realized her intent, she opened her mouth and asked the one question she'd sworn she wouldn't ask.

"How's my dad?"

Chapter 3

She didn't know.

Jack stiffened as the realization socked in. He searched Dani's gaze, praying he'd misheard. But when those soft blue eyes darkened to damp, pleading smoke, he knew he hadn't. Dani had no idea that after she'd walked out on him eleven months ago, he'd finally scraped up the nerve to swallow that goddamned choking case of gratitude and do what he should have done years before. He'd walked out on her father.

It might have taken all his hopes and his dreams crashing down for him to realize she'd been right that last night they'd seen each other, but eventually, he'd accepted the truth. He had been standing between Dani and her father—for ten long years. Whether he'd wanted to be there or not. And now, incredibly, almost another full year later, half a blessed globe away, he was still standing between General Stanton and his daughter. The irony of it would have bitten him in the ass.

If it wasn't already ripping through his chest.

"Jack?"

He swung his gaze to hers, the ache deepening as he watched the fear seep into her eyes. He'd do anything to erase it, he knew that now. Even lie. "Your dad's fine." He waited until the fear began to ebb, then changed the subject before she could question him further and he was forced to compound his lie. Now was not the time to come clean about her dad. And this sure as hell wasn't the place. "How was it supposed to go down?"

She blinked at the sudden shift.

"Your kidnapping case? I'm assuming you had a plan. One my presence in that kitchen interfered with?"

Her gaze cleared. "Yes. My watch contained my tracking device. Unfortunately, it was missing when I woke this morning. I have no idea who took it, or when."

"Maybe one of the other girls—"

"*No.*"

For a split second, her vehemence startled him—until he recalled the mottled bruises on the other girls' faces. She was right. Those girls had had more to worry about lately than petty theft. He was about to confirm her assessment when he noticed the sudden glistening in Dani's gaze. Her stark, distant gaze.

Just like that, the fear surged back into his gut. The cold, nauseating terror. Youssef. She'd sworn the bastard hadn't raped her, but what about Rurik and the rest of his thugs? While Dani was older than Rurik's perverted tastes, rape wasn't about desire. It was about a twisted need for power. A need Rurik had nursed since the siege of Sarajevo years before. Jack sucked in his breath, his own blistering rage. God as his witness, if he could turn back time, he would—and this time, he'd make damned sure that bullet landed deep inside Rurik Teslenko's brain. Jack stared at the bruises mottling Dani's face and neck and forced the words past his bile. "Dani, I know you said Youssef didn't touch you…like that. But something happened here. Something more than a vicious beating. I can see it in your eyes."

Hell, he could see it in the way she'd wrapped

the chain to his dog tags around her hand for the umpteenth time. Only this time, her knuckles turned white. Her fingertips followed. He swallowed the searing acid as it threatened to choke him.

"Dani...what happened?" When she didn't answer, he stepped closer. The folk music he'd switched on to provide cover for their conversation grated through him. He'd have given anything to strangle that shrieking accordion long enough for him to gauge the whisper of her slow, studied breaths. To know if she needed him to pull her into his arms and hold her as tightly and as desperately as he'd ached to hold her since the moment he'd spotted her in that kitchen. Dammit, why wouldn't she look at him? "Honey, you can tell me anything. You have to know that."

She finally raised her gaze...and he damned near died.

"Can I?"

Those two tortured words ushered in a complete and profound understanding for her father he'd never thought he'd hold. *"Yes."*

"I screwed up."

"How?"

For several moments, he didn't think she was going to answer. As he watched the emotions churning through her eyes, he wasn't sure if she could. But then she sucked in her breath and spoke. "When I woke this morning, I was on the floor. Where, I can't be sure, my brain was still fogged from whatever they injected me with. Anyway, the first thing I did was reach for my watch, but it was gone. I had a backup transmitter in my shoe, though. I should have gone for it. I might have made it." She sucked in her breath again. This time it came out in a rush. "Dammit, I was trained to go for the alarm first—because there might not be another chance. I should have *tried*."

"Why didn't you?" But he knew. The blonde. The one the Swede had come for. The one Youssef had raped and murdered. Rurik's *complication*. The tears welling in her eyes confirmed it.

"I heard a girl. The same girl from the clinic. Her name was Lina. She was sobbing on one of the beds, half naked." His heart burned as Dani stopped to scrub the tears from her battered cheek. She swallowed hard. "Youssef was all over her. He was…raping her."

"You went for her instead of the transmitter."

She nodded dully. "Yes."

"Dani—" He caved in to the need burning through him and reached for her, only to clench his fingers into a fist as she jerked away from his touch. From him.

"Dammit, did you listen to what I said? Because of me that SOS was never sent. Because of *me,* a young girl was beaten more severely than she ever would have been beaten. I was too drugged up to help. Youssef was livid with me for interrupting. If I hadn't passed out, I have no doubt he would have strangled me to death. Instead, he turned his rage on her."

Jack forced the latest wave of his own rage from his mind and his heart and locked it deep in his gut. Stored it. Nursed it. Youssef would pay for what he'd done and soon. But not now. For now, he had Dani to deal with. Her grief and her guilt. He ignored her subconscious retreat as he lowered himself to the bed. Somehow, he kept from reaching out as she wrapped the chain about her fingers once again. Though her fingers were bloodless now, he knew that chain was the only thing holding the rest of her together. "Dani, what happened to Lina? Where is she?"

She kept her gaze fused to his tags. "I don't know. Rurik, Zorah, Youssef, none of them will tell me what happened. But I haven't seen her since. The other girls are too terrified to talk to me. Youssef threatened to beat them if they did. I had hopes Lina was in the dairy barn. Maybe to keep her separate as she healed. But given why you're here, it's looking unlikely.''

She was right. But until they had evidence to the contrary, she couldn't be sure. Neither could he.

''I'll talk to Rurik tomorrow. I may be able to get him to tell me what happened to her. Either way, you and Lina may have spared the other girls from Youssef's wrath. The bastard might have threatened to beat the remaining girls if they talked to you, but I don't think he'll dare because I also overheard Rurik ordering Youssef and the rest of the thugs to leave the girls alone. I got the feeling Rurik's worried about something. He may need the money to pull off the embassy attempt.'' Why else had Rurik accepted three hundred dollars? Dani was worth six, seven hundred to the man at least. ''Dani, did you hear me?''

She nodded numbly. Still, she wouldn't tear her gaze from his tags. And her fingers. They'd progressed beyond white. The tips were turning gray. Unwilling to jeopardize her circulation, he reached out, gently but insistently unraveling the chain. That done, he risked reaching for her again, sliding his arms around her shoulders to pull her close. It was a mistake.

She flinched. This time, the recoil wasn't even

subtle. The message was even clearer. *Don't touch.* But at least his blunder allowed her to pull herself together. She drew in her breath and waited patiently, if stiffly, for him to release her. Though it cut deeply, he did, abandoning the bed as she pulled her knees up to tuck them beneath her chin. Her stare evaded his once again, sliding out across the room. Nothing had changed between them. Why had he even hoped it could?

Habit? After all these months—hell, after all these years—it wasn't going to change. She wasn't going to change. She didn't want to. It was time he accepted it. Dani would never see him as anything but the usurper of her father's affections. God knows he'd tried to change that view eleven months ago. Well, he'd failed. Hell, she didn't even know he wasn't with Delta anymore. From her question about her father, she had no idea he hadn't even seen the man but once in the past six months. But that pointed to something even more startling. She hadn't seen the man either.

The rift between Dani and her father was finally complete.

He might never have been able to capture this woman's heart, but he did understand it. He understood her. After the chilling discovery he'd stumbled across last month through an old war buddy of her father's, he understood Danielle Stanton better than she understood herself. If he confessed that he wasn't with Delta, she'd demand to know the rest. What then? She was already hanging by a thread over Lina. There was no way he could bring himself to sever it. If he did, he might lose more than the promise of her heart this time.

He could lose her life.

He shoved his hand into the cargo pocket of his fatigues as he worked to ease the tightening in his chest as well as his growing private terror. Despite the accordion still wailing out from the tiny radio, he caught her sharp intake as he retrieved the open pack of Marlboros he'd brought along for the job.

"When did you start smoking?"

He tapped the base of the pack on his palm. "I don't. Sgt. Jackson's trying to quit." And as far as Rurik was concerned, Sgt. Jackson had just finished one hell of a steamy romp. Might as well use the misconception to strengthen their covers. He shoved his hand in his pocket again, withdrawing the unopened pack. He flipped the cigarettes to Dani, pointing to the sealed cellophane wrapper as she caught it. "That one contains my emergency transmitter. I'll talk to Rurik about your clothes. Maybe we'll get lucky and your shoes and watch will show with them. Until then, hang on to those.

If we get separated and things go south, open the pack and activate it. Hamid will hear the signal and send backup. He's loitering less than a mile away with some distant relatives of his—a band of Roma gypsies.''

She tossed the pack back. "I can't."

Dammit, they'd already established whose mission had priority. As abhorrent as Rurik's slave racket was, Dani's case held three innocent young lives in the immediate balance, if they located the missing soldiers, five. His held hundreds, perhaps thousands. That meant she followed his orders until they figured out how to get out of this mess, not the other way around. He sighed.

"Relax, will you? I'm not defying Gage the Great. I'm being realistic." She dropped her knees, revealing the T-shirt and shorts he'd loaned her. "Where exactly should I hide the pack? Between my breasts?" She was right. With her bra missing, the thin fabric of his shirt clung to every generous curve—right down to the nipples that stiffened beneath his errant stare.

His palms betrayed him, itching in memory. Unnerved, he tapped out a cigarette from the pack in his hands and retrieved his lighter before the rest of his body decided to follow the insurrection. The moment she gasped, he realized his error.

"You *kept* that?"

Talk about getting caught red-handed. His fingers tightened about the silver casing before he could stop them. He loosened them as he shrugged. "Why not? It comes in handy from time to time." He flipped open the lighter she'd presented to him upon his graduation from West Point and lit the cigarette, then tucked the lighter firmly home. "Besides, I heard it was the thought that counts."

And they both knew what she'd been thinking when she'd bought it, didn't they? So had her father. He could still hear the man bellowing at her through the door of his study. Dani turned as beet-red as she had the moment she'd marched out—a barely seventeen-year-old slip of a girl, but the very picture of Betrayed Woman. At least this time she wasn't glaring eternal hatred. "I'm just... surprised you still have it."

So was he. Other than that sultry night a decade later, it was the only gift she'd ever given him. He'd thrown the thing in the trash a hundred times since, only to fish it right back out. Jack shoved the cigarette between his lips and punished himself for each retrieval with a deep, searing drag. He knew from experience it would be enough for the stench of tobacco smoke to cling to him for hours. If only Dani had been as experienced as she'd pretended to be the first time they'd kissed...with cigarettes and with men. Who knows? He might have ended up with her on graduation day instead of the lighter.

Right. He spun around to the dresser and settled the smoldering cigarette over the lip of the ashtray Rurik had dropped off. By the time he turned back to the bed, she was lost in the distant past, too. In the night they'd met and the day after. He doubted she'd ever forget that first weekend. Eleven months ago, he had thought she'd forgiven him, though. Worse, he actually thought she'd cared about him. But she hadn't.

Though they'd parted in a torrid rush in his driveway, he hadn't minded. Mainly because all the way in to Ft. Bragg, he'd reveled in the fact that despite that amazing shower, he could still smell Dani's scent on him. He'd savored the fragrance all morning, along with the memory of her touch. They'd made plans for dinner that night, but he couldn't wait. By noon, he'd decided to stop by Dani's temporary office across post and surprise her with lunch. Unfortunately, another Stanton had opted to head down the hall for an impromptu chat. At the time, it had seemed prudent to forgo lunch with Captain Stanton and dine with the general. In retrospect, it had turned out to be a lousy decision.

By the time evening rolled around, Dani had changed her mind about more than dinner. She'd decided to pass on him.

He still couldn't believe she'd chalked up the hottest night of his life to a case of cold chemistry. *Adrenaline.* Too bad he couldn't lay claim to the hormone. Not then. Those erotic hours they'd spent together on his bed had been anything but a by-product of the flush of a successfully completed mission. Not for him, anyway. He'd long since accepted that this heightened awareness and fiery rush that scorched through him whenever Danielle Stanton was around didn't have a thing to do with some chemical pulsing through his blood. Well, he was just going to have to get over it, wasn't he?

She obviously had. For a few blinding moments at that door, he'd actually believed differently— until he'd pulled away and watched as the adrenaline had worn off—in her. Hell, even now Dani's body language screamed the truth. The woman he'd tried so hard to purge from his mind and his memories these past months would give anything to be anywhere but here with him. He was sure of it when he retrieved the lighter and pack of cigarettes and stepped up to set them on the nightstand beside her.

As she had when he'd tried to hold her earlier,

she flinched. Suddenly, he was sick of it. Of them.
The past, the present. This entire mission. She
wasn't supposed to be part of his present anymore.
And he sure as hell wasn't supposed to be hanging
around on the fringes of this woman's life fanta-
sizing about a future. He'd gotten out of the Army
to get away from Dani and her overbearing father.
Yet here he was, right back where it had all started
a decade before, trapped.

Well, he'd had enough. "You ready to turn in?"

She jerked her gaze to his. Blinked. "Uh…
sure."

"Good." He grabbed the strap to his duffel,
hefting the bag from the bed and dumping it on
the floor with more force than he'd intended. The
duffel skidded to a stop beside the dresser. He ignored the startled brow that arched in his direction
and headed across the room, the hollow thumps of
his combat boots counting off the paces to his
pending incarceration.

He slapped the light switch and darkness flooded
the room. His night vision adjusted to the shadows
and sliver of moonlight bleeding in from the single
bare window as he returned to the bed to remove
his boots and socks. He dumped them atop his duffel and withdrew his 9 mm from the holster at his
hip, chambering a round before extending it butt

first toward Dani who until that moment, once again appeared to be doing her damnedest to look anywhere but at him.

"Tuck this under the pillow."

There wasn't much left to do while she complied but loosen his holster and belt and start in on the buttons beneath. He took a deep breath as Dani stood to yank the quilt to the foot of the bed, then he tugged his trousers down as well, skivvies and all. He dumped the fatigues on top of his boots before he could change his mind and stepped up to the mattress.

"Wh-what are you doing?"

He glanced across the bed. Despite the shadows, there was enough moonlight for him to make out the shock in her face. That, he'd anticipated. But not the suspicion. And, dammit, it burned. Especially when she'd made it crystal clear through every one of those emasculating cringes that she meant what she said when they'd parted a year ago. She felt *nothing* for him. He snagged the sheet from her hand and snapped it to the foot of the bed. "What's it look like? I'm getting into bed. So are you."

"Not like that you're not."

"Dani—"

"Don't 'Dani' me, buster. You're naked."

"Nice of you to notice." The words snapped out before he could stop them. They caused her suspicion to sharpen.

Her frown followed. "It's kind of hard to miss."

"Really?" He turned away to grab the ashtray from the dresser. Ashes from the still-smoldering cigarette puffed up as he slapped the tin on the nightstand. "And here I thought you needed a hit of adrenaline to notice what I was wearing...or wasn't." For the first time that night he wasn't offended when she stiffened; he was pleased. Unfortunately Dani had crossed her arms in her pique. Moonlight glinted off the fabric of his shirt as it strained to contain her pair of extremely generous breasts. A split second later, something else stiffened.

Great. He needed an erection right now like he needed a second terrorist sleeper cell answering to Rurik's own band of thugs. Jack forced himself to ignore his body's reaction, praying Dani would have the tact to follow suit. Then again, this was General Ramrod-and-Ruthless Stanton's daughter.

"If you think I'm crawling in bed with you like that—"

"Don't flatter yourself, sweetheart. It's a reflex reaction, nothing more." That was no lie. "Any woman could have caused it." But that was. It was also a low blow. One Dani didn't deserve. Not given the day she'd had. She was perilously close to breaking. He could see it in her eyes. In the tears that were held just barely at bay. He sighed. "I'm sorry. That was out of line. Look I'm not crazy about bunking down with you either, let alone in the buff. We don't have a choice. That door may be locked, but all it takes is a skeleton key. I wouldn't put it past Rurik or Youssef not to waltz in here during the night to check up on us. Would you?"

Silence. But he knew he'd made his point and made it well, because the tension began to ebb from her body. She finally dropped her arms. "You're right, I wouldn't put it past either of them. Given the conversation around here today, both of those bastards think rape is a spectator sport. Rurik probably only left when he did because he needs you." She sighed. "I was out of line, too. I suppose I should be grateful. The Army could have sent in a stranger. At least we've slept together before."

The moment that last statement left her mouth, she regretted it. He could tell from the way she flushed—dark enough for the tide to show despite the shadows. He knew what she was thinking, because he was thinking it too. They might have shared a bed for four hours but, technically, they hadn't actually slept. They'd been too busy doing something else. Lots of something else. In lots of ways. And every blessed one of them had been incredibly good.

He purged the flood of memories before his body could react to those as well, then clipped the lighter and pack of Marlboros from the nightstand. He crushed the first cigarette into the ashtray and took his time lighting the next, praying she'd use the delay wisely. It would have worked—if the raucous notes of the latest folk song hadn't died out then, leaving just enough dead air for him to make out the swish of fabric followed by two soft plops as his shirt and shorts hit the floor. He cursed the sultry ballad that filled the room as the bed dipped.

Dammit, get it over with.

He dumped the smoldering cigarette into the ashtray and braced himself. By the time he turned, Dani was hugging the opposite edge of that painfully narrow bed, her back to him, quilt pulled firmly to her neck. He snagged the corners of the covers and crawled in, cursing every inch of his oversized, hulking body as he struggled to maintain the microscopic buffer of air between them. Air that was growing hotter by the second. He closed his eyes and forced himself to relax. Everywhere.

Eventually, he felt her relief ease out as his body managed to behave. An eternity later, he felt her yawn as exhaustion scored its first and probably only victory of the night. In this room, anyway. From the moment he'd accepted Rurik's invitation, he'd known he'd be facing a long, sleepless night. But when Dani finally succumbed to sleep—and her warm, silky length gradually eased closer until it was searing completely into his—he also knew it had just gotten a hell of a lot longer.

Chapter 4

The bedcovers were missing.

Even with the sleep-induced mist fogging her brain, Dani was sure. She could feel a cool breeze drifting across her body. Jack must have opened the window when he'd gotten up to turn off the radio. Except for their breathing, the room was quiet. The mist cleared from her brain, only to leave a more disturbing discovery behind. She'd rolled during the night. Even though she'd yet to open her eyes, she was certain. She could feel one of Jack's hands cradling her breasts. That wouldn't have been so humiliating...if her fingers weren't knitted together and tucked snuggly between the man's thighs. His muscular, *upper* thighs. In fact, her hands were all but fused to Jack's—

Maybe he was still asleep. It was possible. They were here, weren't they? Trapped together on a case she'd never have volunteered for if she'd known the man lying two inches away, completely nude, would be on the same continent as her. She held fast to the belief that fate owed her one and opened her eyes. Unfortunately, fate had decided to leer back. Again.

Not only had Jack's lashes parted, revealing dark, knowing pools, but the rest of his body was rapidly waking to the predawn light. Within seconds, the flesh brushing her fingers grew hot and hard. Very hard. Her nipples stiffened in response, pressing directly into his palm. And that made Jack's flesh harden even more. His gaze merged with hers as the air between them smoldered. Ignited. Memories seared in. Another room, another bed. Hopes, dreams. The heady promise of what could have been. Someone's breath caught, then rushed out.

Whose, she couldn't be sure.

In the end it didn't matter, because the half rasp, half groan that followed jolted both of them from the trance. The length of Jack's erection singed her fingers as she jerked her hands from his thighs. A split second later, he pulled his hand from her breast, turned and jackknifed off the bed, snagging his fatigue trousers as he shifted away to don them. She grabbed the reprieve, swinging her legs off the bed and reaching down to snatch his T-shirt and shorts from the floor. By the time Jack had finished buttoning his trousers and turned to retrieve the pack of cigarettes from the nightstand, she'd donned both.

He tapped out a cigarette and exchanged the pack for the lighter she'd never have imagined he'd actually have the nerve to use. But he had. Based on the number of scratches marring the silver casing, more than once. Either that or he'd taken to carrying the lighter with him years before. Both options unnerved her more than she cared to admit. So much so, she took perverse satisfaction in the distaste he didn't bother hiding as he purged the initial drag from his lungs. She hoped he choked on the filthy smoke. God knows she had.

Jack braced his right hand above the open window as he turned away, no doubt to keep that stifling smoke swirling inside the room instead of out. Despite the broad back obscuring her view, she knew he wasn't studying the shadowy hills or even the darkened dairy barn off to the right. He was studying the lighter. The engraving. *Thanks for the lesson.*

Like her father, he probably still assumed those words and that lighter were meant to get back at him for the stunt he'd pulled the day after they'd met years ago. They were. But they'd also meant more. To her, anyway. Of course she'd had to mature a bit before she'd understood her own unconscious dig.

When she'd first met Jack Gage, she'd been a kid. Sixteen years old, newly expelled from Miss Porter's Prison for Proper Ladies and downright desperate for her father's attention—good or bad. Getting caught with a pack of Lynette Cove's cigarettes and condoms on the eve of one of West Point's stuffy spring banquets—specifically, one her father had to attend—had finally earned her the latter. It had also earned her Jack, West Point formal, dress gray uniform and all. Though Cadet Gage had tried to hide it at the time, Jack had been as dismayed as she when his mentor had asked him to play junior jailer for the night. To their surprise, they'd actually hit it off. Or so she'd thought.

Her polite, but too-proper escort had loosened considerably after he'd discovered that she, too, studied jujitsu. By the time Jack had taken her into his arms on that dance floor, her first serious crush was already budding. The next day, it was in full bloom. A late-afternoon movie with a handsome, though still very serious twenty-one-year-old Jack would have turned any girl's head—much less the intimate dinner for two at a quiet, out-of-the-way sidewalk café in nearby Highland Falls. So when Jack had excused himself and slipped inside the café for a moment, she hadn't suspected a thing. Not even when he'd pulled out a pack of Marlboros over coffee. She'd been so full of herself, not to mention too terrified to let him know she wasn't the fallen—or rather, mature—girl her father had accused her of, she'd accepted the cigarette Jack had casually lit for her and inhaled.

She'd nearly lost her dinner on his boots. Even after she was breathing again, she hadn't suspected a thing. Jack was that good, that concerned, that contrite. And she'd been that dumb. It wasn't until he brought her home and she'd snuck downstairs to listen in at her father's study that she'd discovered the truth. The betrayal. The *debrief*. Jack wasn't interested in her. He'd simply been tasked with a mission. Colonel Stanton wanted to know if his daughter smoked, so Cadet Gage had set out to uncover the truth. Mission accomplished. In return, Cadet Gage had earned the gratitude of one of Delta's most respected senior officers. She, however, had received nothing but yet another wave of her father's cold, distant fury…and a broken heart.

Dani waited as Jack tapped the line of ashes from the dwindling cigarette out the window. With no one around but her, he didn't bother with a second drag. Nor did he face her. He simply braced his hand above the frame once again, though this time he actually stared out the window. Silently. Tired of waiting, and definitely tired of avoiding that muscular back and the memories it stoked, Dani turned to the bed. Big mistake.

She'd rather face the man's sleek back than their rumpled sheets. Though white instead of blue, the covers spilling over the foot reminded her of another bed. Another silent, predawn morning. Of her burning need. Not so much for sex. That had been well-sated by then. No, by then she'd been consumed by a searing need to ask Jack if those steamy hours they'd just spent together had been about more than blistering sex. Did he care about her? *For* her? Did they have a future outside the bedroom?

Before she could scrape up her nerve, the alarm had gone off. Jack had suggested they meet after work for the conversation they'd skipped hours before, along with a fresh pizza to replace the cold one still sitting in his oven. She'd agreed, hoping she'd get the answer to her question. She'd gotten it, too, sooner than she'd expected. It just wasn't the one she'd been praying for. But it was one she should have expected.

Fool me once, shame on you. Fool me twice, shame on me.

Well, she wasn't going for thrice. Dani stepped up to the dresser and switched on the radio. The bawdy *sevdalinka* that filled the room was easier on her nerves than Jack's slow, studied breathing. In deference to the thin walls and open window, she nudged the volume down and turned to shake out the quilt before smoothing it over the mattress. She retrieved Jack's Beretta next and fluffed the pillow. The bed made, there was nothing left to do but clear the round Jack had chambered the night before. He finally deigned to turn around as she thumbed the 9 mm's safety and released the magazine onto the bed.

"I want you to carry the extra pack of cigarettes."

She jerked back on the slide, tracking the ejected round's trajectory from the top of the barrel down to the quilt. "We've been through this. Unless my fashion ensemble changes, that pack will stick out like a transvestite in a wet T-shirt contest."

"I don't care."

"Well, I do. Frankly, I've got enough—"

"Dammit, woman, look at me."

She slapped the slide home. "Why? Because you've decided it's time for eye contact, oh Great Delta Master?" His answering growl skirted beneath the fractious folk song. Barely.

She didn't care. Nor did she comply. The three hundred bucks the man had shelled out had obviously gone to his head. Either that or he was still pissed because she'd managed to cut through his lies and beat him to the punch—chalking up the night they'd shared to pure emotionless sex before he could. Adrenaline hadn't driven her into bed with him a year ago. It had driven him. Whether he'd admitted it or not. Jack might have been twenty-one the first time she'd overheard his Benedict Arnold routine, but he'd been thirty-one the second. She might've been able to chalk up the first betrayal to youthful indiscretion, but not the second. There was no way he could have cared about her and then blithely said what he had to her father.

She plucked the bullet from the quilt, ignoring his sigh as she snapped the round into the top of the magazine.

"Dani…will you please look at me?"

She slammed the magazine home as she finally complied. "Why? So you can order me to do something that could very well get me killed? Rurik may like them young, but Youssef doesn't much care. He may not have raped me yesterday, but neither did he keep his hands to himself. Those filthy paws were all over me and I don't just mean my *neck*. His friends aren't any better. Do you understand what I'm saying or must I spell it out for you?"

From the way Jack's jaw locked as his gaze shifted past her shoulder, he'd caught the image vividly enough. Or maybe not. She had the distinct impression there was more to that frozen stare than the sight of Youssef's hands on her body, copping a feel. He continued to stare at the wall as his fingers closed over the smoldering cigarette. They didn't stop until he'd crushed it, glowing ember and all. He didn't even flinch.

"Jack?"

He wrenched his gaze back to hers. "No. You don't have to spell it out."

"Good. Then maybe you can see why—"

"You *need* to carry the transmitter." He pitched the pulverized cigarette to the floor and closed the distance, his gaze burning more fiercely than the flame on that stupid lighter as he locked his fingers to her shoulders. "You have to listen to me. Rurik and I are supposed to finalize our deal today. I may have to leave the farm with him. Not only will I probably not know when, I may not even know where I'm going, much less how long I'll be gone. In other words, I can't guarantee I'll be able to watch your back. If you don't carry that transmitter, Hamid won't be able to watch it either, however distantly."

"And what happens when Youssef corners me by the well and shoves his hands up my shirt and finds cigarettes tucked in my shorts? You think he's going to wait until Sgt. Jackson returns before he opens the pack and steals a 'sample' from there, too?"

Jack closed his eyes.

Dammit, he had to stop doing that. Jack didn't care for her any more than he cared for Lina and the rest of those girls. She was just another component to his increasingly complicated mission. She wished he'd stop making her feel like she was more. He jerked his hand from her shoulder and shoved it into his pocket. The unopened pack of Marlboros surfaced with it. He grabbed the Beretta and shoved the barrel into the waist of his fatigues, then pushed the cigarettes into her palm.

''You can't order me to carry this and you know it.''

He plowed his fingers into her tangled hair, forcing her head and her gaze up until she was drowning in those dark, unnerving pools. ''I'm not ordering you. I'm *begging*.''

Good God, he was. Why? Stranger still, whatever had been in his mind's eye when she'd shoved Youssef's behavior in his face was back. For the second time, she had the feeling he was holding out on her. But as she opened her mouth to question him, someone pounded on their door, then bellowed through the wood.

Rurik.

The doorknob twisted through a wider range of motion than it should have as Rurik pounded on the door again. The bastard was using his key! She jerked her gaze to Jack's, shoving the pack of cigarettes into his hands as his swift nod confirmed her suspicion. The door swung open with the next series of thumps.

The man feigned surprise. ''Excuse me. The lock must be broken.'' Nope, no Academy Award nominations there. Rurik Teslenko's acting was as rotten as his teeth.

She didn't bother disguising the glare she shot Rurik. In deference to their covers, she turned a meeker glance on Jack. "I'll help Zorah with the water as you ordered." She headed for the door before Jack could pretend to change his mind.

"Dani?"

Damn. She stopped, turned slowly back. Waited. Relief washed through her as Jack nodded his permission—until he tossed the pack of cigarettes toward her.

"You forgot these."

She caught the pack instinctively—and promptly tossed it back. "Thank you, Sergeant. But I'm trying to quit, too." She crossed the room, careful to give Rurik the respectful berth he believed his due from the inferior sex. She needn't have bothered. Rurik had latched on to the fact that Jack knew her name.

His decaying grin settled on Jack with grudging admiration. "You *do* persuade better than Youssef, my friend. You will have to tell us exactly how you accomplish this."

Dani ignored Jack's dry response as she snagged the bath towel Zorah had loaned her off the back of the chair and stepped out into the darkened hallway. Jack might not be a criminal, but he could be an arrogant bastard all the same. No wonder Delta had assigned him this mission. The man fit in far too easily. She hurried to the kitchen. If she was lucky, she could forge an inroad with Zorah, convince the woman that despite the rare trust Rurik had placed in her, she didn't fit in. Dani reached the dimly lit kitchen less than a minute later.

Unfortunately, Zorah wasn't there. The back door was slightly ajar, too. Odd. The day before the door had been locked whenever the kitchen was empty—from the outside. She'd checked. Not that she'd had any plans to escape, even before Jack's arrival. But Zorah didn't know that. Nor did it seem in the woman's nature to be so careless. Especially with the radio droning faintly from the guest room above. Dani folded the bath towel and crossed the freshly swept tiles to lay it on the kitchen island, even more intrigued when she spotted the empty pails beside the stove. Zorah couldn't have gone for water, not with all four pails accounted for. Rurik would be bellowing for his breakfast soon. So why wasn't the woman busy making it?

Dani grabbed the opportunity to find out. She hooked a pail over her arm and retrieved the spare kerosene lantern from the shelf above, lighting the lamp with a match as she stepped out onto the path to head for the water pump behind the barn. Ten steps across the cold gravel, she realized how great her opportunity was. The sun might be below the horizon, but there was enough of a glow bleeding up that she should have noticed someone guarding the dairy barn. So far, no one.

Ten more steps confirmed her excitement. The armed thug she'd noted the day before was definitely missing. And there was still no sign of Zorah. Another thirty paces and she was at the man's post—and definitely alone. She glanced at the house. Though the windows on the western side were open to take advantage of the breeze, none of the rooms were lit. Jack had even turned out the light in theirs. Nor was she able to detect any motion within. She spun around to the front of the barn. To those massive sliding doors and the iron links looped about the handles. To that gleaming padlock. Do it.

She dropped the pail onto the grass and stared at the lamp for all of two seconds before extinguishing the flame. While she could have used the flame to peer inside, it also served as a beacon. She set the lamp down beside the pail and tiptoed over the remaining gravel, wincing with every crunch that echoed across the grass. The double doors had been hung from a single rail running across the top. She tried the padlock just in case. As expected, it refused to budge. She tried the left door next. That did budge, but by less than three inches. There wasn't enough give in the chain for more. She jerked the chain in her frustration—and the door moved. At the bottom.

The track at the top had allowed the twin slabs to move away from the barn by a good eight inches at the base. More than enough room for her face. She shot over to the far left only to freeze as she noted the haphazard line of nail heads embedded down the door's frame. Unlike the rusted heads on the wooden doors themselves, these nails were new. She tucked the discovery in her brain, slipping her fingers beneath the bottom edge of the slab as she dropped to her knees. She ignored the splinters stabbing into her fingers as she wrenched the door away from the frame and wedged her face into the opening. Damn. Nothing but dank shadows. She should have risked the lamp.

Five more seconds of squinting and she blew out her breath and sucked up her disappointment—and stiffened.

She purged her lungs and closed her eyes, focusing all her senses on her next breath. Her next sniff. Her stomach lurched as the unmistakable, acrid mix of diesel and gunpowder seared into her lungs along with the stench of old manure and moldy straw. She jerked her eyes open and stared in vain. She couldn't see a blessed thing. But she did hear something. Crying? She closed her eyes again, this time tuning in to sound instead of scent. There…just beneath the buzzing of nocturnal insects. Someone was definitely crying. Or rather, trying not to. *Lina?*

No, that didn't make sense. The muffled sniffs and hiccups weren't coming from inside the barn, but outside. Near the back, near the well. Lina had been beaten much too severely to take on the task of hauling water a day later. It had to be one of the other girls. One of Rurik's thugs must have decided to ignore the moratorium on rape. Her gut told her she'd located the missing guard as well. Dani shoved the barn door against its frame and stood to scoop up the lamp and pail. Jack might not be able to risk interfering, but she sure as hell could. And this time, she wasn't drugged. She stalked around the side of the barn, picking up steam as she rounded the final corner only to jerk to a stunned stop two feet from the heated couple.

The bearded guard froze along with the woman in his arms.

"Zorah?"

The woman's inky hair might be tumbling down her back in disarray, her blouse and the scarf around her shoulders twisted and disheveled, but they hadn't gotten that way against her will. Dani blinked as the guard jerked his arms from Zorah's shoulders as if he'd just realized he'd been cradling the woman to his chest like a lover he adored and not some mere vessel for sexual release. By the time the guard sucked in his breath, almost all the blood in his face had drained down past his beard, leaving his normally swarthy complexion pale and waxy as the silence strung out. The thug was truly terrified—of her. A mere woman.

It would be laughable if she didn't know what this jerk did for a living, or at least, what he turned a blind eye to. The guard tensed as Dani opened her mouth. She didn't blame him. If she screamed and Rurik deigned to investigate, which would be worse? Getting caught raping the man's off-limits cook...or making love to a woman as if she was an equal?

Dani closed her mouth and waited instead. His shirt still hanging half out of his trousers, the guard finally took a step forward, his gaze wary and fixed to hers. And then it wasn't. Even before that dark stare jerked past her shoulder and turned frantic, she heard it too. Or rather, *him.* Youssef. The bastard was bellowing for Zorah, demanding his breakfast like the royal advisor he thought he was. And he was dangerously close.

Dani weighed their collective options against her

case as well as Jack's and made a split-second decision. She shoved the empty pail into Zorah's hands. "Get dressed. Fix your hair. Then fill this." She turned to the guard. "Get back to your post—and shove your damned shirt back in your pants. I'll stall him." She whirled about before either of them could argue and struck out around the side of the barn, the cold lantern all that stood between her and the smack that would undoubtedly follow.

If they were lucky.

Two steps later, she slammed into Youssef's iron chest, deliberately swinging the lantern up into the side of the barn with enough force to shatter the glass. Kerosene splashed into his eyes. A second later, the thug's eyes slammed shut as his fist slammed into her. White-hot pain exploded in her jaw. It ripped into her scalp next as Youssef grabbed a fistful of her hair and used it to pull her close. Her ears still ringing and vision still fuzzed from his punch, she couldn't make out his features clearly, but she could damned sure smell his putrid breath as he vented his twisted opinion of her and every other woman born since Mohammed. She could have handled that. Hell, she *was* handling it. Until the moment he mentioned Lina's name—and promised her the same sadistic fate.

That was when she lost it.

She jerked her right knee up in the classic move her self-defense instructor had taught her when she was eight years old, slamming it squarely into the bastard's groin. Satisfaction seared through her as Youssef doubled over and bellowed like a bull who'd just been gelded. Unfortunately, he'd hauled the bulk of her hair with him as he hit his own knees. He shifted his grip as he staggered to his feet and used her hair to slam her head into the side of the barn. By the second whack, her eyes were watering. By the third, she'd decided that Jack was right after all.

She should have taken the damned cigarettes.

Chapter 5

The second Jack saw Dani's head hit the side of the barn, he knew—Youssef Ben Adnan was going to die. *Now.* He didn't even bother drawing his 9 mm from his holster as he raced out of the compound's kitchen leaving Rurik Teslenko eating gravel. Hell, he didn't even bother retrieving his switchblade or the knives concealed within his jump boots as he tore down the thirty-yard path separating his hands from the bastard who'd dared to strike the one woman he'd never been able to get out of his heart. He simply reached his target and wrapped his fingers around the bastard's throat and let his rage carry him through.

Within seconds, Youssef's skull had followed Dani's fate.

Rurik and his remaining goons were wise enough not to try and stop him as he yanked the dazed thug around, slamming Youssef's shoulders against the barn as he sealed his thumbs to the man's windpipe, mirroring the precise grip the bastard had used on Dani's far-too-slender neck the day before. Only, Jack made sure he clamped down harder as he checked that same slender neck and its owner over. The sun had risen above the foothills beyond, affording him enough light to be sure. Despite her latest beating, Dani appeared fine. Youssef, however, did not.

Jack jerked his attention to the gasping, choking bastard as the thug's hands clawed at the backs of his. A moment later those dark, shifty eyes began to bulge. Another moment, and Dani's fingers dug into his biceps.

"Sergeant, *please,* I'm—"

"Stay out of this, woman!" Jack caught Rurik's stern agreement. He wasn't surprised. Nor did he attribute Rurik's comment to a latent need to protect women. As far as every man here knew, Youssef had touched his personal property. Property he'd purchased fair and square the night before. It was his right to settle this—if he could. And he would.

However, Jack had caught the underlying warning in Dani's voice. She was right. Now was not the time. There was more at stake here than his heart or his rage, or even Dani's battered head and face. He did, however, wait until the very last second. Until he could feel the frantic fury in Youssef's writhing body ratchet to absolute terror. He crushed his thumbs all the way down into the man's windpipe for a single, piercingly satisfying moment—and then released the pressure, slamming the man's limp, wheezing body against the side of the barn as he stepped away.

Youssef immediately twisted to his side and retched.

The show over, Rurik rounded up the members of his motley crew with a jerk of his chin and ordered them to the house. The goons marched off with Zorah, clearly unnerved, in tow. Moments later, the bearded guard Rurik had pegged as C'emal, shouldered his AK-47 and peeled off to resume his post as the group passed the front of the barn. Rurik's gaze returned to the still-heaving man at their boots and lingered. He finally dismissed his fallen stooge with a disgusted shrug.

"Are you coming, Sergeant?"

"You go on ahead—and take this piece of crap with you. I need some fresh air before we leave."

Rurik held his gaze, then nodded. "Agreed."

Not that he had a choice. Not if Rurik expected him to live up to the bargain they'd struck up in that bedroom. Rurik snapped his fingers twice as he turned onto the gravel path. Like any master with a well-trained mutt, Rurik didn't wait to see if it obeyed as he followed the others back to the house.

The mutt wiped his mouth as he stood.

"Youssef?" The bastard stopped, nursing his bloody lip with the back of his hand as he waited none-too-patiently for Jack to finish. Jack did, deliberately keeping his voice soft, "Unlike some cowards I've met, I'm not fond of sleeping with little girls *or* damaged goods. In other words, you even think about touching my woman again and I'll do more than bash your head in. I'll break your neck. *Koji se razume?*"

Oh yeah, Youssef understood. The spurt of bloodred fury rivaling the ripening sunrise beyond the barn proved it. Jack waited until Youssef stalked off before he risked facing Dani. The moment he spied her swollen bottom lip, he knew the decision had been wise. Especially as he reached out to wipe the trickle of blood from the corner of Dani's mouth with his thumb.

"Where's the well?" Christ, his voice was hoarse.

She pulled away, jerking her chin toward the rear of the barn. "It's back there."

"Let's go." He splayed his fingers over the small of her back before she could argue and nudged her along. One of the plastic pails from the kitchen lay upended on the dewy grass beside the hand pump. He scooped it up, dropped it beneath the iron spout and filled it. He stripped off his T-shirt and leaned down to soak up enough freezing water to soothe her cut.

His heart burned as he stood. Her soft blue eyes were so damned big, they filled her face as she stared up at him. And her *body*. The woman was just too slender, too blessed tiny for his peace of mind on this particular mission. Especially given what he'd discovered the month before. Dressed in his spare tee-shirt and shorts, her hair tangled and devoid of makeup save the newest bruise discoloring her bottom lip, Dani looked chillingly similar to her mother in the crime scene photos he'd gotten ahold of. So much so, his hand shook as he carefully washed the remaining blood from her lip. He hadn't been careful enough because she winced. "Sorry."

"It's o-okay."

"The hell it is." He'd meant what he said to Youssef, he'd kill the bastard if he so much as thought about touching her again. He rinsed the end of his shirt and pressed it to her lips again. "Hold this." He relinquished the makeshift compress and threaded his fingers into the tangles on her scalp so he could probe the skin beneath. No bleeding. By some miracle, there were no lumps either. But the skin was scarlet. It had to hurt like hell. He smoothed her hair into place. "What in God's name possessed you to kick him in the bal—"

"I didn't kick him. I kneed him."

"Semantics. *Why?*"

Her eyes glistened as he tucked her hair behind her ears. She swung her gaze past his arm to stare out at the foothills. He took a moment to scan the opposite direction. The massive barn hid them from the house and they were far enough from the guard's post to speak freely, if quietly. Still, he'd have expected C'emal to shift to roving patrol mode by now. This far back, Jack had a clear, straight shot up both sides of the barn. C'emal was oddly absent, affording them complete privacy.

He shifted his attention to Dani. She was still staring past his arm, her eyes still glistening with unshed tears. "Dani? Why did you kick him at all?"

"She's dead."

"Lina? Are you sure?"

Her nod was jerky, curt. The tears barely contained now. "Yeah. He threw it in my face after he slapped me. That's why I lost it. I know, I shouldn't have. But when Youssef told me she died during the night, still sobbing, he was *glad*."

"He's a sick bastard, honey."

"Trust me, I know."

"Then you also have to consider that he may be lying. Rurik didn't mention anything about a girl dying during the night—and we did discuss the remaining girls, though briefly. I found out they're being kept under lock and key in one of the stone crofts. Rurik and his sister have the only keys."

She gaped up at him. "His sister?"

He nodded. "Zorah. Unfortunately, he mistook my question about the girls for interest. He's trying to convince me to take one of the girls off his hands in exchange for verifying a weapons transaction in a couple hours." He shook his head as her eyes lit up. "That's all I know. He wants me to inspect something. I have no idea what."

"I do."

Hope surged. "You got a look inside the barn?"

She shook her head. "It was too dark. But I did get the distinct impression of size—and the stench of diesel and gunpowder. *Plus,* the entire left side of the barn has new nail heads and recent hammer indentations in the wood. As if they had to remove part of the frame and then reconstruct it because something very large wouldn't quite fit through those doors."

He cursed softly, viciously.

She nodded.

Somehow Rurik Teslenko had gotten his hands on a tank, or worse, a goddamned self-propelled howitzer. He'd stake his newly minted DSS shield on it. Based on the fact that Rurik's compound was twenty miles out of Sarajevo—well within range of the U.S. embassy—the worst-case scenario was most likely. A tank would have to be driven straight down Alipašina Street to get close enough to knock on the embassy's door. Even from there, it would take all day to pound it down. But one 8-inch shell from a howitzer would accomplish the same job in under a minute. Two, three more shells and the entire embassy would be leveled.

"Jack?"

He raked his fingers through his hair and dug

them into the base of his neck. Neither helped the knot already throbbing at the base of his skull. "It's not enough. I can't risk mobilizing Hamid and the rest of the team yet." They both knew if he moved on Rurik without enough hard evidence to hang a conviction on, the man would just slip away and spawn a new terrorist cell. One that this time, Diplomatic Security might not be able to locate until it was too late. If it hadn't been spawned already.

"Dani, I have to go though with the meet." Which also meant he was going to have to leave her behind. Unless he could get her to agree to a change in her own plans.

"No."

"I haven't even suggested it yet."

"Don't. I am not taking off across that field. I don't care who you have on the other side. I managed to forge a connection with Zorah. I have to see it through. I owe it to the sergeants I came in after, whether or not they're alive, and I owe it to Lina." She held out his damp shirt. "Don't ask me to leave."

He balled up the shirt to cover his frustration— until the rest sank in. "What do you mean you forged a connection? You were out here ten minutes before Youssef cornered you."

"Youssef didn't corner me. I deliberately ran into him." She tapped her swollen lip. "That's why I ended up with this. I heard crying and thought it was one of the girls so I headed back here. I practically caught Zorah and that bearded guard going at it on this very spot. Before any of us had a chance to recover, I heard Youssef and decided to head him off."

She'd risked her own neck for one of Rurik's thugs?

A fresh wave of fury crashed into him, this one directed at her decision. A decision beyond foolish. He clamped down on to the shirt, ignoring the water that dribbled onto his boots.

"You weren't there. It was a good call. They owe me."

"Like Lynette owed you?"

Her eyes darkened as she glared up at him. He didn't care. Dani might be damned good at her job, but she could be far too trusting. He'd seen it himself through the years. The first, the weekend they'd met. She'd admitted it herself in the café after she'd recovered from that cigarette and finally confessed the pack of Virginia Slims and condoms discovered under her mattress weren't hers. She hadn't even known her best *friend* had stashed them there until the headmaster had hauled her into her office. Lynette never had come forward.

"I was sixteen, Jack. Stupid. I trusted you, didn't I?"

He frowned. This wasn't the time or the place to continue this. Besides, he'd apologized for that.

"What, the guilt not sitting well?"

He checked the barn. She might be on the money about the guard's sympathies because C'emal was still completely out of sight. More importantly, still out of range of their voices. Why not? In deference to her father, they'd danced around the memory of that weekend for ten years. Maybe now was the time.

She was staring at him, her smooth brows arching when he glanced down. God help him, her arms were crossed. Rurik had better produce the woman's bra soon—before he went insane. Jack sucked in the cool morning air, hoping to purge the unwelcome, but not unexpected, rush of desire searing through him. "Like you said, you were *sixteen*. Someone had to get to the bottom of what happened. You wouldn't talk to your father."

"So what was your excuse the second time?"

Second time? "I have no idea what you're talking about."

"Whatever." She shrugged sharply and stepped

past him, clearly intent on returning to the main house. Oh, no. She was not dropping a cryptic comment like that and walking off on him. He had enough to occupy his brain today. He slapped his shirt over his shoulder and snagged her arm, ignoring the warm silk that replaced the damp, clammy cloth.

"Explain."

She stunned him by wrenching her arm from him. The low growl and whisper she ground out next were just as fierce. "Let's get one thing clear right now, Captain. You don't outrank me and you sure as hell don't *own* me. So unless someone's watching, keep your goddamned hands to yourself."

Instinct forced him to do the opposite. This time, he locked both his hands to her arms.

"I'm warning you—"

"Fine, warn me. But while you're at it, do me the courtesy of explaining. I don't know what you're so fired up about, but I'd like to be filled in now. Before this mission ends and you sneak right back out of my life without so much as a goodbye."

Jesus! What was with him today? He did not need this woman knowing he'd hung around Ft. Bragg for an entire month following that blissful night before he'd found the strength to murder his empty hope and put his plans back in motion. Not when she had accepted an assignment that sent her to the opposite end of the globe the very next day—and didn't even bother to inform him. Eventually, he'd come to accept that when Danielle Stanton said, *Thanks for the sex. It was great, but it's over and I'm outta here,* she meant it. Especially when she stared at his dog tags as if she'd dearly love to use them to strangle him with.

"Are you going to release me?"

"No." There wasn't a blessed thing she could do about it either and she knew it. Not given the crowd up in that house.

"Jack...this isn't fair."

He had to laugh at that. Curtly. "Fair? Don't talk to me about fair, lady." He leaned low so he could grate the rest directly into her ear. Not because he was afraid C'emal would remember who he worked for any time soon, but because *he* still didn't even want to admit it to himself. "You're not the one who twisted your life into a pretzel only to find out afterwards that while you thought you had something great going, the other person had been driven by nothing more than a mix of good old-fashioned lust and surging *adrenaline.*"

She flinched.

He dropped his stare to her throat as he dragged his mouth away from her ear, maintaining his hold on her arms as he stared down at the pulse now thundering at the base of her neck.

"Go to hell."

"Been there, done that, sweetheart. You ought to know, you're wearing the T-shirt."

"Screw—"

He anticipated that one, tightening his grip just enough to cut the rest off. "Done that, too, honey. Again, with you. At least I was honest about it the morning after." The smoke in her gaze grew so dark and so thick, he should have choked on it.

"Honest? Oh, that's rich. Even for you. You're the one who slept with me to further your precious career."

"I did *what?*" He stiffened as the accusation ripped through his gut like a fragmentation grenade. She glared at him as he struggled to stanch the shock. The fury.

The absolute confusion.

"Oh, kill the innocent routine. It didn't work the first time and it won't work now. I was there. Again. Outside *your* office this time. I heard it all." She flicked her gaze at the barn. "I hope you're keeping a better lookout this time because frankly, for a Delta operative, your stealth skills suck. Or maybe I'm just better at my job than you and my father think.''

She *had* been there.

And the shrapnel was still pinging around inside him.

He released her arms, slowly, deliberately, knowing she wouldn't stalk off. Not now. Not even when he turned away to stare out over the gradually warming hills to try and absorb the blow. The shock. The goddamned irony of it. Dani was wrong. She hadn't heard it all that day. She couldn't have. If she had, they might still be standing here, but it wouldn't be like this.

Eleven months. He'd wasted eleven long months. Hell, he'd changed his career. Yeah, he'd have switched it anyway. But she might have been at his side while he'd done it but for that overbearing, meddling man. He might finally understand why the general had treated his daughter the way he had her entire life, but he couldn't forgive it. It had caused too much damage. To Dani and to them. Jack reached for the pack of Marlboros inside his cargo pocket, tapping out a cigarette before he remembered he didn't even smoke. He shoved the pack home and hooked his T-shirt around the back of his neck, gripping the damp ends hard to disguise the trembling in his fingers as he turned.

"You misunderstood what you heard."

The fire cooled in her gaze. Shadows replaced it. Pain. Resignation. And a host of uglier emotions he'd give every last one of his concealed weapons to ease. But the most insidious was doubt. He watched it invade that soft gaze before she turned away from him to stare at the barn beyond. To hide. He knew then that not only had Dani heard her father tell him she never belonged in the Army and never would, but that she'd also heard the deliberate, resounding silence that followed—*his.*

At the time, he hadn't argued with the man. Too much had been at risk. So he'd said nothing. Talk about a minefield of a conversation. He'd just finished confessing his professional and personal intentions to the one man who had the power to destroy both. With the Army short of special operators, as his commanding general, all Ramrod-and-Ruthless would have had to do was *not* support his request to resign from Delta and then blackball his invitation to join Diplomatic Security. The man had enough buddies in the Army and the State Department to pull it off. Then where would he and Dani be? She wasn't the only soldier her father had trapped beneath his iron thumb during the past thirty years. Nor was he. He was just the one willing to risk it all to get out.

She was worth it. Not that she'd believe him if he told her. The acid of her father's subtle but continuous undermining had finally eaten its way into her confidence. He'd watched Dani stand up to the man for years. It was one of the reasons she'd managed to steal his heart as a sixteen-year-old kid. But it wasn't until this mission, until Lina's death that she'd finally succumbed to it. And she had succumbed. It was in the way she'd bowed her head. The silent quake of her shoulders. In each hoarse rasp as the warming air around them ripped in and out of her lungs.

''Dani?''

She ignored him. He couldn't blame her. He was too busy cursing himself. He was the one who'd screwed this up. Screwed them up. Adrenaline. What should she have said? *I heard my lover agree with my father that I was incompetent?*

''Danielle.''

She flinched. Again, he couldn't blame her. He'd used her given name only once before in ten years—during a four-hour stretch in his bed and in his shower.

''Please, honey. Just look at me.'' She did. His fingers shook as he smoothed them across her bruised cheek, then her perfect one, erasing the tears from her flesh. More than anything, he wanted to ease them from her heart. "I didn't agree with your father. I just didn't…disagree."

He watched her suck in her breath, her pride. "That I know. What I don't is why you even discussed me with him at all?"

In the terse moments that followed, he came perilously close to giving her the truth. But he didn't. He couldn't. Not with that fresh bruise on her face and the memory of her head slamming into that wall. Not with Youssef in the house up on that rise, nursing the hatred he'd seen burning in the bastard's eyes, more determined than ever to dog Dani's every step, waiting until she was alone, distracted, before he pounced. The hell with his mission, it was too critical to her *life* that she remain completely focused—lest she end up dead. All he could do was give her as much as he could and pray she still cared enough to stick around when this was over and listen to the rest.

"Well?"

He sucked in his own breath. "Your father got in earlier than I did that morning, Dani. He'd driven by my house. He recognized your car. You and me, standing—kissing—beside it."

Her lashes flew wide as she blanched.

He knew the feeling. He'd felt it himself. His surprise had quickly deepened to shock, however—over the depth of her father's. That any man, even him, had dared to sleep with the general's little girl. The man's initial, barely suppressed fury hadn't even made sense. She'd been twenty-six at the time. Old enough to make her own decisions regarding where she spent the night and with whom. Jack shrugged. "At first, I was hoping to keep the peace. At least until I'd had a chance to talk to you."

She just stood there, those huge eyes filling her face. Those damned bruises on her cheek and jaw, the marks on her neck, the tears still dampening the ivory skin that was left. He brushed at them again, this time with his right thumb, trying to brush the salt away before it slid down to burn the split in her lip. Before he realized what he was doing, he'd leaned down and dried the rest with his mouth. He heard the catch in her throat, felt her soft, swift exhale bathe the stubble on his cheek and jaw. When she didn't pull away, he took a chance and trailed his mouth to hers. He forced his lips to hover. To wait.

Relief, hope and desire blistered through him all at once as he finally tasted her bittersweet sigh. The years fell away as he reached out and slowly slipped his tongue into the tentative warmth of her mouth. He was twenty-one again, responding to a thank-you kiss he'd known was innocent the moment he'd tasted it, well aware he had no business accepting it, much less in that café for all of West Point to see. For her father to see. It was a miracle the man hadn't. Though he wouldn't touch these lips with his for another ten years, he'd never forgotten that brief, mesmerizing caress.

That kiss, like this one, was why he'd really gone Delta.

Dani was so wrong. He hadn't forged a relationship with her father through the years and then slept with her to further his career. He'd chosen his career track and his mentor to stay close to her. He slowly lifted his head, determined to tell her.

"Good God, Sergeant—aren't you done *yet?*"

They stiffened together as the shout reverberated across the grass and around the side of the barn—and she finally spoke.

"Rurik."

Jack nodded. As much as he wanted to force her down the hill to link up with Hamid, it was too late. He couldn't see Rurik yet, but the man was bound to be headed straight for them. He tugged on his damp shirt as he rushed through the rest. "It's time. We've got a drive ahead of us, into the mountains. I may not be back until dinner. Don't worry about Youssef, he's coming with us. If Rurik changes his mind, I'll refuse to go."

She smoothed the collar of his T-shirt as he crammed the damp hem into the waist of his fatigues. "Is that wise?"

He checked the sides of the barn, the path. Still no sign of Rurik. "Don't worry, Rurik won't call my bluff. He's desperate for whatever I'm supposed to inspect. Think about it. I've written my own game plan twice now. Playing basketball with Youssef's head this morning and last night, with you. He never should have let you go for three hundred dollars. Not even to a man who saved his life. It's just not in his nature. Not when you're worth two, three times that amount to these goons."

To him, she was priceless.

Deep down, he'd always known that.

He checked the barn again. Rurik was on this end of the gravel path now. Jack tipped her chin, captured her stare. "I asked for your clothes. Rurik says he doesn't remember a watch but he promised to produce your shoes. Zorah should have them. Swear to me you'll go for the transmitter this time if you need to." Relief seared through him when she nodded. "Good. I left a leather belt under the bottom of the dresser along with my cell phone in case someone searches my duffel while I'm gone. Flip the belt over. There's a small, razor-sharp knife sheathed in at the buckle.'' God willing, she wouldn't need that either.

He shot off another furtive glance. Rurik had sauntered halfway down the length of the barn and he wasn't even close to being done. *Damn.* He cupped his hand to Dani's neck and dragged her body to his as he had eleven months earlier, standing beside the door to her car. But this time, he was forced to twist his torso to shield her from Rurik's stare as he lowered his mouth. He put everything he'd ever felt for this woman into a brief, searing kiss. The way her pulse thundered beneath his thumb, the way her eyes darkened as he lifted his head, gave him hope that someday she might feel the same.

''Honey…we need to talk.''

She licked the split at her lip as she nodded slowly, cautiously. ''I agree.''

Before he could kiss her again, Rurik's rotting grin fouled his peripheral view. Jack forced himself to release Dani as he turned to face it. She'd agreed to talk. If everything went down as he hoped today, they might even get the chance.

Chapter 6

Jack was late.

Dani finished scrubbing the last of the earthen bowls and stacked it to the right of the sink with the others as the reality of the hour locked in. Jack had promised to return by dinner. The Spartan dinner of leek stew and bread had ended an hour ago. The sun would be setting soon. So where *was* he?

Was he safe? Had the arms deal soured? Or had Youssef decided to try and even the score from this morning? Yes, Jack was extremely good at what he did. But she'd also learned firsthand that Youssef turned downright rabid when thwarted. So had Lina. Once Jack completed his part of the arms deal, would Rurik bother to keep Youssef leashed? Dani purged the terror from her heart, but before she could concentrate on the next set of questions, the source of most of them appeared beside her.

"We need water. Come."

Zorah ignored the thugs nursing their coffee at the island and passed an empty pail over as they left the kitchen. As with most of the chores they'd accomplished together, they headed down the path silently. While Dani had begun to suspect sometime during the dinner preparations that Zorah might be ready to open up to her, she didn't push. She'd already plied the woman with questions the day before. Zorah would decide to answer or not.

She was surprised at the soft smile Zorah sent C'emal as they reached the front of the barn, though. Especially when the guard nodded. The exchange had been subtle, but it was telling. Had anyone but her witnessed it, there would be hell to pay. Dani waited until they were out of C'emal's earshot before she voiced her concerns. "Was that wise?"

Zorah simply shrugged as they rounded the dairy barn. Dani dropped her pail into place as they reached the well. She was about to lift the handle on the pump when Zorah spoke, so softly she'd almost missed it.

"Lina is dead."

Regret shafted through her as she jerked the iron handle up and down several times. Water splashed into the pail and up over the sides, soaking the toe of her left shoe. She shifted her foot—and the emergency transmitter—out of range. "I know. Youssef…told me." Dani sucked in her breath as Zorah reached out, smoothing her callused fingers down the side of her mouth.

"I am so sorry."

She shrugged, uncomfortable accepting compassion from a woman whose life wasn't much better than those of the girls locked up in that hovel awaiting their new masters. Zorah might not be raped regularly, but she lived in fear just the same. Dani had seen the faint bruise at the base of her jaw during the light of day, the old burn marks on the woman's arms when she'd pushed up her sleeves to scrub her brother's clothes. C'emal hadn't put those marks there, Rurik had. "You didn't hit me, Zorah. And you didn't kill Lina."

"But I stood by and did *nothing*."

She didn't know what to say to that. She certainly couldn't bring herself to pass judgment. She hadn't survived four years of starvation and a daily barrage of shelling and sniper attacks during the siege of Sarajevo with nothing but a rosary to cling to in an attempt to keep the horror at bay. Zorah had. She finished filling her bucket and hefted it away from the pump's spout. Even now, given what was left of the Bosnian culture, what options did Zorah really have?

"C'emal says I should leave with him."

Water sloshed over the rim as the bucket hit the ground. She captured Zorah's now-terrified stare. "When?"

"Tonight."

"Why?" But she knew why. She'd seen the answer this morning. Love had won over constant fear and familial loyalty. It also complicated things. Jack's mission as well as hers. God willing, it wouldn't compromise them. Dani scanned the path. It was empty. By the time she turned back, Zorah had picked up her own bucket and tucked it beneath the spout. "Zorah?"

The woman finished filling her bucket, her heavy sigh merging with the cooling evening air as she faced her. "I do not know where the women soldiers are. Rurik does not share this with me. Nor does C'emal know. He only guards the doors. I am sorry. But I can give you something for what you tried to do for Lina. For the courage you have given me.''

Despite her searing disappointment, hope surged—for the other girls trapped down in that croft. ''The key?''

Zorah nodded.

It was better than nothing. Especially if Jack returned in time to cover for her and maybe even coordinate with Hamid. If Zorah and C'emal were leaving, she might be able to release the girls at the same time. Make it seem as if the lovers had liberated them, thereby preserving both their covers. But when she picked up her pail and held out her hand, Zorah shook her head. ''I must give the key to you later, just before we leave. Rurik will return soon. He will want to check on the girls with me before *Isha Du'a*. I must have the key then.''

Stunned, Dani dropped the bucket. The contents splashed over the rim, soaking her shoes and the calves of her jeans. She stared out at the hills and the fiery sun that had just set. She gaped at the bearded guard next. The one making his way to them via the path. With every confident step C'emal took, another piece of the puzzle fell neatly into place. Rurik, placing his sister off limits from sexual advances even though he didn't give a rat's ass about her. Zorah and C'emal's shock at being interrupted after sunrise; their obvious freedom to steal a few minutes at midday, then late afternoon and now, just past sunset, even though Rurik's men were still in that house.

It didn't matter. The thugs were occupied. Just as Rurik and his goons would be occupied later tonight with *Isha Du'a*. The evening prayer. Despite the fact that Rurik, an ethnic Bosnian Croatian, had been baptized Catholic like his sister, the man would not be clutching a rosary. She'd bet the emergency transmitter in her shoe he'd be secreted in his room along with his men, kneeling on an Islamic prayer rug instead.

''Rurik's Muslim.''

Jack jerked his hand from the radio, leaving the volume on that earsplitting accordion where it was as he whirled about to face Dani, hoping he'd misheard her. Praying. Either that, or she was severely mistaken. Frankly, he'd take either option. Her steady gaze as she stared up at him strangled his hope.

''Yes, I'm sure. Zorah confirmed it. That crucifix hanging from his neck is as phony as the dog tags on yours, at least to him. He converted during the siege of Sarajevo. Rurik's as much a Catholic as you are an artillery sergeant.'' Jack followed her revelation with a curse that would have stunned an Army priest as she sank onto the edge of the bed. ''I know. It changes things, doesn't it? At the very least, the level of the game.''

She didn't know the half of it—yet. ''This is no game.''

''He's got the rounds, then?''

''I think so.''

She blinked up at him. ''You think? I thought that's why Rurik brought you along. So you could inspect them.''

''So did I. All he had me do was check the charges.''

''How many?''

''Nine.'' He nodded, agreeing with the sentiment behind her own blue curse. Nine bags of premeasured gunpowder. Just enough to lob an 8-inch shell smack into the embassy courtyard in downtown Sarajevo. But that wasn't all. ''Dani, the warhead was there. He just wouldn't let me near it.''

''But that doesn't make sense.''

''It does if you recognize the guy who sold it to him.''

Her brow shot up.

''Farid Vlaldosta. He's a former army artillery officer from Azerbaijan. I recognized him from a mug book a few years back. Farid's dirty as hell and *very* well-connected.'' Jack fell silent as the accordion shrieked out its final, wailing notes. Stark, dead air filled the room as he pushed off the dresser and paced his way around Dani's shoes. The beginning notes of a less raucous, more romantic *sevdalinka* filled the room as he reached the window. Despite the cooler breeze outside, he kept the window shut and turned to lean against the frame.

Dani twisted around to face him, shifting her legs over the foot of the bed as he sighed. She didn't respond. She didn't have to. They were thinking the same thing. Why Azerbaijan?

If Rurik needed howitzer ammo, he could have gotten the shells from any number of black-market weapons dealers. Why go all the way east, past half a dozen NATO countries including Turkey? Hell, Rurik could have gotten the shells right here, from some UN peacekeeper in Bosnia…unless he hadn't been after conventional rounds, but something a lot deadlier. A special version of the 8-inch shell that'd been removed from the U.S. inventory years before—say around 1991—but hadn't been removed from the inventory of some of America's lesser-known allies.

From the chill that'd slipped into Dani's gaze

when she finally lifted her gaze, he knew she'd made the same connection. Her question confirmed it. "You sure there were only nine?"

"Yup." Just enough powder for one single lob. That's all Rurik and his thugs would need.

"You suspect Farid of selling Rurik a chemical warhead…or a nuclear one, don't you?"

He nodded. The former—a chemical round— would take out a couple thousand citizens along with the embassy. But a nuke? That, as she'd so succinctly put it, raised the game to a whole new level. With a one-kiloton yield, the round would not only obliterate the embassy but pretty much everything else within the city limits, including Sarajevo's half a million citizens. Most of which, interestingly enough, were Muslim. However, without getting a look at the round itself and the color-coded band around the base, he had no idea how twisted the man's interpretation of Islam was. Nor did he have proof.

Suspicion wasn't enough. They still needed hard proof. They needed the warhead itself, conventional, chemical *or* nuclear. Otherwise, Rurik would do a couple years for possession of the howitzer—if that was even in the barn—and the powder. When he got out, he'd set up camp elsewhere and finish the job if another terrorist cell didn't already have the warhead. Today's transaction could have been a feint. Rurik could be a decoy.

Christ. Jack raked his hands through his hair. It didn't help. Tension had been eating a hole through his gut since he'd been forced to leave Dani behind that morning. Worrying about her dodging some thug's hands all day hadn't helped. Neither had sitting next to Rurik in the front of a rusted truck, faking small talk during a five-hour ride home while Youssef baby-sat nine bags of gunpowder and a possible unconventional warhead in the rear. He never should have stopped that bullet in Mostar. Except if he hadn't, he—and DSS—wouldn't have had this in with Rurik and he knew it. Jack paced his way to the door, his boots muffled by the lively folk song that kicked in. He took advantage of the noise level and paced back to the bed. Back to Dani. "I've got to get in there."

To his surprise, she cursed.

"What's wrong?"

"Nothing. I've just been so stunned, I forgot to tell you. What time is it?"

He glanced at his watch. "Eight-ten, local. Why?"

"Because we're already scheduled to go in. About seventy minutes from now. Just before Rurik and his thugs retreat to their rooms for *Isha*

Du'a. Once Rurik checks the slaves, Zorah will slip two keys under the door—one for the lock on the croft where the girls are being held.'' She tipped her head toward the window. ''And one for that padlock down there on the barn.''

''Why the hell would she risk that?''

''Because she won't be sticking around to suffer the consequences. Neither will C'emal. The keys are a parting gift.'' Her lips curved briefly. ''I told you it would pay off.''

She had. ''I'll be damned. I've got to call Hamid.''

Adrenaline surged into his blood as he turned to the dresser and the cell phone he'd left secreted beneath in case she needed it. Dani snagged his hand, her fingers threading into his as he turned back. She shook her head.

''I took care of it. Hamid will be waiting for our signal. The transmitter in your pack of cigarettes or the one in my shoe. If either goes active, he'll descend on the barn with everything you guys have—including the chopper you stashed in his cousin's tent. They'll be here in five, ten minutes tops.''

Relief seared through him, displacing the adrenaline—and yet, not. The mix ended up tumbling though his gut—right into the waiting tension.

Trapped in this room for the next hour, there was no way to expend any of it. He dropped his gaze to their hands. Not smart. Their fingers were still linked.

And he was still clutching on to the urge he'd been trying to suppress since the moment he'd walked into that kitchen. The one that made him want to haul this woman into his arms and kiss her—without an audience present. The urge that made him want to finish that kiss up here, right now. He tugged his fingers from hers and shoved his hands into his pockets—and hit metal. He grabbed the insignia and jerked his hand out. Dani wasn't the only one who'd forgotten to mention something.

"What's wrong?"

He shook his head. "Another gift. While you were adding a piece to my puzzle, I managed to locate one of yours. Here." He laid the flat-black U.S. Army Specialist Fourth-Class insignia with its missing clasp into the center of her palm, waiting as she turned the tiny shield over. She stiffened as she read the numbers scratched into the back—*42.*

The female sergeants Dani was tracking had been attached to the 42nd Field Hospital before they'd disappeared.

Jack nodded as her gaze shot up. "The prong

was stuck into one of the bags of powder. I didn't see money change hands. Rurik must have handed over the girls along with the down payment. I'm guessing one of your sergeants hoped someone would understand her coded SOS. I've got someone tailing Farid. They'll locate the hole he crawled out of. If the girls are there, we'll find them." But they both knew it wouldn't happen—couldn't—until they took Rurik down. Not unless they wanted Rurik warned.

His chest began to burn as Dani dropped her gaze to the insignia and closed her left hand over it. She smoothed the fingers of her right across her bottom lip. The swelling had gone down and the split was healing, but it was still visible. So was the one in her heart. When she wouldn't raise her gaze, he lowered himself to his knees and took her hands in his.

"We'll get them back." Nothing. "Honey?" He slipped a hand to her neck, hooked his thumb beneath her jaw and nudged it up.

It was a mistake. Her lips parted.

And, God help him, he stared. Touched. Caressed. Her lips were smooth beneath his thumb, warm. Her breath swirled between them, deep into his lungs. He closed his eyes against the scent. Fought the urge that crept up on him whenever he was in the same room with this woman. He opened his eyes and stared into the soft blue invitation. *No.* This was not smart. Not now. He didn't give a damn if the door was locked with the chair wedged beneath the knob. He had too much tension coiled in his gut, too much raw adrenaline pulsing through his veins. So did she.

If they acted on it, they'd both be guilty of doing exactly what he'd blamed her for doing eleven months ago—using the rush to experience an incredibly enhanced sexual release. But, Lord, he wanted to. So did she. He tensed as she lifted her fingers, sliding them across his lips. "Dani, we need to talk."

She leaned close, her warm whisper filling his ear. "I don't want to talk…do you?"

No. "Yes." They might not get another chance. She was right. The fact that Rurik was Muslim changed everything. Especially if the man's benefactor was who he now suspected it was. C'emal's cooperation and *Isha Du'a* notwithstanding, there was a high probability that when they walked into that barn tonight, they wouldn't be walking back out. She threaded her fingers into his hair as she pulled away—not far enough. He was staring directly into that mesmerizing gaze. "I don't suppose you'd consider—"

"No. I am not leaving. This is bigger than anyone thought and you know it. You need backup. On site. Now, regardless of how the rest of tonight plays out, the fact is we've got seventy minutes to kill. How do you really want to spend them?"

"Inside you."

Oh, that was smooth. About as subtle as that cat-in-heat accordion grating down from the dresser.

She laughed anyway. "I like the way you think, soldier. Now get rid of those boots and that uniform along with the pistol you've got tucked at the small of your back." She leaned forward and pressed her lips to his ear once again, the promise in her voice throbbing just beneath the music. "I'm much more interested in the gun you've got tucked inside your front."

He might not be in the Army anymore, but he remembered how to follow orders. He was off his knees, Beretta in hand and round chambered before she could draw her next breath. He tossed the pistol on the rickety nightstand. It had the grace not to go off. He grinned down at her T-shirt—*his* T-shirt—as she blinked. "Seventy minutes, huh? Race you."

Her smile spread. "You're on."

He tore his shirt off as he headed across the room. By the time he'd hit the light switch and made it back to the bed, she was minus his shirt, her shoes and her jeans, looking too damned gorgeous in the moonlight in a plain white bra and matching panties. She was also ahead…but only because of the knotted laces on his jump boots. When she reached back to unhook her bra, he knew he had to do something, and quick. He shoved his trousers down and made his move, snaking his right arm around her slender waist as her bra fell away. He dragged her forward as he sat down on the bed, swirling his tongue around the plump nipple that filled his view. He absorbed the first, heady taste and instinctively reached for seconds.

She gasped…and he groaned. It had been too damned long since they'd done this. But it all flashed back in an instant. He gave his lips, teeth and tongue free rein as he sent his fingers down to yank at the laces on his boots—sucking, licking, and nipping greedily, taking up the rhythm he'd learned drove her insane during those hours on his bed.

She moaned as she lost her grip on her panties. "That's *cheating.*"

He grinned as he kicked off his boots and peeled off his socks. Completely naked, he slid his hands up her thighs, teasing his fingers beneath the elastic as he stood. "You complaining?"

"Hell, no."

"Good, 'cause I won."

"Really?"

Oh, no. He knew that look. Then he remembered.

She grinned—because this time, she had him. He ought to know…because he'd made up the rule eleven months ago. During their heated rush up his stairs, she'd confessed she needed to go to her SUV and grab something from her rucksack. He'd been so aroused, the euphemism hadn't registered at first. Until he remembered that *his* ruck was in his closet—along with the stash of condoms some soldiers carried to keep the barrel of their M-16 dry in the rain. Unwilling to wait the minute it would take her, he'd scooped her up in his arms and insisted during the detour to his closet that providing protection was the man's job. And now that protection was across the room, in his duffel bag.

"Don't move. I'll be right back."

Not only did she move, her panties were dangling from the tip of her index finger as he turned. She nodded to the packet in his hand. "Did I forget to mention I'm safe right now?"

"What?"

Her grin gleamed in the moonlight.

"You *cheated.*"

She shrugged. "You complaining?"

"Hell, no." Not with those lush curves beckoning to him. But he did intend to even the score. He stalked across the room as she laughed, backing her up to the wall, trapping her there as he lowered his head and captured her mouth. Her lips were as soft as they'd been out behind that barn this morning, as hungry as he'd dared to hope. She drew him in quickly, thoroughly, feeding off him. Meeting him as easily and squarely as she had that night in his bedroom. She didn't give an inch. He didn't want her to. And then they were both demanding more.

Hotter, deeper. Harder.

He grabbed the panties from her hand and flung them somewhere over his shoulder. The condom followed. He dragged his hands up her waist, cupping her breasts, squeezing, pinching and pulling her nipples as her hands seared down his chest. A second later, his stomach bottomed out as she stretched up to bite the side of his neck and suck *hard.* Adrenaline, abstinence and the truth in his heart slammed into him at the exact same moment, rocketing him straight up to the edge of the abyss.

He growled and plowed his fingers into her hair, tugging her head back to the wall as he struggled for sanity, for control—for *air*. When he finally found it, it was short and ragged, coming in and out as rapidly as hers as he stared into those fathomless eyes, now smoke-blue with passion. Like that first time in his kitchen, they were going way too fast. He didn't care.

She hiked her right leg against his restlessly, and he took the hint, grabbing her bottom and lifting her up to his level. His hoarse groan rivaled that blaring music as her fingers raked down his back and around to his groin. He lost his air again as she wrapped her hand around his erection and pulled—firm, hot, guiding. And then his entire world was wet. And tight.

Sweet heaven, he did not remember Dani being this tight.

He shuddered right along with her, into her, gripping her gorgeous bottom with his left palm as he slammed his right into the wall above her, bracing both of them as the brunt of their need rocked through them. He was piercingly aware of her legs hiking higher, locking around his hips, drawing him in deeper, holding him right there, as he pounded into her liquid heat again and again. He tried to slow down, but he couldn't. She moaned into his neck, he groaned right back into hers. It was fast and it was furious—and, dammit, he was almost *there*.

No! Not yet.

But it was too late. It had truly been too long. It was her scream that did it. He caught it in the nick of time and swallowed it whole, praying it would help drag the moment out, at least a bit. But it didn't. The moment her short nails ripped into his shoulders, down his back, and dug into his naked ass—one last racking shudder—and it was over. He was still gasping for air when she pressed her forehead into his sweat-slicked neck and sighed. He was pretty sure that was satisfaction. But still. He tipped her chin and stared into those huge eyes.

"I'm sor—"

Her fingers came up, pressed to his lips. She glanced at the Beretta he'd dumped on the nightstand. "If you apologize for that, I'll put a hole in you before Rurik can."

His lips twitched, but he could still feel the heat creeping up his neck. "Dammit, Dani, I didn't even get you to the bed."

She stared past his arm again, her beautiful, sated smile quirking. "Nice bed. Bit narrow, though." Her gaze skimmed to his thighs, then up, stopping at the juncture of them. "Nice—ah—gun, too. The caliber's as impressive as I remember."

The caliber increased. He dropped his forehead to hers, confessing the truth as he shifted his hands to cradle her bottom in his right. "Yeah, well, it's been a while since I've been out on the range. Eleven months to be exact. My grip's rusty, not to mention my trigger was a bit...quick. But that's nothing a little practice can't cure, I swear."

She snagged his left wrist and tugged it close, turning it until she could read the dial on his watch in the moonlight. "We still have fifty-six minutes. Care to reload and fire again?"

He didn't wait for her to ask twice. He just wrapped both arms around her and swung her about to the bed. If they had fifty-six more minutes to kill, he intended to murder each and every one of them slowly this time, sweetly. Because if they did make it out of that barn alive, he wanted to make damned sure she came back for more.

Chapter 7

They still had nineteen minutes to go.

Dani glanced across the room. Despite those minutes, Jack was already dressed, boots, fatigues, concealed weapons and all. He slipped his Beretta into the waist of his trousers as he turned to stare out the window at the barn below. He retrieved the open pack of cigarettes and tapped one out, the flame from the silver lighter she'd given him all those years ago flashing to life for a brief moment as he lit the end. The tip of the cigarette glowed as he tucked the lighter home and braced his hand against the top of the window frame. It wasn't until she finished wrapping his belt around her waist twice and watched him take his second, searing drag on the cigarette and then saw his hand tremble before he anchored it firmly back on the frame, that she realized what was really going on.

Jack Gage, a man legendary among even the Shadow Warriors of Delta for his calm, cool composure, no matter what the risk, what the job, let alone the nonexistent odds, was nervous. Scared. Because of her. That's when it hit her. Actually, when it punched into her fist-first, straight into her heart.

She loved him.

Even as the mind-numbing aftershocks continued to pummel into her, she knew it was true. Finally. For ten long years she'd managed to convince herself that what she felt for the man standing across this darkened room with his back to her, staring out that window, was infatuation. Even during this past year, ever since that murder-for-hire case had forced them to pose as man and wife, she'd still managed to avoid the truth, chalking up this familiar feeling in her heart to a searing case of lust. It was both. And neither. It was love.

And maybe, just maybe, he'd hung around so long, not because of her father…but because he was in love with her, too. Oh, God, she hoped so.

Prayed so. The mere thought made her knees tremble, her stomach churn. But she had to know. Tonight. Now. Before they walked out of here and into that barn. She needed to know if Jack loved her, too. She crossed the floor silently as the smoke from his third drag filled his lungs and then the room, reaching out to close her hand over his as he brought the cigarette back for a fourth.

"You don't smoke."

He stood there for a moment, silent amid the music still blaring out across the room. Still staring out the window at the barn. At C'emal, who was doing his best not to pace as the man waited for his lover to finish her chores so he and Zorah could leave…and she and Jack could begin.

He finally sighed and turned. "We have to talk."

She nodded. He was right, they did. He opened his mouth, but instead of words coming out, his sigh filled the space between them. She waited as he shook his head and crossed the room, recognizing the distance he was putting between them for what it was and not some concern about his status as a guest who cleaned up after himself as he stopped at the nightstand to grind the cigarette out in the ashtray. He retrieved his Beretta, released the clip and checked it before slapping it home. Then he just stood there and stared at it.

Maybe she should say it first? God knows she'd made this hard enough on him as it was. She stepped out to follow him, only to halt as he finally spoke.

"Dani…if I don't make it toni—"

"No." She shook her head as she stepped out again, grabbing his hands as she reached him, clamping his fingers into the cold steel of the Beretta's barrel. "Don't start like that. Start *any* other way. Just don't start like that."

"Dammit, just listen to me."

She dropped her hands. Swallowed hard. "Okay."

He sucked in his breath. "If something happens to me tonight, I want you to promise me—" He broke off. Drew in another breath, this one deeper. "I need you to promise me…"

What, dammit? That she'd remember he loved her? That she'd move on, find someone else? Bull. She'd do neither. Nor could she do this. She could not stand here and look into that expression on this man's face. She'd rather go another round with Youssef than stare into that torture. She opened her mouth, took a deep breath, and said it for them.

"Jack, I—l—"

"Promise me you'll talk to your father."

What?

She blinked. Waited through an entire verse of that god-awful folk song until, finally, somehow, she managed to speak. "Tell me you didn't just ask me what I think you did."

But he nodded.

She stood there, for what seemed like eons as she struggled to absorb the blow. The heart-wrenching disappointment. The iron fist of truth. Memories slammed into her. The past, the present. A future she was so stupid to believe could ever be. Just like that, she was sixteen and yet twenty-six, standing in front of both those doors at the exact same time. Listening to both those men. She wanted to cry. She wanted to scream. She wanted to slug the man standing in front of her for daring to make her dream. But most of all, she just wanted to curl up into a ball. In the end, she just did what she'd always done. She turned away. Only this time, he knew she was there—and he stopped her.

She whirled around, wrenching her arm from his. *"Don't."*

"I have to. honey, you don't understand—"

"Oh, I understand. You're still doing his dirty work."

She could make out the fire smoldering within

his gaze, despite the dark. "Wrong, I'm trying to help."

"Well, guess what? We don't need help. I don't need it. Neither does he. Hell, he doesn't even love me. I've known that from the time I was twelve. One day, the man just shut down. I guess I must have used him up because all I've gotten from good ol' Daddy Dearest since is ice-cold silence. You, on the other hand, got to become the surrogate son. The Chosen One. You got to go fishing with my father, have dinner at his house any damned day you wanted, gather his professional pearls of wisdom. And, of course, you got to hear firsthand how I never belonged in *his* man's Army and how I never would." With that she spun around. But again, Jack grabbed her. This time, with both arms. And this time, when he twirled her around, she couldn't break loose.

Damn him. Damn the both of them. She renewed her struggle with a vengeance.

"*Stop.* Dani, just listen to me for once instead of shutting down. And quit running away. The two of you are so alike it's not even funny. There are things you don't know. Things I didn't know, let alone understand until last month. Until this week—this case. But I know now. I understand. But that's not enough. You need to understand. All

I want you to do is promise me you'll talk to him.
Ask him about your mother.''

Her mother?

Just like that, the fury she'd held on to for so
long with this man—that she'd been using to shield
herself from him—just shattered. Rippling fear replaced it. She couldn't explain, let alone understand the chill that slithered down her spine before
snaking into her belly—simply because he'd mentioned her mother. And when the frustration bled
out of Jack's gaze, and the fear slid into him, she
wasn't sure she wanted to explain it. She had no
idea what to say, so she just said the obvious.
''Jack, my mother was killed when I was three. I
barely remember her.''

''I know.''

He did. She'd told him in that café. She'd de-
scribed her one and only memory of her mom. A
hug. And then she told him how her mom got into
her car and came home in a box. ''Then what are
you trying not to say? Please, I want you to be the
one to tell me, not my dad. What do you suddenly
understand?'' Instead of answering, he released her
wrists. He cupped her face, the torture locking
back into his gaze as he smoothed his fingers over
the bruises he'd gently kissed one by one on that
bed not more than twenty minutes ago. ''Jack,

please. You started this, now finish it. Tell me what my mother's murder has to do with my father and me.''

"Everything."

She opened her mouth—and froze instead. So did he.

The door! She hadn't so much as heard the tentative knock over the music, as felt it. And then she saw them. The keys. Whether she wanted it to be or not, their conversation was over.

Because it was time.

The howitzer was in the barn. She could sense it.

They both could. Dani waited until Jack slid the door shut before she risked turning on his red-filtered mini Maglite. A moment later, he slipped the flashlight from her hand and snagged her elbow, drawing her along with him as he took off across the moldy straw. Even without the red illuminating their path, the acrid stench of gunpowder and diesel would have led them right to the roughly 25-foot-by-10-foot artillery piece. Though slightly narrower in girth than a tank, the howitzer's massive, towering gun barrel hung over the front of the tracked wheels by another ten feet, forcing Rurik to run the rear scooped stabilizer almost flush with the back of the barn.

Dani stopped with Jack as he swept the scarlet wash in front of the metal beast and pointed. "There. To the left of the gun barrel, at the base of that narrow door."

She saw them. Nine bags of pre-measured gunpowder, the size and shape of one-pound coffee cans. But it was the two-by-four-foot wooden crate behind the pyramid that held their attention.

"Here."

She took the flashlight from Jack's hand as he hunkered down, bathing the oversized bullet with red as Jack removed the lid. Unfortunately, she couldn't make out the colored band near the base of the round. Jack flicked his gaze to hers. The tension that'd been winding through her gut ever since that unfinished conversation in the bedroom five minutes earlier fisted tighter as he shook his head.

"I can't tell, either. We need white light."

Great. She wasted precious seconds unscrewing the filter from the flashlight, then flashed the Mag again. A split second was all it took for both of them to blanch—and curse.

"It's a nuke."

Jack nodded as he stood. He took the flashlight

from her and quickly reattached the filter before pressing the lighter as well as his switchblade into her palms. He kept his Swiss Army knife for himself. "Go see if you can crack the track's control panel open and disable the battery. I'll take the warhead."

"You sure you know how?"

"In theory, yeah. In practice?" His grin flashed amid the red light washing the scruff covering his cheeks and jaw. "We're about to find out, aren't we?"

Or not.

They must have heard it—or rather them—at the same moment because he grabbed her arm, hauling her with him as he spun around. A split second later, light flooded the barn, blinding them. By the time they'd blinked off the effects, Rurik stood ten feet away, just under the howitzer's barrel, the phony cross still hanging around his neck. Youssef stood several feet to the right, Zorah in his arms…and a Makarov pistol to the woman's head. One look at the agony in her brown eyes and Dani no longer wondered where C'emal was. It didn't matter. The guard was dead.

While her heart and nerves were still screaming in concert, Jack had already reverted back to cool. He reached down and casually shifted his hand behind him, retrieving the switchblade from her fingers. She clamped down on the lighter as he tucked the blade into his back pocket and spoke, "I guess this means *Isha Du'a* has been canceled for the night, eh?"

Rurik laughed. Youssef scowled.

Zorah all but fainted. "I am sorry, Dani. I tried to warn you with the knock. They—" She received a vicious knock of her own for her efforts, compliments of the pummel master himself.

Dani stepped forward without thinking—only to run smack into Jack's torso as he shifted to block her path. She took the hint and pulled herself together. Jack, meanwhile, capitalized on her mistake, slipping the sealed pack of cigarettes into her fingers. She hadn't even realized he'd palmed it from his pocket. He shifted again, covering her movements as he nodded to Youssef. "I see you're still hiding behind a woman's skirt."

The man stiffened. *"Nečist!"*

"Silence!" Rurik smoothed out his scowl as he faced Jack. "And you, my friend, be careful. I do not need you anymore."

"You never did."

That decaying grin spread wider. "Very good. Correct, as well. But when you stumbled across my path, I could not turn down the opportunity. I should thank you. Your sacrifice will ensure my name is exalted all the more long after you and I— and naturally, all of Sarajevo—have passed from this earth.''

''But why, brother? Why kill so many? Your *own* people now?'' Dani winced as the pummel master rewarded Zorah's impertinence with a harder whack. They wore matching split lips now.

''Dammit, leave her alone!''

Rurik ignored his sister—herself too, continuing to focus on Jack. ''You know why.''

Jack kept his gaze on Rurik as he nodded, but he answered Zorah. ''Your brother hopes to unite the Muslim world. He thinks if he murders half a million Muslims and makes it look like a Catholic Croat and an American soldier are to blame, that ought to do the trick. Maybe even kick off World War Three.'' They both even knew why the man had been careful to keep up his slave trade until the bitter end—so he wouldn't arouse suspicion.

For an insanely calculating monster, Rurik's shrug was remarkably sheepish. ''A lofty goal, yes.''

But one that might come to pass…since Dani couldn't seem to get the pack open. The irony of fumbling around with a pack of cigarettes six inches from Jack while trying to look cool about it bit into her. But this time, he wasn't about to lean over and snag it from her hands and help her out. Relief seared though her as she finally located the tail of the plastic strip embedded in the cellophane. She peeled it off and wrenched the pack open, shoving her right fingers into the box to feel around for the switch as Jack shifted to maintain his block on Rurik's view. She was almost there when—

"You *stupid,* bitch!" Youssef dragged Zorah with him by her braid as he vaulted towards her. Before Dani could blink, he had his free hand locked to her wrist. "What are you doing?"

She blushed as Jack turned and settled his cool gaze on the pack and lighter in her hands. She went with her jangled nerves, used them to make her stammer real. "I—I need a s-smoke." She welcomed the downright amused brow that followed. The one that asked, *Now?* It succeeded in firing the temperature in her neck to roasting—and let him know that, no, she had not had a chance to throw the switch. "Sorry. I guess I'm a little nervous."

"Hell, Rurik. Let her have one. I could use one myself. 'Specially since it'll be the last smoke and all." He pointed his chin toward the far side of the howitzer. "We should probably take it over there, though. Away from the powder."

Rurik's grin should have startled her, but it didn't. He really should have melted that cross down and capped those teeth a long time ago. "A last cigarette to go with the last screw? To repay the debt for a careless bullet in Mostar?"

Jack held the man's gaze. "You gonna have another chance?"

His grin actually split wider. "Why not? It will take ten minutes to ready the weapon. I have always said you should take your pleasure when and where you can. The when is now and the where must be within my sight, not the shadows. But first, your pistol if you will...and that blade you like to carry." Rurik waited as Jack tossed his Beretta and switchblade over. The man pocketed both, then waved Youssef off. "Remember, my friend, the smoke and pleasure only. For old time's sake. Your last supper, if you will. You and I both know an accidental fire will prevent nothing. Farid assures me the warhead will still explode. The damage may not be as great, true—" He shrugged. "But the end result will be the same. My goal will be met."

Jack nodded as he slipped a cigarette from the pack along with the silver lighter from her hands.

He nudged her toward the center of the barn, beneath the howitzer's massive barrel, careful to keep his body between Rurik and Youssef as he stopped to light the cigarette. The scarlet tip glowed as he inhaled deeply, holding the smoke in his lungs long enough for her to locate the emergency transmitter and throw the switch.

Rurik was wrong. They didn't have ten minutes. They now had five. *She hoped.* Dani forced herself not to cough as Jack's smoky breath filled the air between them as he bent to fondle her bottom while he pretended to kiss and nuzzle her neck.

"If we have to, we torch the straw."

She knew what he was asking. Was she with him? It was 500,000 innocent residents of Sarajevo—Muslim and scattered Christians alike—or it was the five of them. This barn. And, if they were lucky, 100,000 of those citizens. Rurik was right, a fire would engulf the warhead along with the bags of gunpowder and ignite both. A split second later, there'd be nothing but a five-mile-wide crater where the barn should be. But enough of Sarajevo and her citizens would be safe to make it worth it.

"Okay." She clenched her fingers around the lighter, hiding it as Jack tugged her T-shirt out of her jeans. She couldn't help it, she flinched. Surely, he didn't actually intend to—

His breath filled her ear. "*Relax*. Work with me, honey." A moment later, smoke filled her lungs as he brought the cigarette to her mouth. Piercingly aware of their audience, she let him slip the end between her lips. She'd never know how she managed not to wheeze and choke as the smoke seared into her mouth and lungs, then out. But she did. Jack leaned down to capture the remaining puff along with her grimace with his mouth.

The kiss was pure ash at first, nasty and stifling, but then it was all Jack. Dark, heady and very smooth. Just as he had on that narrow bed he took his sweet time, delving deep inside her mouth as the howitzer's diesel engine fired to life behind them—his slow, languid kiss matching the sluggish churn of the track's internal hydraulic system as it turned over and warmed the pressurized oil needed to raise and aim the massive barrel. She was dimly aware of Jack switching the cigarette to his left hand as he worked her belt with his right.

No, not her belt. *His*. The knife concealed within. She forced herself to do as he'd asked, dragging her hands to his waist as Jack deepened the kiss and groaned loud enough for the Bosnian bastard now leering two feet away to hear.

"I should have charged you more, I think."

Jack ignored Rurik, working the buckle loose as

they continued to kiss. Her fingers finally cooper-
ated with her brain and she managed to unbuckle
his as well. She started in on the buttons beneath,
praying he'd hurry up and get to that damned knife
before she got to *him*. They reached their respective prizes at the same moment. His buttons now
undone, she held his pants up for him as Jack slid
the knife from its sheath with his right hand, still
kissing and caressing her with his left.

His left? Then where was the cigarette?

And then she smelled it.

"Fire!" The shout ripped out across the barn as
Youssef jerked the Makarov from behind Zorah's
disheveled back. That was as far as the thug got.
A split second later, the blade that'd been in her
belt speared the man directly above his left eye—
piercing Youssef's skull to plunge deep into his
brain. He didn't even scream. He simply fell, any
thud masked by the howitzer's engine still growling behind them. She spun around to help Jack take
out Rurik. She didn't get the chance.

Neither did Jack.

They stiffened together as the shot reverberated
through the barn, displacing the track's rhythmic
rumble for a brief, deafening moment, then Rurik
joined his henchman, falling face first into the
straw. Before Dani could blink, Jack shot across

the barn and reached Zorah, the Makarov still pointed straight out from her heaving chest, hanging above the flames.

The flames.

Jack grabbed the pistol and the woman's shawl. By the time he'd joined Dani at the fire, she'd stripped off her T-shirt. Together they thrashed the flames spreading across the concrete floor, devouring scattered ancient straw, mold and all. A pair of bare, swarthy arms joined them, shirt in hand. Then another pair and another. And another. She jerked her gaze up, half-expecting to discover C'emal alive. No such luck. But she did welcome the squad of half-dressed American soldiers turned fire-stompers beating out the remaining flames alongside an ethnic Muslim she didn't recognize. Hamid and the cavalry had arrived.

And the fire was out. It was over.

Jack buttoned his pants as she stood. From the look that flashed between him and Hamid as he buckled his belt, Jack was going to have explain his state of undress eventually. She did not want to be around when he did. Jack captured her gaze and stripped off his T-shirt, tossing it to her along with a devilish wink before he turned to link up with Hamid. The men headed across the barn to check the warhead and seal the crate so they could get it and the bags of gunpowder under lock and key. Anywhere but here.

Someone must have been assigned to kill the howitzer, because the roar of diesel engine died out. Adrenaline still simmering though her veins, Dani dropped Jack's singed T-shirt and donned his fresh one as she headed across the barn. She found Zorah slumped on a pile of straw. "Are you okay?"

"C'emal. After all our plans. He is..." Dani's heart broke as the woman's tears slipped free, finishing for her.

"I know." She did. It had taken her eleven years to find Jack, even though he'd been right in front of her face the entire time, or at least near her side. She could have lost him just as easily tonight. She wrapped her arms around Zorah, holding her tightly as the woman's sobs broke free. "I'm so sorry."

"Dani?"

She raised her head. But Jack was looking at Zorah, not her. Hamid stood beside him.

Jack smiled. "One of the guys located our friend. He's got a nasty knife sticking out of his chest, but the medic thinks he'll make it. Anyone want to hitch a chopper into Sarajevo?"

Zorah blinked up at Jack for a full two seconds.

On the third, it sank in. She shot to her feet and threw herself into Jack's arms. By the time Hamid led her out of the barn, everyone was teary, including Jack. Dani turned to follow Zorah to check on C'emal and thank him when Jack stopped her. His smile faded as he snagged her hand with one of his and cupped her cheek with the other.

"What's wrong?"

"You should probably hitch a ride, too. I just got off the phone with the embassy. They've got a guest." Even before he squeezed her hand and nodded, she knew. "It's your father."

Chapter 8

Across an empty, darkened ballroom with his back to her, he should have looked like any other soldier in Army Greens. But he didn't. She'd recognize that stiff, unyielding stance anywhere. Even here, in Bosnia. Jack was right. Ol' Ramrod-and-Ruthless himself had flown halfway around the world just to track her down. Amazing. Hell, she couldn't even get the man to drive a hundred miles to visit her at boarding school. Maybe she should shower first. At least change into the uniform the marine escort had offered. Oh, hell. She stepped into the room before she chickened out, wincing as her tennis shoes squeaked.

That was all it took. He spun around. But he didn't say a word. It was too dark to make out more than the flash of triple stars running across his shoulders—and those didn't reveal any clue as to his mood. She locked her spine to attention and marched forward, stopping five feet away, just shy of a pair of hardwood chairs left beside the French doors.

"Sir."

He returned her nod. "Danielle."

The seconds ticked out the silence—just like whenever they got together. It was usually like this too, with him in uniform and her feeling like a basic trainee washout. Before long they were into a minute, then two. *Screw it.* She was tired. Jack was on his way, if not already here. Not exactly eager for the scene she was now enduring she'd disobeyed the general's implied orders and headed to the hospital with Zorah. While she was there, she'd even made a call to her command and spent an hour or so coordinating Farid's takedown. Okay, two hours. All right, so the sergeants she'd gone in after were already tucked in their unit's welcoming arms, safe and sound. But from the black leather bag blending into the dark beside the chairs, it looked as if her father hadn't even unpacked, much less settled in.

Another minute of silence and she'd truly had enough.

She cleared her throat. "Well, general, it's... been a long day." Now there was an understatement. "I'd like to find a shower and a cot before it gets any longer." *Nothing*. Fine, she'd had enough anyway. She executed an about face and stepped out—

"Turn on the light."

She stopped, stared at the French doors now to her left. She leaned over and twisted the dimmer switch beside them, wincing as light from half a dozen chandeliers flooded the room. She took a deep breath and turned...and nearly gasped out loud.

"You look like hell," he informed her.

Yeah? Well, he didn't look so great either. His Greens might be crisper than they'd ever been, the silver that passed for hair cropped shorter than usual, but the jagged lines tracking across his forehead and down his cheeks were anything but. They were fresh, too. She'd swear the man had aged eleven years in the past eleven months. And he'd been crying. Though his steel-blue eyes were bone-dry now, they were bloodshot and puffy. Only two things made this man look like that. Tears and Scotch. She'd never known him to indulge in either one except on the anniversary of her mother's death.

No, her mother's exceptionally brutal murder.

During the chopper flight, she'd figured out what Jack had been trying not to tell her. He'd been right about that, too. It did help her understand. She just didn't think it could change anything. Hell, look at them. The way her dad's gaze was fused to the bruises on her face, they were both thinking it.

So say it. She drew in her breath.

"Mom wasn't just murdered. She was raped, too."

His eyes weren't dry anymore. They were glistening. He didn't cry though. But that wasn't new. He never did when he knew she was looking. His heavy sigh flooded the room instead.

"Jack told you."

"No." Not in so many words. "He tried really hard not to." Until that moment, she hadn't realized how hard. "But this was...a difficult case." *Lina.* No, even as hurt and angry as she was with her father, he didn't need to hear that. She swallowed the pain and regret and chose her words carefully, knowing if they were ever going to get past this, ever heal, it would have to start now. "Jack did push it though. He pushed me to talk to you. I think—I hope—it was because he cared too much to walk away. I'm also thinking...hoping...that someone else came here...*is here*...because he cares, too.''

Relief swamped her, displacing the biting fear as her father nodded. ''He does care.''

Just say it. ''We're not just talking about Jack, are we?''

''No, we're not.'' But then that damned awkward silence settled back in and they weren't talking about anything anymore. As usual, neither of them seemed able to cross it. She swore her father was as relieved as she when the marine who'd shown her in entered the ballroom. The sergeant apologized for the interruption and greeted her father first, then held up a slip of paper in his gloved hand.

''A message, ma'am. From Special Agent Gage.''

Special Agent who? *What?* For the first time since she'd entered the room, she was truly glad her father was standing in it. While she was busy gaping, he retrieved the sheet and dismissed the sergeant. ''I take it you didn't know.''

She shifted her gape to him.

''Guess not.''

She blinked. ''Jack *left* Delta?'' Duh! How

many special agents had she met in Special Forces? But...why? More importantly, "When?"

"Couple months back."

"How many?"

"Nine. But he put in his request earlier."

Even before she asked, she knew. But she still asked. She had to be sure. She swallowed hard. "How much earlier?"

"The day after you two wrapped up the murder-for-hire assignment. I'd stopped by his office to ask him to lunch. To see if—" He broke off, ran a hand down the silver at the side of his head. "That's not true. I wasn't interested in lunch. I was interested in answers. I saw you two out by your car that morning. I wanted to know his intentions." It was one thing to hear from Jack that her father had seen that steamy kiss. It was quite another to stand in front of the man and look into those steel-blue eyes while she heard it from him.

She flushed. "And—ah—what were those intentions?"

His gaze turned so desolate she almost took the question back. Especially when her father turned slightly to retrieve his hat from one of the chairs and stare at the gold leaves embroidered along the brim. "Jack asked for permission to marry you. I told him..." He traced his fingers around the edge, then dragged his stare to hers. "I told him he could have it—"

"If he got me out of the Army."

"Yes. I'm sorry."

She nodded. It was all she could give him.

He took it. "If it helps, I've finally admitted that I'm the one who drove him out. I think he's always known it would come down to you or me. And I've always known you would win."

"This isn't a contest, dammit. And Jack's no prize." It wasn't until it came out that she realized how bald it sounded. But it succeeded in lightening the moment and, frankly, they both needed it. Though slight, they shared their first smile in years. "You ever tell him I said that, I'll shoot you."

"Coming from an expert shot, I'll take that seriously."

"You'd better."

Her father's smile faded as, once again, the silence settled in. The seconds ticked off until she couldn't handle it anymore. She had to know. "What happened?"

He didn't pretend to misunderstand. "You left. He'd gotten the invitation to work for the State Department the year before. I know, because we discussed it. He was flattered, but he wasn't interested. We never said it, but we both knew why.

I've always known. Even before he did. I'd been there myself with your mom. If I was the man you both deserved, I'd have pushed it. But I didn't. I knew Jack would never make you choose between him and the Army. I guess I was holding out for someone who would.''

There wasn't much she could say so she waited. He turned his hat in his hand and stared into it for a good minute. He finally sighed and met her gaze. ''That day in his office, Jack told me he was going to take the job. After the way I'd seen you two kiss, not to mention his stated intentions, it didn't take a genius to figure out he wasn't getting out of the Army. He was getting away from me...so he could finally go after you.''

He dropped his stare again. This time, he kept it fused to his hat as he continued, ''I'm sorry I'm not as brave as you. If I were, I'd have accepted your choice years ago. Logically, I know you're not her. But the older you got, the more you started to look like her, and, well, the more confusing it got. And the more terrifying. At first, I didn't tell you because you were too young. And then I couldn't tell you because I'd never told you. But when I got word you were missing...possibly raped and murdered like her...and I didn't even know you'd gone in, much less had a chance to say g-goodbye—'' He broke off. The knot in his throat bobbed as he swallowed hard. He finally tore his gaze from his hat and met hers square on. ''I'll try harder, honey. I swear it. On your mother's love.'' Once again, the silence settled in. But this time something came with it.

Tears.

She watched, transfixed as they welled up in those stark blue eyes, until he'd hoarded so many, they finally spilled down. She swore she could feel every one of them searing into her heart. She stepped forward without thinking and reached out, capturing them as they continued to slide. Or she tried to. There were too many. So she stepped closer and slid her arms around his neck and pulled him close. He stood there for what seemed like eons, and then he snapped. When his arms came up to crush her to his chest, she started crying. She wasn't sure how long they stood there, but eventually they both realized it'd been long enough. They pulled away at the same time.

He reached out, his hand shaking as he wiped the tears off her cheeks before she could. He cleared his throat, but his voice still came out hoarse. ''The Army lost a good man because of me. Don't you lose him.''

Somehow, she managed a smile. ''Trust me. I

have no intention of losing Jack. Not after I had to smoke another cigarette to keep him.''

His brow shot up. But then that damned heavy, awkward silence saturated the air again. Would they ever get rid of it for good? Maybe. Because he cleared his throat again. He was trying. He even spoke, ''You've got somewhere to be, don't you?''

Yes. But Jack would understand. ''No, I'll just—''

''Link up with your old man tomorrow?'' He shrugged off her surprise. ''It's late. Long flight. Man's gotta sleep.''

Her heart lurched. He really was trying. Dammit, then so could she. ''A man's gotta eat, too.''

''Lunch?'' He looked so uncertain, the tears threatened.

She nodded slowly. Smiled. ''I'd like that.'' His answering smile was slower and a bit stiff as she turned to leave, or maybe just rusty. She figured she'd find out soon enough.

''Just a minute, young lady.'' Startled to hear the general's voice and not her dad's again, she whirled around. He'd donned his hat and snapped to attention. He wasn't her dad anymore. He was General Ramrod-and-Ruthless Stanton in the flesh. Especially when he popped the sharpest, crispest salute she'd ever received. "I've been briefed. Outstanding work today, Captain."

Damn him. He just had to send her to Jack in tears, didn't he? Again.

He'd waited so long, he was starting to worry. Jack stared at the silver lighter clenched in his hand. Worried, hell. Six hours earlier, trapped in a barn with Dani wrapped in his arms while he waited for the right moment to flick a cigarette into fifteen feet of straw separating them from nine bags of gunpowder and an 8-inch tactical nuclear round, he'd been worried. Right now, he was pretty much terrified.

So much so, his stomach roiled when he heard the knock. He tossed the lighter on the coffee table and strode across the guest suite's carpet. His feet knew the way. They'd paced it out a hundred times already. He sucked up his panic and wrenched the door open. Dani was loitering on the other side, leaning against the wall, her loose hair still tangled, his T-shirt tucked into her jeans and his oversized belt. Soot still streaked across her right cheek, the purple bruise and split lip still marred her left. At least the marks on her neck had faded.

His heart burned as she smiled. "Hi. I'm sorry, I know it's late. But it's kind of important. I'm

looking for a man who goes by the name Special
Agent Jack Gage?''

''That would be me.''

''Hmmm...so I heard.'' She cocked her brow
toward the room behind him. ''Mind if come in?''

He threw the door wide, making way as she
stepped inside.

''This isn't a bad time is it, Agent?''

He blinked.

Her gaze swept his dark-blue robe. ''You look
like you were getting ready for a shower...or
bed.''

''Whichever comes first.'' At the moment, he
wasn't sure he'd have company for either. Not
when he spotted the note he'd sent via the marine
as she retrieved it from her back pocket. The paper
was still folded. The creases still sharp. Had she
even opened it? Did she even want to? Every time
he'd thought he'd gained ground with Danielle
Stanton, her father got in his way, whether or not
the man intended to. And she'd just spent half an
hour with him.

His heart burned once more as she set the square
of paper on the coffee table, right beside the
lighter. And this burn wasn't good. It seared in
deeper as she pulled a wad of bills from her back

pocket and carefully smoothed them. He stared at the stack as she held it out.

"Sorry about the twenties. The bank machine was out of hundreds. It's all there, though."

Christ. His heart blistered. "I don't want your money." He hadn't wanted a goddamned thing from this woman for eleven years now—except one simple statement. He was so sure he'd have heard it from her up in that room of Rurik's if they'd just had a little longer. But now? Staring at that stack of bills? He wasn't sure of anything. Maybe it had been adrenaline after all.

"Take the money, Jack."

"Dammit, Dani, I—"

"What? Three hundred's enough for a lowly army captain, but not some lofty special agent?" She tsked her tongue as he blinked, gaped. "My, my, just what agency are you with?"

"State Department."

"Diplomatic Security?"

He nodded.

"Mobile Security Detachment?"

He nodded again.

She frowned. Her low whistle filled the room, invading the bedroom beyond. "I hear they travel quite a bit. Never home. Understand the work's pretty dicey on occasion, too."

"It can be."

"I guess you're right then. Three hundred won't cut it." She sucked in her breath and squared her shoulders. He sucked in his own as that gorgeous gaze darkened with determination. "Unfortunately for me, I've decided that—special agent or not—I like what I see. So, how much is it going to take?"

Just like that, the burning in his heart eased.

"One word." His heart swelled as her gaze softened and slid to the square of paper. His hope swelled.

"Which word would that be?"

"The right one."

He stood there, his bare feet fused to the carpet as she slowly smoothed the bills and folded them before tucking the wad back into her pocket. His pounding heart timed the silent, excruciating seconds as she leaned down and picked up the note, unfolded it, then carefully smoothed that out, too. She took her sweet time reading the short statement and burning question he'd scrawled after. She took so long, he not only knew what her answer would be, he was certain she was enjoying every raw, bloody second of his torture. Christ, could this woman be cruel! He didn't care. Especially when he knew what was behind it. She might understand his silence at Rurik's, but she also intended to make him earn his forgiveness. Fine with him. He wasn't about to give up now. But he would have to make her pay, too.

"Yes, I'll marry you."

His heart exploded with joy. He had no idea how he managed to stand there and calmly nod as he absorbed the sheer ecstasy that showered back down, but he did. Nor did he have any idea where he found the strength to slowly shake his head. But again, it was there. He used it. "Sorry, that's four words."

When her gaze widened slightly, he knew she knew he was on to her. "Oh." She blinked. "Well, I guess the deal is off then."

She spun around—and got precisely *nowhere*. His hands whipped out before he could stop them. He hauled her in close, locking her wrists together with one of his hands as he swung her around with the other. He leaned in closer, staring directly into her eyes. "As long as you've overpaid, give me the rest."

"You're cheating."

"This isn't a game anymore, Danielle."

She nodded solemnly. "I know. I also know I shouldn't have walked out eleven months ago. I should have decked you and *maybe* given you a chance to explain. But I shouldn't have left."

"No, you shouldn't have. But I shouldn't have waited so long to tell the old man off, either."

"Why'd you finally do it?"

"Because once I got you alone, in my house and in my bed, I knew I'd never be able to let you go again. I should have said then, before we left for work, what I wrote in that note."

"Why didn't you?"

"'Cause I was scared, honey. We've known each other for so long. Hell, I've always known you were attracted to me. But what if that was it? What if you didn't feel the same way deep inside your heart? What if it *was* just adrenaline?"

"You really think adrenaline can cause what happened on your bed and in your shower? Beside my car? What happened against that wall tonight? What happens between us whenever we're *this* close?" She dragged her gaze down to his mouth and dragged her husky whisper even lower. "What's happening between us right now?"

"Hell, no. But I need to know what you think. What you feel. Dammit, Danielle, I need to hear the words."

"Come closer."

He leaned in until the tips of their lashes meshed. He was so close her very breath was turning him on. He could feel the soft, cool suction against his lips as hers parted, inhaled, and then the warm, slow wash as she exhaled. He felt each and every excruciatingly slow breath that followed, every single sensation as she shifted to scrape her lips across the individual hairs that formed the scruff on his cheek—until she stopped, and then finally, mercifully, filled his ear with her throaty whisper.

"I love you too, Jack."

The burn returned. This time, not just to his heart. The ache spread out, searing through every single inch of his body as he turned his head and leaned down to sweep her up in his arms. He carried her into the bedroom, right up to the bed he'd turned down almost an hour before, claiming her lips as he laid her out and sank into her curves. He delved deep inside her mouth, capturing the sigh from her heart and dragging it into his own, savoring it for so long that when he finally poured it back into her, it had turned into a hoarse, needy groan.

He didn't care.

It might have taken him eleven years and he might have had to cheat a bit along the way, but every blessed moment had been worth it. Because he'd finally won the most precious prize of all. The complete, unconditional surrender of Danielle Stanton's heart. He intended on treasuring it and her for the rest of his life.

* * * * *

Don't miss Candace Irvin's next book,
A DANGEROUS ENGAGEMENT,
part of her Sisters-in-Arms *military miniseries, in October 2003, only from Silhouette Intimate Moments.*

Only love could renovate the hearts
of two rough-and-tumble architects!

#1 *New York Times* bestselling author

NORA ROBERTS

brings you two classic riveting tales of romance.

BY DESIGN

Containing LOVING JACK and BEST LAID PLANS

And coming in October, watch for

LAWLESS

by Nora Roberts.

Available at your favorite retail outlet.

Where love comes alive™

Three men of mystery, three riveting classics from the incomparable mistress of romantic suspense

#1 *New York Times* bestselling author

NORA ROBERTS

Available at your favorite retail outlet.

Where love comes alive™